THE SECRET OF THE India Orchid

Other Proper Romance Titles by Nancy Campbell Allen

My Fair Gentleman

Beauty and the Clockwork Beast

Other Proper Romances

Julianne Donaldson

Edenbrooke

Blackmoore

Heir to Edenbrooke (eBook only)

Sarah M. Eden

Longing for Home

Longing for Home: Hope Springs

The Sheriffs of Savage Wells

Josi S. Kilpack

A Heart Revealed

Lord Fenton's Folly

Forever and Forever

A Lady's Favor (eBook only)

The Lady of the Lakes

The Vicar's Daughter

THE SECRET OF THE India Orchid

PROPER ROMANCE

NANCY CAMPBELL ALLEN

SHADOW MOUNTAIN

To Dad and Maryellen, because this book owes its life to the solitude of your basement. Love you.

© 2017 Nancy Campbell Allen

All rights reserved. No part of this book may be reproduced in any form or by any means without permission in writing from the publisher, Shadow Mountain®, at permissions@shadowmountain.com. The views expressed herein are the responsibility of the author and do not necessarily represent the position of Shadow Mountain.

Visit us at ShadowMountain.com

This is a work of fiction. Characters and events in this book are products of the author's imagination or are represented fictitiously.

Library of Congress Cataloging-in-Publication Data

Names: Allen, Nancy Campbell, 1969– author.
Title: The secret of the India orchid / Nancy Campbell Allen.
Description: Salt Lake City, Utah : Shadow Mountain, [2017]
Identifiers: LCCN 2016046609 | ISBN 9781629722931 (paperbound)
Subjects: LCSH: Man-woman relationships—Fiction. | India, setting. | LCGFT: Detective and mystery fiction. | Romance fiction.
Classification: LCC PS3551.L39644 S43 2017 | DDC 813/.54—dc23
LC record available at https://lccn.loc.gov/2016046609

Printed in the United States of America
Lake Book Manufacturing, Inc., Melrose Park, IL

10 9 8 7 6 5 4 3 2 1

Chapter 1

Anthony Blake, the new Earl of Wilshire, stepped from White's Gentlemen's Club with a light heart and a smile on his face. Soon—that very evening, in fact—he was going to approach his good friend, Jack Elliot, Earl of Stansworth, and formally ask permission to court Jack's sister, Sophia. Once he had made the decision, he could think of nothing else.

To say Sophia was beautiful was the grossest of understatements. She possessed a face and figure men dreamed about, the kind that inspired poetry and duels at dawn. But in the six months since Jack's marriage to Lady Ivy Carlisle, Anthony and Sophia had been, by virtue of their respective relationships to the happy couple, placed together at balls and soirees, and for rides in the park, picnics, and quiet evenings around the hearth in the comfort of the Stansworth townhome.

Time spent with Sophia had become a habit to Anthony, and a very pleasant one at that. Although her physical beauty was a thing to behold, her inner core and her personality traits were beyond what Anthony dreamed could be housed within one physical frame. She was delightfully sharp-witted, possessed a no-nonsense air that served well in times of stress, and had a keen mind and a perception of people that was accurate to a deadly degree. They were friends at the root of it all, and he'd shared parts of his soul with her that he'd never divulged to anyone.

In short, he was truly, madly, passionately in love with Sophia Elliot, and he wished with all his heart for her to accept his hand and become the next Countess of Wilshire. He thought she might be amenable to the idea. He recognized the spark of awareness in her eyes, the subtle shift in her physical proximity to him when they were together, the genuine delight in her laughter when he said or did something she found humorous.

Even so, his nerves were strung taut as the coach bearing his distinguished family crest drew alongside him in front of White's. He felt certain Jack would offer his blessing to the union; he had come to respect Anthony as a good friend and, Anthony hoped, one he would trust with his beloved sister. But what if Sophia was reluctant? Perhaps she hadn't seen enough of the marriage mart to have decided which of the many men available to her as the sister of an earl would suit her best.

Anthony climbed into his coach, confident that he had done his best to stay out of her way when the flurry of men, both young and old, vied for a spot on her dance card or sought to sate her thirst with numerous cups of punch. The fact that his jealousy burned hot every time she favored another man with her attention was something she need never know. She always saved a dance for him—a waltz, no less.

She often penciled his name onto her dance card before the male masses descended, showing the small paper to him with a light laugh and an admonition that he remember which dance was his.

As if he would forget.

He would dance with the young debutantes shoved at him by grasping mamas. He would attend to the more mature women of the *ton* who were bored with their own marriages and viewed Anthony as some sort of prize as a war veteran. And he would smile and say all the expected things while his heart was truly and firmly entrenched at the feet of his best friend's sister. He was always aware of her, he knew where she was at any given time, and he was fairly certain he could sense her presence in a room before knowing for a certainty she was there. He had taken to wearing small flowers in his lapel, different colors and types for different meanings. She would smile, seeing him across a crowded room, knowing a sprig of lavender meant devotion, and that it was for her.

His well-sprung carriage made the trip to his well-tended townhome situated in the midst of London's finest neighborhood and not far from Jack and Ivy. He dismissed the driver and made his way inside with the intention of immediately climbing the stairs to his suite to change into his evening attire.

His butler, Dillington, cleared his throat when Anthony's boot touched the bottom-most stair. "My lord, you have a visitor."

Anthony frowned. "I am not receiving now, Dillington. Whoever is waiting must return tomorrow."

Dillington approached the stairs, forcing Anthony to

pause. "Sir, it is the Viscount Braxton. He would not be put off. He is in the library."

Anthony looked at his butler for some time, his heartbeat increasing a fraction. The last time Lord Braxton had demanded an audience, Anthony had found himself spying for the War Department in Napoleon's France. "No, I don't suppose he would be put off." Anthony changed direction, heading for the library. "Don't bother announcing me, Dillington. And please see that Faring lays out my evening clothes. This meeting will not be lengthy."

Anthony entered the library and took note of the man who had sent him to war a handful of years back. Anthony's elder brother, Alfred, had been alive then, as had his father and mother, and as the spare to Wilshire's heir, military service was Anthony's natural course. Lord Braxton, though, had reviewed the battery of tests Anthony had taken upon the purchase of his commission and pulled him aside for "a deeper cause."

Braxton stood at the hearth, examining the portrait of Anthony's late mother that hung above the mantel. He turned at Anthony's footsteps and offered his signature smile, the one that so easily influenced other members of various organizations to see his way of things. Anthony's instinctive guard came out of retirement and slammed into place. Braxton could charm a shilling from a street vendor, and Anthony always wondered about the man's true motives.

"What do you want?"

Braxton's brows shot up, and he laughed. "Direct as ever, I see. Perhaps I'm merely stopping by to renew an old acquaintance."

"Forgive my abruptness. The last time we spoke I believe I made myself clear. I want nothing more to do with the War Department."

Braxton's smile slipped. "Sometimes the past has a way of coming home to roost—I believe that's the saying."

Anthony studied the man and finally gestured to a pair of chairs near the hearth. "What past is coming home to roost?"

Lord Braxton paused after taking his seat. "Someone stole the Janus Document."

Anthony's breath left his lungs, and he stared at the viscount for a long moment before finally blinking.

"I need you to find it."

Anthony shook his head, regarding the man who had, with one sentence, disrupted his entire life. "How did this happen?"

Braxton sat back in his seat and sighed. "A man named Harold Miller works as my subordinate. He has access to my offices, but not to the documents under lock and key." He rubbed his forehead. "I don't know how he did it, but the document is gone. I tracked him as far as France before I lost him completely. I believe he intends to sell it to the French military."

Anthony frowned, an uneasy sense of dread settling into his stomach. "You wrote the document in a code nobody knows but you, though. At least, that is what you told me when you first created it."

Braxton shifted in his seat. "I had intended to. Time became an issue, and I was obliged to focus on weightier matters, so I found it simpler to create it with our code already in use."

Anthony stared. "There are dozens of agents who know that code," he bit out. "Any one of us could be bribed or threatened into revealing it." He ground his teeth together, wanting very much to thrash the man. "We are as good as dead—all of us. Your operatives."

Braxton's brow wrinkled and he winced. "Not only the operatives, I'm afraid. The document is a composite of detailed information intended for my use only, but it is exhaustive: names of operatives, their families, addresses, associates both business and casual." He spread his hands wide. "You see the implications. Even encoded as it is, the document must be retrieved or hundreds of people are at risk of abduction, torture, or worse."

Anthony shook his head. "I've not been in France for more than a year. I assume you have people still in Paris, Marseilles. You can use operatives already in place."

Braxton shot him a flat look. "They are young, amateurs in comparison to the skills you possesses, Anthony. And we haven't operated abroad with nearly as much success since your return home. Before, as the son of a distinguished earl, to parade you as a diplomat was the perfect tactic. Now you actually are the earl with the freedom to travel, to do as you please, to convince the enemy you're still a ne'er-do-well with naught on his mind but pleasure-seeking. The cover has grown even more effective with time."

Anthony's lips tightened. He'd been well aware that he'd risked life and limb each time he was sent as an "emissary" for the military. His duties had required him to listen well, use his considerable charm to flirt with dignitaries' wives and daughters, and quietly pass messages to double agents on the French side. For three years he'd been tense, his muscles knotted, his appetite sporadic. One misstep would find him captured, tortured for information.

And then his brother had died suddenly. As much as Anthony grieved the loss, the change in his station to assume the role of heir had required his immediate return home. His relief at bringing the subversive activity to a close had been nearly palpable. Braxton's very presence now in his home engendered emotions that had no place in his current life, a new life he'd planned to begin that very evening by announcing his intentions to court a beautiful woman who had become his dearest friend.

Braxton broke eye contact and stared instead into the banked fire in the hearth.

Anthony studied him, suspicion nagging at the back of his mind. "You would have me believe your only concern is for the welfare of those on the list? The war effort? What else is there?"

Braxton flushed. "Is it not enough that I fear for the lives of dozens of people? Come, Anthony, you know me."

"I know your first concern is usually you."

Braxton leaned forward in his seat, impatience showing on his face. "I am the only one with access to the document. Nobody else—*nobody*—is allowed anywhere near it."

Anthony smiled without humor. "Ah. And there it is. If something happens—*when* something happens—and it becomes common knowledge that the document was taken out from under your nose, *you* will be the one to bear responsibility for it."

"That document has your information on it, Wilshire. As

well as that of dozens of others, many of whom are still serving abroad. Multiple lives are threatened, as well as families, friends, loved ones. Rumor has it you've become close to a young woman—the sister of an earl relatively new to the *ton.* I hear she has caught many an eye, most notably yours. Now, supposing I were one of your former French associates who came into the knowledge that you had been a spy, someone you had duped or fooled; I might take great interest in your current social situation. You know very well that loved ones are used as leverage for information. Nobody in your circle is safe, especially one to whom you now show special favor."

Anthony's eyes narrowed, hot rage boiling in his gut. "You will not speak of her, and you will not use her to force my hand."

"And yet you know I speak the truth!" Braxton threw up his hands, his frustration clearly mounting. "Yes, I am concerned for myself." He sighed, and his shoulders slumped. "Not only do I bear sole responsibility for the document, my information is contained in it as well, as your governmental liaison, the mastermind of the entire operation."

Anthony allowed himself to fully absorb the conversation and, along with the pervasive anger, felt a deep and sharp stab of fear. If the Janus Document did indeed find its way to his former French associates, nobody was safe. His friendships with Jack, Ivy, and Sophia were well-known. Anybody with an ounce of investigative skills would soon realize that although Anthony's blood relations were dead, the Elliots had become his family.

Anthony inhaled and exhaled slowly and shook his head. "Believing my life was my own was too good to be true. I ought to have known. Where am I to start looking for the blasted thing?"

"As I said, I traced Harold Miller as far as France. He has disappeared."

"Are you certain he is the one who has it? Why do you suspect his intentions are to sell it?"

Braxton frowned. "He's a bright lad, but destitute and from difficult circumstances. He commented once on the amount of money the document would bring—" He rubbed his face though clear evidence of his stress remained in the lines around his eyes and mouth. "He was the only one with access to my office. I saw him in it less than an hour before I realized it was gone. I immediately started tracking him, of course, but lost him in Paris. And it isn't as though I can approach French authorities with the situation. *Pardonnez-moi, mais je requiers l'aide pour trouver une liste des espions Anglais.*"

"Is he working alone? How has he gained access to resources?"

Braxton shrugged. "I don't know. I wouldn't have believed he could mastermind something of this magnitude, but as I said, he is an intelligent sort."

"Are we to assume it hasn't already fallen into the wrong hands?"

"I know it hasn't. I still communicate with our people on the inside, and very few are even aware of the theft." Braxton shook his head. "If the French get the list, I suspect we will know soon enough. An experienced agent will eventually see the patterns in the code."

"Or one of our own could be turned," Anthony warned again.

"I don't believe that would happen. Our people are carefully investigated before serving. But should the worst happen, I suspect our operatives past and present will likely begin disappearing. Of course you see the urgency."

Anthony sighed and rubbed his eyes. The evening was now colorless, joyless. Not only would he be forced to leave Sophia, but he wouldn't be able to tell her the reason. She would hear Braxton's carefully placed rumors that Anthony Blake, the new Earl of Wilshire, was back to his old tricks. It left a sour taste in his mouth, and his eyes burned at the thought of her inevitable feelings of betrayal. Because aside from the fact that he wanted her in every way he possibly could, theirs was a genuine friendship. They had spent countless hours in meaningful conversation, sharing confidences in the library over a game of chess while Jack and Ivy read or played cards. He had grown accustomed to being with Sophia.

Before, when he had served in France, the secretive nature of his role had been unpleasant but it hadn't upset anyone else. Then, there had been no one with whom he cared to share the details of his life. Now, Sophia was the one person on earth who knew him without his protective wall of cynicism.

"I am sorry, old boy." Braxton did indeed look regretful. "Dreadfully sorry. If it weren't so critical, I wouldn't ask. You're truly the only one who can do this—you have the knowledge, the resources, the persona already in place."

"With any luck, I won't need to use it for long." Anthony stood and gestured toward the library door. "You should leave. I find I'm not much in the mood for company."

The corner of the viscount's mouth lifted. "You were never in the mood for my company anyway."

"Is it any wonder? A meeting with you never did carry good news."

"Be at my office in the morning. I'll have more for you then." Braxton clapped a hand on Anthony's shoulder and took his leave.

Anthony rubbed a hand over his face and stared for a moment at the empty room. He poured himself a drink at the sidebar and wandered slowly to the mantel where the image of his late mother looked down on him benevolently. *All will be well.* He heard her familiar refrain echo through his thoughts and rolled his eyes. She'd lived for years with a lying, philandering husband that Anthony honestly couldn't say he missed, an arrogant firstborn son, and a floundering second son who had made a general nuisance of himself trying to find his place in the world. All had not worked out well for her, and he marveled that she'd ever believed it would.

He braced one hand against the mantel and hung his head, frustration clawing at him until he felt he'd explode from it. With an oath, he hurled his glass into the fire and closed his eyes, steeling himself for what lay ahead. Because as much as he hoped he would find the Janus Document quickly, he had a feeling it would be some time before his world was set to rights again.

Chapter 2

Sophia—

This letter is one of farewell as I find myself yearning for the Continent. I have shared with you the stresses the earldom has thrust upon me, and I find I am simply not ready to embrace my responsibilities. Perhaps I am merely postponing the inevitable, but I am stifled here in Town. I must get away from London, from England, from all of it. I am hoping to rekindle former acquaintances and perhaps gain some much needed perspective.

I count you among my dearest friends and appreciate our association of the last several months as would a very fortunate elder brother. Indeed, if I could choose a sister for myself, it would be you. Jack is fortunate, and I envy his relationship with you. Perhaps in some small way, I have joined him in that affectionate, familial role, in seeing you launched successfully into your place in society. You glitter like the brightest of stars, and I am so glad to call you "friend."

Ever affectionate,

Anthony

It had been almost two years since Sophia had received the letter that had crushed her heart into small pieces, and she still remembered every word. On occasion she wondered how she could have been so terribly wrong in her assessment of their relationship. *Friendship*, he had called it. He regarded her with all the tender affections of a *brother.*

Her mind circled back, unbidden, to their time together. Waltzes where he'd held her perhaps just a bit too closely, the stolen moments on London's finest balconies and in her most beautiful gardens, silent communication with flowers both sent to the house and worn on his lapel, glances across the dinner table, picnics with Jack and Ivy, parties at the Stansworth country estates and at Wilshire, flirting over card games, and long conversations in the drawing room after dinner, quietly confiding things she'd never told anyone.

He had helped her and Ivy establish their school and had extended his compassion for the indigent women they sought to empower. She had listened with her whole heart as he unburdened himself to her about his troubled relationship with his father, his brother. She had grown to love so many things about him, not the least of which was the flutter she felt deep in her stomach whenever he entered a room, bowed over her hand for a dance, or scribbled his initials on her dance card with a wink.

Her *brother* most assuredly did not inspire similar feelings.

Sophia now stood on the deck of a sleek ship that sailed the Arabian Sea, approaching the west coast of India, and wondered for the millionth time how she could have so totally misread Anthony's intentions. And more to the point, if she could ever move beyond the sting of having been firmly and definitively assigned the title of *friend.*

Sister!

For the love of Heaven.

The wind blew across the deck and tugged at a few curls that escaped her bonnet. The humid sea air wreaked havoc on her coiffure, and while she had appreciated the benefit of curly hair at home in London, somehow the added heat left her with an unmanageable tangle. Her maid, Briggs—how strange was life that Sophia Elliot had a maid!—did the best she could but often grumbled at Sophia for spending so much time topside in the wind and sea spray.

It would be good to arrive, finally, on solid land. The ship itself was commodious; a good majority of Fishing Fleet expeditions traveled from England to India in much poorer conditions. Jack had not been thrilled when Sophia had announced she wanted to go to Bombay with the Fleet, which had a reputation that wasn't altogether positive, but she had to get herself out of London and every cursed drawing room and dance floor that reminded her of Anthony Blake. Her brotherly friend.

Jack had finally relented, insisting that Sophia travel with not only her lady's maid but also an older woman who was traveling to India to visit her family. He'd also made arrangements with one of his former sea captain associates to transport this particular batch of women in comfort. Belonging to one of England's wealthiest families had its advantages.

As a member of England's Fishing Fleet—the contingency of single Englishwomen who, unsuccessful at securing husbands in London, traveled yearly to India to appeal to England's military men and civil servants—she would be among people whose culture matched her own and yet could still enjoy the benefit of visiting a new country with all its wonders.

And if she happened to find a handsome man along the way, so be it. She'd had offers in the two years since receiving Anthony's letter, but this was a fresh start, a new beginning, a grand adventure.

The ship continued its quick clip, and each nautical mile took them closer to Bombay. Sophia's heart skipped in anticipation, and she looked upon the coastline with a thrill she'd not felt in some time.

Just before Sophia left London, Jack had received a letter from Anthony, who was in South Africa, of all places, and on his way to Bombay and then Calcutta. France must have proven too small, she supposed, for "rekindling relationships with former acquaintances" and the like. Of course he had associates in South Africa and in Asia. Where didn't he? The *ton* buzzed with rumors of "that scoundrel, Wilshire" and his latest liaison with yet another actress or opera diva. The lords chuckled and elbowed each other, the ladies sighed, the matrons and chaperones pursed their lips, and Sophia fumed.

The letter Jack received from Anthony wasn't the first,

but it was the first time Sophia realized they had been communicating. She couldn't very well voice any sort of outrage about betrayal or her hurt feelings that Jack had sided so clearly with the enemy, because she had outwardly downplayed Anthony's desertion to such a level as to appear negligible on the scale of Things That Mattered to Sophia. Of course she missed their *dear friend*, but a lord must do what a lord must do, and really, the earldom was apparently much too stressful for one such as Anthony, a man who clearly was not yet prepared to *be* a man.

As much as she craved the sight of him, she hoped he would have moved on to Calcutta by now. If so, she could have her adventure, make her own way, and find a clean break from an earl who was too handsome and charming for *her* own good. Perhaps she might actually allow herself to develop fond feelings for another man, someone else to make her heart race, wondering if that night would be the one where he finally kissed her. Scandalous, to be sure, but Sophia had never had the pleasure of a kiss she welcomed. Those she had experienced could hardly be considered kisses; instead she had suffered from aggressive, unwanted attention from men who sought to take advantage of her servitude in their grand houses.

And then Jack had inherited their grandfather's earldom and Sophia had been transformed from lady's maid to lady, literally overnight. She had had six glorious months with Anthony before he left, and she worried the sting from his abandonment would never fully leave.

The ship was still more than a mile away from shore, but the sights and sounds from the exotic country began subtly wafting from land to sea, and Sophia's eyes widened at the foreign but pleasant stimuli as the country grew larger in her vision.

Jack had been to India several times during his days as a sailor, and she wished he and Ivy were with her now. She would have loved to see the country through his eyes, and she missed Ivy and their daughter, Catherine, like mad. Jack and Ivy were still as besotted with each other as they'd been on their wedding day. They were a lovely couple, despite their differences in both temperament and background, as natural together as if God Himself had introduced them to one another. And perhaps He had. All Sophia wanted from Him at this point was to strike a certain earl dead.

There had been a time when she'd imagined children of her own playing alongside her niece, Catherine—children with black hair and green eyes who looked like their handsome father. Her smile faltered, and she turned her attention outward, focusing instead on the lush landscape that grew ever larger in her vision. She was torn; she was finally embarking on a new adventure and it was eclipsed by images of an English lord who may or may not be within a few miles of her now, and who may or may not be in the company of an actress or an opera diva.

She narrowed her eyes, her nostrils flaring slightly, much preferring anger to heartache. Perhaps it was time to petition God again about striking him dead. That thought cheered her immeasurably, and she looked forward to the coastline with a smile.

Chapter 3

The early morning sunlight was warm, but not uncomfortably so. Winter was far and away the best time to be in India, and residents and visitors alike knew they had until roughly the end of March before the heat began its oppressive and deadly descent.

A bead of sweat trickled between Anthony's shoulder blades. He stood in the shade of a large banyan tree outside the Resident's mansion and looked down the long tree-lined drive at the approaching carriages with his heart in his throat, wishing he could blame the heat for the reason he perspired.

Dylan Stuart, his friend and a military major with the First Cavalry Light Brigade, stood next to him. He was tall, blond, and handsome, with an unapologetic smile on his face. "I do not believe I've ever seen you quite so undone, old man."

Anthony scowled. "I am most certainly not undone."

"Who is she?"

"I do not know what you mean."

Dylan laughed. "Come now, Blake, I am no fool. I have

known you for more years than I care to count, and I have never seen you rattled."

Anthony glanced at him askance before returning his attention to the three carriages that grew closer. "The sister of an old friend might be with this Fleet. I am simply seeing to her welfare for his sake."

Dylan's lips twitched. "Of course."

The only bright spot thus far concerning his time in India had been renewing his friendship with Dylan Stuart. The First Cavalry Light Brigade was headquartered less than a mile from the British Residency compound, and the area boasted nearly as many British citizens as Indian. Anthony had spent the bulk of his time over the last few weeks trying to pin down Captain Miller—uncle of Harold Miller, the man who had stolen the Janus Document—but the captain was proving as elusive as his nephew. He was frustrated and tired, and looking forward to the next few minutes with equal parts excitement and dread. He couldn't decide if he wanted Sophia to be in one of the carriages or not. His task was unfinished, so he was still obliged to play his role, as distasteful as it was to him.

The carriages rolled to a stop at the front steps, and Anthony shoved his hands deeply into his pockets to keep from fidgeting. The first carriage, and then the second, deposited their occupants onto the sprawling front yard of the British Residency. Young women of all ages gathered on the lawn with exclamations of delight at the sight of the enormous mansion, the trees dripping with moss, the vegetation awash with colorful splendor. India was a country that invariably evoked an excess of stimulation to the senses—Anthony well remembered his first impressions.

He knew he should favor the ladies with his attention, if only to keep up his appearances of being an unconnected bachelor, but his heart wasn't in it. Not when Sophia might be the next woman to emerge from the carriage.

Sophia was not among the number of women gathering so he moved slowly to the third carriage, well aware of Dylan hovering behind him like an amused shadow. The carriage held six occupants, and he began to wonder if Sophia had changed her mind about joining this Fleet. Jack had written to ask him to see to Sophia's welfare, if possible, though he'd warned Anthony that Sophia had been hurt by his desertion. Anthony knew Jack was also frustrated by Anthony's sudden departure from England to France, and it chafed that he was unable to enlighten his friend fully.

It also chafed that Jack had included a postscript to his note, casually informing him that Sophia had had offers aplenty for her hand since his departure.

Only one woman remained in the final carriage, and he moved forward to nudge the footman out of the way when her head finally appeared in the opening. Anthony's heart pounded in his ears. *Sophia.* More beautiful, more radiant, more *everything*. His memories, hoarded and jealously reviewed in the quiet of his private hours over the last years, hadn't done her justice. Before he did something foolish, like weep, he extended his hand and wondered what she was thinking as she stared at him, unblinking.

He cleared his throat. "Miss Elliot, such a surprise and delight to see you here." His restraint was tested to its fullest as he fought the urge to grab her from the carriage and clasp her close. There had been a time and place in their relationship when such overt affection would not have shocked those who knew the two of them well. That time had passed, though, and now all he could do was wait to see if she'd ever take his hand and step out of the conveyance. He tried to smile but fell well short of the mark. His heart thumped, and a sheen of sweat broke out on his forehead.

The color had leeched from her face, and he wondered if she would faint. It would be a first—Sophia was one of the steadiest people he knew—and he couldn't decide if he was pleased or upset that the shock of seeing him rattled her nerves. Her face flushed as blood returned to her cheeks, and she clasped his fingers, stepping out of the carriage.

He was at a complete and total loss for words. An ache in his chest bloomed and climbed into his throat, and he felt his eyes burn. He kept hold of her hand when he should have released it, tugging her closer by small degrees, trying in vain to truly read her.

"I have missed you," he murmured.

He was gratified to hear the slightest hitch in her breathing, and after one . . . two . . . three long heartbeats, she withdrew her fingers from his.

Who could blame her for maintaining distance? He'd left her with the impression that they were very good friends and nothing more. He'd never confessed the depth of his feelings, his intentions to court her, and she'd never learned the true reason he'd left. The devil of it was, he still wasn't at liberty to enlighten her. Until his business was finished, nobody could safely know the full extent of his mission.

"Sophia, I . . . that is . . ." He placed a finger under his collar, cursing the humidity, the starched shirtfront, the cravat, all of it.

"Jack mentioned you might be here, but I suppose I had assumed you would have moved on to Calcutta by now." She took a quick breath. Her expression brightened and she smiled. "It's been such a long while. I do hope you've enjoyed your adventures. I suspect we shall have time later at dinner, perhaps, and you can entertain me with your tales."

So that was how it was to be. He'd been relegated to the status of Admirer; he'd heard that tone in her voice and seen that expression on her face more times than he could count, directed toward gentlemen whose feelings she didn't necessarily want to bruise, but whose attentions she didn't necessarily want to encourage. He supposed he was fortunate she hadn't smacked him upside the head with her fan—it was no less than he deserved.

"I look forward to it." He smiled and regained his equilibrium with practiced playacting that had kept him in good graces more than once. He turned to Dylan, who stood at his elbow and watched with unabashed curiosity. "May I introduce my good friend, Major Dylan Stuart, who is currently stationed here in Bombay with the First Cavalry Light Brigade. I've known him since our early days at Eton, and we spent time together in France during the war. Major Stuart, Miss Sophia Elliot, granddaughter of the deceased thirteenth Earl of Stansworth and sister to the current earl."

Dylan took Sophia's extended hand and bowed, placing a kiss on the back of her fingers. "A pleasure, my lady."

Sophia smiled, at her charming best. "My, that certainly

is a long association! How wonderful to renew a friendship after so many years. Lord Wilshire is nothing if not constant in his affections for dear friends."

Anthony winced.

"I believe we share an additional connection, Major Stuart," she continued. "Your cousin, Miss Rachael Scarsdale, is also among our number, and we became friends on the voyage over." Sophia craned her head to look at the crowd of young women. She called out to one with a beckoning motion.

The woman approached, as blonde and pretty as the major himself, and her face broke into a wide smile. "Dylan!"

"There she is!" Major Stuart grinned and clasped the woman, swinging her off her feet as she laughed. "Your mother mentioned your intentions to join the Fleet, but I did not know you were coming this year." He set her down and drew Sophia into their conversation with a conspiratorial wink. "Now ladies, I realize the goal of such an expedition is true and everlasting love—preferably within the bounds of holy matrimony—"

Rachael slapped his arm.

"However," he continued, "as you are both apt to receive multiple proposals daily, I urge you to be selective. And ask me specifically about the suitability of any potential suitor." He gestured a thumb at Anthony. "This one hasn't been here long enough to offer any useful help, but I know every eligible bachelor between here and Calcutta." He smiled. "And there are many."

Rachael laughed. "You are clearly following my mother's

instructions. She cannot help but interfere in my affairs, even a world away."

Dylan shook his head, a wry smile still in play. "That may or may not be true, I confess nothing; however, I would be remiss in my duties as your doting protector to neglect the warning."

By this time several of the other ladies present had gathered around them and Anthony spoke to the group at large. "Lady Pilkington will be thrilled to know you've all arrived. We have a veritable house party in full swing at the moment. Several of Lord and Lady Pilkington's friends from England are guests here at the mansion for a time, and we daily enjoy the company of soldiers from the First Cavalry Light Brigade. I trust you won't miss Society in the least."

A general exclamation of glee went up from the crowd.

"You truly are just in time," Dylan added. "Lady Pilkington's biannual costume ball is to be held tonight."

Additional squeals of delight filled the air, and the group began moving *en masse* toward the wide front steps of the Residency. Two additional carriages approached via the tree-lined drive and drew to a stop near the crowd. A number of ladies' maids disembarked, and Sophia and Rachael moved to speak with them.

Anthony watched as Sophia spoke easily with a young woman and elicited a smile from her. Of course Sophia would be kind to a maid—she'd been one herself. She had balked at having one when Jack had first come into the title, but she'd finally acquiesced when Ivy convinced her she would be doing any young woman a favor by offering her generous employment and a kind mistress. Good work was not always easy to come by, and to be treated well by the family was a blessing. Sophia knew the truth of that altogether too well.

She and Rachael returned to Anthony and Dylan and climbed the front steps to the main house. Anthony was curious about Jack's willingness to allow Sophia to travel with the Fishing Fleet, but he didn't feel he had the right to ask her about it. The Fleet had become notorious for carrying women far below Sophia's station who had been unable to secure a good match at home. There were also rumors of shipboard dalliances with other single gentlemen during the voyage that scandalized proper society. He was saved from giving voice to the awkward question when Dylan asked it instead.

"A little surprised my aunt approved of your travel with the Fleet, my dear cousin." He grinned. "How did you manage it without me there to charm her?"

Miss Scarsdale rolled her eyes. "It took some doing, I must admit." She sighed. "And Mrs. Stilton, my hired companion for the voyage, was most reluctant to allow me association with any of the other ladies, but when she realized Miss Elliot also traveled with a respectable companion and was the sister of an earl, besides, she finally relented."

"Traveling with a respectable companion is a wise course of action," Anthony said. "I would recommend it if any female relation of my own were traveling with the Fleet." He managed a smile for Sophia, but then braced himself at the quick glint in her eye he knew was but the briefest of warnings before her veiled sarcasm struck.

"And how apropos! I am, after all, your surrogate sister, yes?" She dimpled at him, her lovely face the very image of a charming debutante well versed in the art of harmless flirtation. She would set the wife-hunting populace of British men on their collective ear. "And I am the most fortunate of women to have *two* such strapping men to look after my well-being. I simply cannot imagine making my way through life without the guiding hand of elder brothers. Or *dear* friends."

Anthony searched for something to say from a well of charming platitudes that had suddenly run dry.

Sophia linked arms with Rachael, asked her something he couldn't hear, and they entered the mansion, laughing.

Lady Pilkington, a trim woman approaching middle age, and striking in both dress and ornamentation, received the group in the front hall. She clapped her hands with a wide smile when she singled out Sophia. "My darling Miss Elliot, what a pleasure to meet you in person! The likeness your brother sent with his last letter hardly does you justice. What a beauty you are, and what fun we shall have! I've never been a sponsor—it shall be grand!"

Sophia smiled and accepted the woman's quick embrace, and then introduced Rachael Scarsdale and several of the other women in the group. Lady Pilkington clucked after the bunch, showing Sophia, Rachael, and a handful of other ladies to the guest rooms. The remainder of the young women were to lodge either with other British families and dignitaries near the Residency or in one of the larger nearby British compounds. The butler, Himmat, directed those not with Lady Pilkington to the drawing room for tea before they were to leave for their own quarters.

Anthony took the opportunity to ask Dylan to join him in the library. Dylan had been in India for some time, though he had arrived at the Residency only a short time before the ladies, and Anthony was eager for a more in-depth conversation with him.

Dylan was one of very few people who had been aware of Anthony's actual duties during the war. Dylan had even saved his life more than once. It would be a relief to finally confide in someone, to share the burden of the true reason Anthony was in India.

The library was an airy room with whitewashed walls and ceilings and plantation shutters on the windows. Shelves along the walls held a variety of leather-bound volumes on subjects ranging from history to horticulture to politics. A thick, red Turkish rug anchored a seating arrangement in the center of the room where he and Dylan sat.

Dylan leaned back in his chair. "Why are you here, then? I hear the rumors, of course, that you're back to your carefree days, but I'm inclined to believe those rumors are more of a screen than the truth. You and I both know they weren't true the first time, either."

Anthony sighed. "Braxton sent me."

Dylan nodded. "And what is it that endangers the Realm this time?"

"The War Department has lost a confidential document that contains information about His Majesty's servants—detailed information, I am afraid."

Dylan's brow raised. "And Braxton has sent you to recover it."

"Yes. He believes the document was stolen by a young man named Harold Miller. I tracked his movements from England to France, where he secured passage on his uncle's merchant vessel. However, by the time Captain Miller put ashore at the Cape, he'd lost several of his crew—including his nephew, Harold—to illness." Anthony lowered his voice. "The captain is here as a guest of the Residency. I assume he is in possession of the document, though I do not know where he might be keeping it."

"One hopes the document is in code?"

Anthony nodded. "It is, although the code is not exclusive to Braxton. We can assume the information is secure, for now, at least. Our operatives in France have remained safe, though depending on what the captain does with the document, that could change in an instant."

"Do you believe the captain could break the code?"

"Doubtful, but he could find someone with the necessary skills. Or, he could sell it to an individual or a government who might have an interest in holding the document ransom. Either way, I have tracked the thing for two years now and am quite at the end of my rope." It was an understatement, truly. He went to bed at night cursing the document, and he awoke in the morning cursing the document. He had begun to wonder if he would spend the rest of his life chasing the thing.

"When did the captain arrive at the Residency?"

Anthony sat back in his chair and lifted a shoulder. When he spoke, he kept his voice down. "He arrived several days ago, just before I did. I've tried to pin the man down, but have not been able to find the right approach. And my hands are somewhat tied by the very reputation designed to keep me safe. I am not here in an openly investigative capacity; I am here to fritter away my time and attention on inconsequential matters and to flirt with pretty girls. I cannot abandon my cover now—the world is very small where it concerns the British Empire. I've already encountered several people I know from home and military service."

Dylan nodded. "Happens here more often than not." He paused. "And now you find yourself in the company of a woman for whom you have obvious affection. What does she think of your ne'er-do-well reputation?"

Anthony leaned forward and braced his elbows on his knees. "She is hurt." He rubbed his eyes with his thumb and forefinger. "I had intended to formally court her, but then Braxton arrived at my door. I was instead obliged to downplay my devotion to her, not only to complete the task at hand, but to keep her safe." He looked at Dylan. "The document contains privileged information not only on our operatives, but on their friends and family—anyone who could be used as leverage against us."

Dylan whistled low.

A headache settled behind Anthony's eyes. The woman who haunted his dreams was now under the same roof as he. Being able to court her openly was motivation enough to put the Janus Document business to rest. Perhaps if he could find the thing she might find a way to forgive him for deceiving her.

Chapter 4

Sophia came to some rather quick conclusions about Lady Pilkington. She was like many English women in that she held a definite sense of British superiority and she believed her worth lay in furthering her husband's career and hosting the most impressive parties. She had been born to privilege and, despite marrying slightly below her station, still found herself in a position to be envied by many. Her husband was a Resident, sent to act as a liaison to one of India's many regional princes. The mansion was grand—larger than most of the other families' bungalows, she was quick to point out—the servants plentiful, and the environment lush and exotic.

She was now Miss Sophia Elliot's sponsor, and she couldn't have been more proud of the fact, as she mentioned numerous times before reaching Sophia's room. She'd always wished for a daughter, she said, and was honored to temporarily stand in for Sophia's dear mother for a time.

For her part, Sophia felt a sense of cautious fondness for the woman, who seemed, above all things, sincere.

The women's guest rooms were situated adjacent each other on the far north end of the mansion's second floor. Thatched screens—*tatties*—on window shutters that in the summer were continually wet to catch crosswinds and cool the rooms, were absent now, which provided an unobstructed view of the grounds. Shade trees and flowers were abundant, and the world outside the windows was a splendid wash of vibrant color.

Sophia cast an appreciative eye about her own room, which was soothing. Relaxing. The walls were white, the floors a deep cherry color; decorative accents on the walls and pillows on a window seat overlooking the back of the property provided beautiful flashes of color. Mosquito netting hung around the bed, and the white cotton bedding was offset by the same bright pillows that graced the window seat. The whole of it looked very comfortable and, though she was tired, she was determined to avoid sleeping until nightfall.

Loath as she was to admit it, she didn't want to miss a potential moment spent in Anthony's company. Perhaps if she were with him, she might divine some clue as to his reason for his abrupt departure. She desperately didn't want to believe he had left London to escape her company. Since his desertion, the fear at the back of her thoughts was that *London* wasn't smothering him, *she* was.

She made her way to a small vanity that also doubled as a writing desk and sat down. Had she known for a certainty ahead of time that Anthony was going to be here, would she have still wanted to come? As much as she desired answers, she feared them. She also felt a flash of anger that her own get-away-from-England plan was now for naught; she had wanted to leave to distract herself from memories of Anthony, which were everywhere, only to encounter the man himself a world away.

And oh—

Sophia looked at herself in the mirror and shook her head. "You are hopeless," she muttered to her reflection. He was so handsome it took her breath away. When she had climbed from the carriage and saw him standing there, she thought her heart might burst. The familiar sound of his voice had washed over her like warm rain, and it had taken true restraint to keep from launching herself at him. Whether her intention would have been to envelope him in an embrace or to pummel him, she wasn't certain.

He had been affected by her appearance; she knew it without any sense of guile or conceit. There had been a flash of something in his eyes that he had quickly masked. She was forced to admit he was good at it. Apparently he had been masking the truth for a long time. Perhaps from the very beginning.

She put her chin in her hand and tried to decide whether or not to let herself sulk. Had he ever been honest? About *anything*? She thought back to the first time they'd met. Jack had taken a nasty fall from a horse, and Anthony had been standing at Jack's bedside, elbow deep in blood-soaked towels and grim as anyone she'd ever seen. His fear for her brother's life had been genuine. That much had been true. She didn't doubt Anthony's authentic affection for Jack, and truthfully, he had said he held *her* in affection as well. Why should she punish him for her own misunderstanding? He'd never claimed to be anything more than her friend, had never even kissed her. He may have occasionally pushed the bounds of propriety but had certainly never crossed them.

She tried to believe his attention had been nothing more significant than that which he paid to other women, but he had spent nearly all of his free time with either her or with the Elliots together as a family. She closed her eyes against a sudden sting as memories flooded and threatened to swamp her: humorous observations regarding certain ridiculous members of their social set, the deep timbre of his voice spreading warmth through her limbs and igniting a slow burn in her abdomen as he murmured in her ear; the way he took her elbow as they walked, placed her hand on his arm, brushed against her at the dinner table; the light touch of his hand on her back as they left the theater or made their way through the crowds on Bond Street; the touch of his hip against hers as they rode in his phaeton through Hyde Park; the lingering manner in which he bowed over her gloved hand with the slight pressure of his fingers against hers . . .

Was it all done in the name of platonic friendship? They were small things, but between men and women in the courting stage of life, they meant much. At least, she thought they had.

Sophia shook her head and straightened in the chair, focusing on the tranquility of her bedchamber through blurred eyes. Enough, already. She had cried her tears over the Earl of Wilshire. Her pride demanded she pull herself together and lift her chin. She would not beg for a man's affections. Perhaps she might fall in love with another man someday, but she had her family, her niece, her girls' school with Ivy, and now a holiday to an exotic location—she had much for which to be grateful.

"Sophia?" Rachael stood in the doorway, her brow creased with concern. She crossed the room. "What is it?"

Sophia shrugged and turned back to the mirror on the vanity. She tried for a smile that was wobbly, at best. "Men are rather awful, are they not?"

Rachael smiled. She looked at Sophia in the mirror. "You love him still."

Sophia nodded miserably, not bothering to prevaricate or pretend she didn't understand what Rachael meant. She'd confided in her new friend during their ocean voyage and felt a sense of relief that she had someone to talk to now that she was thousands of miles away from Ivy. "He bid me good-bye as a friend. In the letter he gave me before he left."

Rachael winced.

"He so firmly placed me in that category that he couldn't have been more clear had he said straight to my face, 'I will never have a romantic interest in you.'"

Rachael let out a breath, and gave Sophia's shoulders a gentle squeeze. "You and I both know that is a lie. We are women, and we are not stupid. I took note of the way he behaved outside. Nary a glance for anyone but you."

Sophia's brows came together, and she didn't even care that it would leave a crease. "Then why did he leave me?"

Rachael's eyes narrowed, and she drummed her fingers absently on Sophia's shoulders. "There is something afoot, Sophia. I shall ferret it out of my cousin. I have methods."

Sophia's lips twitched, and she met Rachael's gaze in the mirror. "Blackmail, perchance? Secrets from childhood?"

Rachael grinned and winked. "Dylan may not be privy to all the details of Anthony's life, but whatever he *does* know, *we* shall also know before long. Sad, really, that he fancies himself so invincible."

"My lady?"

Sophia and Rachael turned at the sound of Sophia's lady's maid. "Yes, Briggs?"

"Lady Pilkington asks that you and Miss Scarsdale join her in the drawing room to meet some of the other ladies who have just returned from the bazaar."

"Please tell her we shall be there straightaway."

Rachael met Sophia's gaze squarely. "Now, then. We shall solve this mystery of the mercurial earl and discern every last one of his secrets."

Sophia laughed—how could she not? She grasped Rachael's fingers and gave them a quick squeeze. "Thank you, Rachael. How lucky I am to have found such a friend."

Rachael put her arm around Sophia as they walked to the door. "Besides, what we cannot discover by coercion, we can certainly gain by force."

Sophia choked back a laugh as they made their way to the drawing room. "You frighten me, Rachael Scarsdale. What will you do? Make use of medieval torture devices?"

"Oh, Sophia, what nonsense." They reached the drawing room and Rachael smiled. "I don't have access to any of those."

The next several hours passed fairly quickly as Sophia and Rachael met a few of Lady Pilkington's bosom friends. Some were married to military officers, while others were visiting from home. Many of the other Fleet women joined the group, and Sophia knew their names from time spent with them on the long voyage. The women were a varied collection, ranging from pretty to plain, charming to gauche, quiet to loud. In short, much like society anywhere. Many were delightful, and Sophia regretted for them the necessity of traveling across the world merely to secure a husband. Surely something must have been amiss with the men in England who overlooked them. And there were also a few girls who, like Sophia and Rachael, had wanted simply to get away, to see something beyond the borders of their own island.

When time came for an afternoon rest, Rachael asked Sophia if she would like to accompany her to the nursery. Rachael had several nieces and nephews in England and held them in the highest of affection, and she missed them terribly. Sophia felt a pang in her heart for her unmarried friend—Rachael wanted so much to have a family of her own, and as Sophia watched her interact with the guests' children, she realized Rachael was as natural with the little ones as anybody she'd ever seen.

The little master of the house, Charles Pilkington, or Charlie, quickly became Sophia's personal favorite. He was six years old but slight of stature and possessed an irrepressible smile and a quick laugh. He was charmingly articulate for one so young, and, unlike some of the other boys, he was comfortable sharing his toys and playing companionably with the other children. There was a spark in his eye, something bent on perhaps a small amount of mischief, that spoke to Sophia's spirit, and she sat near him and his *ayah*, Amala.

The nanny was nearing middle age and clearly enjoyed the delight of playing on the floor with a child. Her hair was drawn back in a long, thick black braid with a few wisps of gray at her temples. Her face was gentle; her smile easily given. She wore a traditional Indian sari, made from a beautiful combination of orange, yellow, and purple silk. Charles had called her "Amala Ayah" and the name stuck, and she laughed when Sophia said, "Amala Ayah, it is a pleasure to make your acquaintance." The woman's English was very good, and her affection for Charlie was evident.

Lady Pilkington, who had accompanied Sophia and Rachael to the nursery, espoused the virtues of having a retinue of Indian servants who were extremely devoted to the children. So devoted, in fact, that they often were lax in disciplining their charges and created little terrors who tended to "run amok."

Amala Ayah smiled, but remained silent.

"I also instruct the Indians to speak only their native tongue to Charles. I don't want him adopting the *chee-chee* accent with which they speak English."

Sophia glanced at Amala Ayah, whose expression hadn't changed. Lady Pilkington's attitude evoked a familiar emotion in Sophia—frustration. Here was another lady of the house making comments about her servants as though they were not present or were void of feeling or the finer emotions that made one a human.

One of the other toddlers playing in the nursery, Ruth, suddenly stumbled and fell, resulting in a bloody nose and much wailing. Lady Pilkington vacated the nursery immediately, murmuring something about checking on dinner preparations.

Charlie's attention riveted on the little girl with the

bloodied nose, and his face paled. Amala Ayah put an arm about his shoulders and pulled him close, whispering in his ear, followed by a gentle smile and a tap on the nose. She looked at Sophia and said, "Master Charlie does not so much like to see blood."

"Ah." Sophia smiled at him. "I do not care for the sight either, Charlie. I noticed earlier this wooden toy horse you were playing with. Will you tell me his name?" She ran her finger along the smooth edges of the horse's back. "He's a very handsome horse, to be sure. If he were mine, I should name him Lightning because I'm certain he is very fast."

Amala Ayah caught her eye and missed only a beat before nodding. "Yes, indeed. He is very fast. And while Lightning is an excellent name, this horse already has a different one. Charlie, will you tell Miss Elliot the name of your horse?"

Sophia looked at Charlie and then at the toy as though she did not mean to pressure the child to speak. When she glanced up again, Charlie met her eyes and nodded.

"His name is Chestnut," Charlie said, and Sophia shifted closer to him with the toy, effectively blocking his view of Ruth. "My father had a horse named Chestnut when he was a boy, and he gave this toy to me for my second birthday." Charlie scrunched his nose. "I do not remember, of course, because I was quite young."

"I think this is the finest toy horse I have ever seen." Sophia extended the toy to him. "Thank you so much for allowing me to hold him." She smiled gently as Charlie took it from her and cradled it close to his chest. The color slowly returned to his face, and the red splashes standing out in stark relief to the white pallor of his cheeks gradually faded into a healthy pink.

Charlie's eyes regained some of the spark and he grinned at Sophia. "Captain Miller has come to visit again, and he promises not only new stories but a toy for each of us. I hope it is a wooden cutlass. When last he visited, he said he would bring a wooden cutlass."

Amala Ayah retrieved a wet cloth that she used to gently sponge Charlie's brow. She murmured to him, the sound comforting and the bangles on her arm tinkling together quietly. Once Charlie was settled, she sent him back to play with the others.

"Is this a common occurrence?" Sophia asked Amala Ayah quietly.

"No, my lady." The nanny shook her head. "He simply cannot abide the sight of blood. Inherits it from his father, I understand."

"Well, there is certainly no shame in it." Sophia smiled again at the sight of Charlie playing with Chestnut. Her lady's maid, Briggs, appeared at the door to summon her to prepare for an early dinner to precede the costume ball. "Charlie, I should love to visit you again and see Chestnut. Would that be acceptable to you?"

The boy smiled, a small dusting of freckles stretching across his cheeks as his face brightened. "I would welcome the visit, my lady. Perhaps by then I shall have lost this tooth." He wiggled his front tooth, which was indeed loose.

Sophia ruffled his hair, her heart most effectively melted, and motioned to Rachael, who reluctantly bid a pair of young twin girls good-bye with promises to return. As Rachael left the room with Sophia, her eyes were bright and liquid. "Alice and Annie are of an exact age with my sister's children," she said. "Thank you for indulging me with the visit, Sophia. I know it is not at all the thing one does, but children are sweet, and I do adore them."

"My pleasure, truly. I confess I find myself entirely charmed by young Master Charles. What an adorable child. I know little about children, other than the bits I have observed. My own niece, Catherine, is still quite small. I suspect I shan't recognize her when I return home."

Sophia and Rachael parted ways outside the nursery, and Sophia returned to her room to change and freshen up for the early dinner. But rather than anticipating the costume ball, she felt like a schoolgirl eager for a glimpse of a handsome lord. Even in his absence, Anthony proved himself irritating.

She made her way to the drawing room, where she waited with the other ladies until, after what seemed an eternity, Lady Pilkington announced that the time to dine had arrived.

As she descended the stairs to the main floor, Sophia saw Anthony chatting with Major Stuart and Lord Pilkington. She imagined he must have felt her gaze, because he looked up and immediately found her in the group. He swallowed noticeably before managing a nod to her. Then his eyes moved past her and he smiled at the other ladies behind Sophia.

How awkward it was—knowing she held him in higher esteem than he did her. She smiled, determined to reestablish their relationship according to the boundaries he had set. They would be friends, lighthearted and fun, and if he blurred the line by standing a bit too closely or allowing his hand to linger on her back when the waltz was finished, she would admonish him that such was not appropriate for *friends.* Because in truth, it hurt too much, and if he didn't intend for a deeper level of association, she wasn't about to allow it. She didn't think her heart could manage the strain.

They entered the dining room in pairs by rank, matched with their social equals. Lady Pilkington had made matters perfectly clear from the moment Anthony arrived that formalities and rank were as strictly observed in her household in Bombay as they would be in London. Though Lady Pilkington consulted her copy of *Warrant of Precedence* religiously, as did any self-respecting British woman of important rank and status in India, she told him as an aside, she did, on occasion, mix the arrangements according to her own whim once they were actually in the dining room. It would never do to have her guests complain of dull dinner company, and as she knew quite well nearly each guest attending, she was adept at orchestrating the mix of people to the benefit of all.

Thus Anthony found himself paired with Sophia, a fact he had actually guaranteed beforehand by paying Lady Pilkington a few carefully chosen compliments and offering a single pink rose. The lady had blushed and giggled and told Anthony that she had intended to pair him with the sister of an earl anyway, of course, but a little token of affection went a long way to securing the match.

Sophia grasped his arm lightly, and he fought the urge to place his hand over her fingers. He glanced at her, wondering if she would set the tone for their evening or if he should attempt something to set her at ease. To set himself at ease. In the end, she decided the matter for him.

She gave him a smile that seemed genuine and void of her earlier discontent. "I've spent the time since your departure from London looking high and low for a friend and confidante to replace you, Lord Wilshire, and I've had a most vexing time of it. I do hope you're prepared to apologize very prettily to me."

Humor sparkled in her eyes, and he realized, his heart sinking, that she must truly believe every word he'd written to her in that awful letter. She seemed to have accepted it, to have found the wherewithal to move forward, despite what Jack had mentioned about the state of her heart. It was for the best, of course, because her safety was paramount, but Anthony had hoped, somewhere in the back of his mind, that she would come to him in fury, demand to know what he was about, why he'd left, express her hurt and dismay and anger, thereby proving that she cared for him as much as he did for her and that perhaps when he found the Janus Document they might resume their path.

He returned her smile and dredged up a show of charm, hoping it didn't sound forced. "I shall put every effort into such an apology then, my dear lady, and hope that in time you will find it in your heart to forgive me." He wanted nothing more than to take her by the hand down the hallway and into the library where they could speak alone, where he could explain.

Anthony pulled out Sophia's chair at the table and waited until the footman had seated her before taking his own seat.

Conversation buzzed around the group, which was large enough to require two tables that accommodated twenty-four people each. Usually skilled in monitoring several exchanges at once in a small crowd, Anthony found himself struggling to pay attention to anything but the woman seated next to him. Sophia said something to him, but he was at sea like a fool. Had her dark lashes always framed those tawny eyes so beautifully? Had her expressive face ever truly looked at him with joy and affection? Might he, even now, be her husband if Lord Braxton hadn't interrupted his life that fateful night and thrown his plans awry?

He blinked. "I'm sorry?"

She wrinkled her brow. "Are you feeling well, my lord?" She paused. "I asked if you have enjoyed your time in India thus far."

"Yes, very much." He scratched under his collar with one finger. "Sophia, please no 'my lording.' There was a time when I believe we considered ourselves the very best of—"

"Friends. Yes, I know." When she reached for her glass and took a swallow, her eyes narrowed. Or perhaps her expression hadn't changed, for when she looked at him again, she was all things flirtatious and light. "I suppose I shall make an exception in your case. Propriety would insist we address each other more formally, given the time that has passed since we last were together, but as Jack holds you in such high regard, I will not take you to task for using my Christian name without permission."

Blast. Was she in earnest? Were they truly reverting back to the beginning of their relationship? They had very likely had a conversation similar to this one right after Jack and

Ivy's wedding when they began to spend more time in one another's company. His frustration mounted, his anger at Braxton and the Millers reaching new heights.

He had no choice but to follow her lead. "I thank you for your permission, of course. How crass of me to have made presumptions." He managed a tight smile and a wink. *This is ridiculous.* They were speaking as strangers. The woman knew more about him, about his views on life, and his struggles as a youth with his family, than anyone alive or dead. There was nothing he hadn't shared with her except for his status as a spy during his war years. And keeping that from her had been more force of habit than anything, an instinct to protect her from the espionage and danger that had dogged his heels. He had put it behind him. It was finished.

Except now it wasn't.

Anthony stifled a sigh and leaned back slightly as the footman placed the first course before him on the table. He ran his customary glance around the room, unconsciously taking note of who was seated where, who conversed with whom, who seemed out of sorts. He looked for anyone who acted differently than they had in the short time he'd known them.

The clergyman and his wife seemed stiff, but he couldn't truly say it was an anomaly. Mr. Denney ruled his congregation and—one might assume—his family with an iron fist. Mrs. Denney was a woman of relatively few words and no strong opinions.

The First Cavalry Light Brigade was represented by its usual cast of characters, mostly favorable fellows with a few rowdies thrown into the mix. Lady Pilkington was firm about rules of conduct at the Residency. Where their military training left off, her edicts took over, and according to Dylan, there had been no incidents of note at the Pilkington mansion.

There had been a time when Anthony would have shared every detail with Sophia and solicited her opinion on the characters in play. Perhaps in the coming days or weeks, he and Sophia might find their way back to that place where they knew what the other would say, would think. And she would tease him for bothering to care about mundane details of elite social gatherings, and he wouldn't tell her that he didn't truly care, but he only wanted to hear her laugh, to listen to her talk, to gauge her assessment of people that was as good as any operative he'd ever worked with in the field. There was the ultimate irony, he supposed with a small shake of his head as he spooned the last of his soup. Sophia would have made an excellent spy.

Chapter 5

Sophia forced herself to relax her grip on the dessert spoon. She'd suffered through dinner making inane conversation with several of the people surrounding her. She longed for the days when she and Anthony would have debriefed afterward in Jack and Ivy's library over a hand of cards. They would have compared notes, made predictions, assessed people. Sophia would tell him about the young lady fresh from the country who had quietly admitted that her family despaired of her ever turning a gentleman's head, much less making a suitable match. And at the next ball, Anthony would confirm the young woman's identity with Sophia, would show an interest in the painfully shy girl, and ask her to dance. Other young men in the room would take note, would wonder what they'd missed that the dashing Earl of Wilshire clearly saw—he was known to have exacting taste in women, after all—and the awkward young debutante would suddenly find her dance card full.

It had happened on multiple occasions, and Sophia had continually been in awe of the power Anthony wielded that could turn the tide of a person's future. The first time he subtly maneuvered events to spark interest, to plant favorable impressions, or to improve the odds, Sophia had fallen a bit in love with him. And with each successive "rescue," she slipped a little bit more in love until she found so many things about his character to adore that she couldn't count them all.

And then he had left Town, said that he was restless and needed to take up again with people from his past. It hadn't made sense to her then and it still didn't. Something was amiss, and she wondered yet again what had caused Anthony to throw their whole world into disarray the way one might overturn a chessboard.

Somewhere in the course of seating her guests, Lady Pilkington had taken liberties with social status because Mr. Gerald, a professor at the newly founded English university in Bombay, was seated across from Sophia despite his lower rank. He conversed easily with a matron, Lady Finch, on his right and Rachael Scarsdale on his left. He had engaged Sophia's attention politely throughout the course of the meal and seemed pleasant. He was the son of an Indian mother and a British father, a tea planter who had made his fortune providing England's drawing rooms with delightful oolong. The handsome professor had a thick head of black hair and deep blue eyes. Why couldn't she fall in love with someone like him? She highly doubted he would ever form a close and tender attachment with a woman and then bolt for the Continent.

"Mr. Gerald," she asked during a lull in conversation as the guests enjoyed dessert, "what works of literature do you most enjoy teaching?"

"Hmm," the professor replied as he finished chewing. "I

suppose I favor Shakespeare's comedies, but I confess a scandalous preference for Chaucer."

Lady Finch gasped.

Mr. Gerald placed a supplicating hand over his heart. "My apologies, of course." He did not look at all apologetic. "But when one spends one's energy in dusty tomes day after day, one must search for spots of delight, yes?" His smile eventually won the woman over, and she shook a finger at him in remonstration that was clearly all for show.

"Only because your manners are beyond reproach, professor, do I forgive you for discussing such shocking reading preferences."

"Have you read Chaucer, my lady?"

Her eyes widened. "Certainly not!"

"But you are familiar with the content?"

"Well," the older woman hedged, "my late husband, Lord Finch, spoke of reading *The Canterbury Tales* at school, and he emphatically stated it is material unfit for a lady's gentler sensibilities."

Sophia poked at her dessert and refrained from comment. Her father had died when she had been an infant and Jack had gone to sea shortly afterward. Her mother had worked as a seamstress all hours of the day and most of the night but she had taught Sophia the basics of reading before leaving her to her own devices. Without a consistent male figure in her life to dictate what she could and couldn't read or do, Sophia read everything she could find, whether from a lending library or discard piles at local charities.

There were times Sophia felt the need to defend a woman's right to learn. And then there were times when she hadn't the energy. If she weren't feeling so emotionally drained from *not* acknowledging the imposing physical presence of the man seated to her right, she might have taken a small amount of delight in suggesting she would be happy to offer a summary of Chaucer's finest. Since Lady Finch hadn't read him, of course.

"I detect a glimmer of something, Miss Elliot," Professor Gerald said, and she heard the smile in his voice.

She looked up from her dessert, realizing her mouth was turned in the ghost of a smile so something of her thoughts must have been visible on her face.

"Perhaps you are a woman who has read extensively of fine English literature?" Mr. Gerald held up a palm. "And please, do not suppose I suggest it to cause embarrassment. My sisters who live in England read and write exhaustively. I believe current education opportunities for females are sadly lacking."

She heard Anthony mutter something that sounded suspiciously like, "Of course you do."

Sophia raised a brow and smiled at the professor. "I daresay that is the most refreshing thing I've heard all day. My sister-in-law, Lady Stansworth, and I own and operate a school for indigent females. We train them to be ladies' maids and governesses, and we are working to expand the teaching curriculum to include more extensive mathematics and sciences."

Lady Finch made a sound of censure under her breath.

"We find our ambitions opposed from certain corners, of course." Sophia smiled.

The professor's lips twitched, but he remained admirably diplomatic. "And yet the fight must continue. I laud your efforts." He tipped his head to her in salute.

Sophia also inclined her head. The movement to her

right was subtle, but she sensed Anthony leaning infinitesimally closer to her side. She felt the warmth of his arm as his sleeve brushed against her.

"The school is indeed a godsend for many young women," Anthony said. "I look forward to witnessing its growth upon my return to London."

Sophia turned to Anthony, her eyes widening slightly. "You do intend to return, my lord? Well, this is news indeed!"

Anthony's nostrils flared slightly, and someone who hadn't spent such copious amounts of time studying his face might have missed the subtle expression. "Of course it was always my intention to return, my lady."

"Yes. To accept the duties and responsibilities of your title."

"Quite so."

"How long will you be staying in India, then?"

One corner of his mouth quirked. "Are you hoping I'll leave soon, or hoping I'll remain longer?"

She shrugged. "Oh, I haven't a preference one way or the other. But your absence from the House of Lords has been noted. And I'm certain your steward wonders if responsibility for your estates and tenants will be his into the eternities."

Anthony leaned an elbow on the table and turned fully to her. "I have kept in constant contact with my steward, and he is well aware of my imminent return."

Lady Finch tutted from across the table. "Young lady, you presume to lecture his lordship, as though you have a right to do so? Perhaps you misunderstand your role in society."

"Oh, it is no impertinence on my part, I assure you! Lord Wilshire and I are the dearest of friends, you see. He is rather like my own brother. We are truly family."

Sophia thought she heard Anthony grinding his teeth, but she wasn't certain.

"Oh, is that so?" Professor Gerald looked from Sophia to Anthony and back again. "Well, what a delightful association! I know I find great joy in my friendship with my sisters. There is something special about a bond between siblings. Isn't it interesting that such bonds are not always defined by blood?"

"Fascinating." Anthony regarded the man, unsmiling, and Sophia realized Lord Wilshire had dropped any pretense of charm or finesse.

Sophia tilted her head and took in the nonverbal aggression of Anthony's posture; his body was still turned fully toward her and their chairs were completely flush. She laid her fingers on Anthony's arm and turned to Mr. Gerald. "I know I count myself as the most fortunate of women to have two such wonderful brothers to look after my interests. And if that relationship lends itself to familiarity on my part with Lord Wilshire, well, he appreciates my counsel on his duties as the steward of one of England's oldest earldoms." She patted Anthony's arm. "Is that not right, dear friend?"

Anthony's eyes narrowed fractionally. She felt a thrill course through her limbs and caught her breath. He was irritated. Well, let him be. He had made this friendship bed, and now he could lie down in it.

"I heed your counsel above all others, Miss Sophia." He smiled but it looked grim. "And without a doubt, I have been away from London far too long."

Chapter 6

Two hours after dinner, Anthony stood in the Residency ballroom wearing a black mask he desperately wished he could remove. His vision was inhibited by the thing, and he wanted to spot Sophia as soon as she made an entrance. He had no idea which persona she would don, but he had it on good authority that Lady Pilkington had an entire room dedicated to nothing but ball gowns and costumes of all shapes and sizes. Sophia and the other Fleet ladies would be well accommodated.

Dylan Stuart had helped Anthony pull an ensemble together. His mask complemented not only the cape he wore, but his trousers, shirt, and waistcoat, all of which were black. He was a highwayman, and while it was not the most original of disguises, he was grateful for even that much. He didn't care for costume parties, but he needed to attend to flirt with the young ladies in order to preserve his cover. He hoped, though, that he might also observe Captain Miller, should the man make an appearance. He had been frustratingly elusive, but during the after-dinner port and cigars, Lord

Pilkington had confirmed the man would be in attendance at the ball.

"You do make a convincing highwayman, what with the scowl and all." Dylan grinned and saluted Anthony with a glass of punch from the refreshment table.

Anthony shot him a glance and turned his attention back to the crowd, which grew in number with each passing minute. "My attention is divided," he muttered. "I now watch for two people as opposed to just one."

"I should be happy to keep watch for the prettier of those two."

Anthony flared his nostrils as he gave his friend the benefit of his full regard. Dylan was dressed as a handsome prince from a young girl's storybook. "Tread wisely, my friend, or I shall be forced to describe to the young ladies the true nature of the Brothers Grimm and their fairy tales. The reality is rather grizzly."

Dylan blinded him with a dazzling smile. "You will do no such thing. You are too much of a gentleman to sully a party with such unpleasantries."

"Have you not heard?" Anthony looked again toward the ballroom's entrance. "I am all things licentious and debauched." A flock of brightly dressed women strolled past, and Anthony smiled at each for a moment. He was already exhausted from maintaining the façade, and the evening had just begun.

Dylan snorted. "That anyone who knows you might actually believe such a thing is something I cannot quite make sense of. Never could."

Anthony lifted a shoulder. "People see what they expect

to see. Most are easily led by rumors." He scanned the crowd from left to right, hoping to locate the burly sea captain. His nerves were taut. "Provided the captain does make a showing here," he said quietly to Dylan, "it may be our one opportunity to search his cabin. Do you know how many will guard the ship tonight?"

"No fewer than four, according to my sources." Dylan shook his head. "I do not see a way around discovery. When was the last time you snuck aboard a guarded ship and broke into a captain's cabin undetected?"

He was correct, of course, and it did Anthony no good at all. Sooner rather than later, he would be forced to admit the true nature of his mission to the captain and demand answers regarding the late Harold Miller's belongings. The ship was scheduled to leave port in three days. The window for discovering whatever the captain may know about the Janus Document was quickly closing.

A series of feminine gasps and laughter drew his attention to the entrance and he blinked. Sophia stood there looking trim and petite in a blue soldier's uniform, down to the last button and meticulously shined boots. And breeches. She could have passed for one of Major Stuart's men if . . . well . . . she were a man.

Her honey-colored hair hung in a long braid over one shoulder, tied at the end with a frothy blue bow that stood in direct contrast to the masculine attire. When Anthony finally drew a breath, it escaped again on a laugh.

Dylan whistled. "I don't know that I've ever seen a woman in military garb. Leave it to your unconventional friend to imagine the impossible."

And unconventional it was. The uniform fit her body like a glove, accentuating rather than hiding her feminine form. Whispers spread around the room, accompanied by exclamations of surprise and laughter, and finally a smattering of applause. Sophia curtseyed as beautifully as any well-bred lady, which brought another round of laughter and hoots of approval.

Anthony's gaze swept the room again, noting the fact that nearly every male eye was glued appreciatively to Miss Elliot. "It isn't as though a woman has never worn a man's attire to a costume party before," he muttered under his breath.

"Ah, but how many of them looked like *that*, old boy?" Dylan placed his empty glass on the tray of a passing waiter and grinned at Anthony. "I can honestly say that before this evening, I have never wanted to dance with a fellow soldier. I haven't seen Cousin Rachael yet, so I shall I offer my services to keep the young lady occupied while you search for the other object of our interest."

Anthony narrowed his eyes. "You were supposed to help me with that, too."

"Oh, I shall. There is much to be observed from the dance floor."

Anthony had to admit a grudging respect for his friend's abilities, which had always proven effective. Dylan would be able to dance with the most beautiful woman in the room and still gather intelligence necessary to the investigation. That he looked every inch the handsome prince rather than the second son of a baron who had volunteered for the military merely spread the icing on the proverbial cake.

Anthony watched as Dylan worked through the crowd,

subtly, neatly, almost invisibly reaching Sophia's side and effectively nudging all others out of his way without seeming to have done a thing. He grinned and bowed to Sophia, saluted her, and made a comment that caused her to laugh. He offered his hand, which she took, and walked with her to the middle of the floor.

Anthony noted that the couple claimed the attention of most of the guests, which gave him better access to make his way around the room and search closely for the sea captain, who could be disguised as just about anyone. He glanced at Sophia and Dylan, trying and failing to muscle his jealousy into submission as they made their way through the steps of the quadrille. At least it wasn't a waltz.

Lord Pilkington nodded as Anthony approached. He was dressed as Caesar, which made sense, as Lady Pilkington was attired as Pompeia. Anthony could only assume theirs was a salute to the happy couple's beginnings, before Caesar had decided his wife must be above reproach.

"Lord Wilshire! A highwayman, I see?" Pilkington waved a staff in Anthony's general direction, only to entangle it in the folds of his white toga.

Anthony's lips twitched. "Indeed. And a fine Roman you are, Pilkington."

Pilkington moved closer and spoke in an aside, "Must please the wife, you know. I never question her directives at these things. She does host quite the most popular parties."

"Of course." Anthony paused. "You did say you expect Captain Miller to make an appearance this evening? I've promised to pass along felicitations from one of his former sailors."

Pilkington's brow creased. "He committed to attend, but I've yet to see him. I do hope he hasn't left the Residency so soon. He quite entertains the children with stories of his adventures, and I do not believe he has done so, yet. My own son looks forward to Miller's visits with much anticipation. I often sit in on his storytelling, as well. Must keep a finger on the pulse of the happenings in my home, of course."

"Most assuredly." Anthony struggled to keep the smile from his face as he pictured Pilkington sitting on the floor next to his son and the other British children, paying rapt attention to the merchant captain's tales of piracy and derring-do on the high seas.

Pilkington's features brightened. "Ah, but he cannot have already left—not two days ago he asked if he might store a packet of papers in the safe in my study and he has yet to retrieve it."

Anthony's heart skipped a beat. "Must have been something quite valuable to not simply have left it locked aboard ship."

Pilkington shrugged. "I suppose so." He accepted a glass of champagne from a footman. "Lady Pilkington quite likes this stuff. I'd much prefer a stiff whiskey myself, eh, Wilshire?" Pilkington nudged Anthony, who managed a murmured assent as he cast an eye about the perimeter of the room.

"Oh, drat, not that one." Pilkington edged slowly backward and tossed the champagne down his throat in one long swallow. "Clergyman Denney. I presume we shall hear quite a fiery lecture this Sunday on the evils of drink."

Anthony looked in the direction of Pilkington's nod and

saw Mr. and Mrs. Denney, dressed as a cardinal and a nun. Anthony tipped his head in question. "They are not Catholic, are they?"

Pilkington shook his head and looked for a place to set his empty champagne glass. "No, however this marks the third costume ball they've arrived thusly attired." Pilkington finally tucked his empty glass in the pot of a large plant nearby. "But what is a costume party if not to be splendid for the evening?"

Or perhaps the man fancied himself a religious icon. Anthony turned his attention from the clergyman to the couples on the floor. A number of young women attempted to catch his eye, and for once he was grateful for the mask he wore. It allowed him to focus on Sophia without anyone taking note of his interest. Sophia—in pants—was making her way through the last of the set with Dylan. It was all his layers of clothing, Anthony supposed, that accounted for his sudden rise in temperature. The highwayman cape was heavier than it looked and trapped in his body heat.

Pilkington muttered something under his breath as the clergyman and his wife approached, but managed a smile and a bow when the cardinal and nun joined them.

"Splendid gathering, as always, Pilkington." Mr. Denney gestured to the crowd as though offering benediction.

"My thanks, Your Eminence, and I shall pass your compliments on to my wife. And might I also remark upon your costumes! Mrs. Denney, again you make a very lovely nun."

Mrs. Denney smiled and managed a "Thank you" before glancing at her husband and falling silent.

"And your daughters, Mrs. Denney?" Anthony asked. "Surely they are also here?"

She nodded, genuine happiness crossing her features. "They've spoken of nothing else for days, now. Beatrice is dressed as the Mona Lisa, and Charity is a princess."

"Is she now? Well, it so happens I know of a handsome prince in attendance. I shall introduce them." He smiled at the woman.

"Needn't bother." Mr. Denney frowned. "They're going home to London to find husbands next Season."

The light expression fell from his wife's face, and she was silent. Anthony glanced at the clergyman and forced his expression into neutrality. Mr. Denney was much in spirit like Anthony's father had been.

Pilkington cleared his throat. "Of course, Denney, of course. But certainly it can't hurt the girls to enjoy some association with other youngsters until they leave."

Denney's answer was a noncommittal grunt, but he refrained from further rebuke. Instead, he turned his attention fully on Pilkington. "I do notice a fair amount of spirits circulating, my lord. I would assume you are keeping close watch on your guests? Nothing good comes from inebriation."

"Most assuredly." Pilkington nodded. "Which is why Lady Pilkington has also provided fruit punch at the refreshment table."

Anthony gave Lord Pilkington a head bow and excused himself from the conversation, breathing a sigh of relief as he moved away, hoping to intercept Sophia as the set finished. His reprieve was short-lived, however, as he was waylaid by four corporals dressed as a shepherdess and three sheep. He found it oddly fitting.

"Corporal Mailor." He managed a bow for the shepherdess.

"I said you would be recognized straightaway, Mailor!" said one of the sheep as the other two guffawed.

"And Corporal Larson. What a delightful ewe you make." Anthony smiled at the young man as his fellow flock elbowed and laughed.

Mailor, who had flushed at his friends' laughter, now joined in. "Stowcroft and Carlton wanted to be pirates, but I convinced 'em to try something new."

"You certainly managed that." Anthony glanced past the four young men and caught glimpses of Sophia's blue uniform as Dylan escorted her from the floor.

"Not as unique as he might have thought!" Corporal Carlton also watched Sophia's movements. "Seems you weren't the only one to try something new, Mailor. And might I add, the lady looks much better as a soldier than you do as a shepherdess."

The three sheep and the shepherdess turned as one toward Sophia, and Anthony scowled at the lot. One of the sheep whispered something to the others, and Anthony was fairly certain the boy should have his ears boxed. He couldn't be sure, though, and he wasn't about to ask the lad to repeat himself, so with a brief eye roll, he left them and headed for Sophia.

Chapter 7

Sophia caught her breath as the highwayman made his way through the crowd. She would know him anywhere, in any disguise. His fluid movement was graceful and athletic, not a gesture wasted, his focus complete. It was centered completely on her, and for a moment she forgot everyone else in the room. Rachael had just entered, dressed as Joan of Arc, and Sophia had intended to join her at the refreshment table. Instead, she stood rooted to the spot.

"My dear Miss Elliot, what a dashing figure you cut." Anthony smiled and bowed over her fingers, his eyes very green against the black of his mask.

"I must return the compliment. You must be the world's most handsome highwayman." Sophia heard the breathless tone of her voice and mentally chastised herself.

"Might I interest you in a turn about the room?"

"I should be delighted." *Friends, friends . . . friendship is fun.*

She placed her hand in the crook of his arm, and he bent his head to comment on the ballroom's elaborate décor, which resembled the Roman Colosseum. That voice, his very scent. She closed her eyes for the briefest of moments and felt as though she had truly come home.

"It is most creative," she managed to respond. "Have you seen our hostess?"

"Yes, indeed, and she is a resplendent Pompeia."

"And most assuredly above reproach." She smiled at her sponsor, who held court among her guests as though born to it.

As they neared the refreshment table, Sophia noted a man lavishly attired as a maharaja, his clothing a blending of purple, orange, and blue silks. "Who is he?"

"That is the prince's cousin, Taj Darzi. He is soon to ascend the throne, as his cousin, Prince Ekavir, is reportedly gravely ill. Lord Pilkington speaks highly of Darzi and says his approach to relations with the British is one of cooperation with an eye to future success."

Sophia studied the man in question as he accepted a pastry from Lady Pilkington, who was all smiles. He was much younger than Sophia had thought at first glance. "Suddenly the chatter begins to make sense."

"Which chatter is that?"

"The women of the Fleet have been exchanging gossip with the ladies of the Residency. It seems the prince's cousin is quite the catch, but has yet to show preference for any one woman despite his frequent visits both here and at other British enclaves. Rumor has it he would prefer a British wife to further Anglo-Indian relations, but it could prove problematic."

Anthony nodded. "Their offspring would face resistance

from either culture. I suspect Professor Gerald may have felt some of the sting. Though Mr. Darzi and his potential bride may have an easier go of it than some, as Mr. Darzi will soon be royalty."

Sophia frowned. "Rather unfair. People are often cruel." She looked at Mr. Darzi with a woman's discerning eye and found him very pleasing in form and aspect. Tall and handsome, with strong features and both wealth and influence to aid his cause. He would likely have his choice of brides and she said so to Anthony.

"Would you number yourself among those vying for the title of princess?"

Sophia looked at Anthony, wondering if there was something in his face that would mirror the slight edge to the tone she thought she'd heard. The corner of his mouth quirked up in a smile, and she dismissed the notion that she might have heard jealousy in his voice.

"I just might. Imagine that—Sophia Elliot, former lady's maid, becomes a princess."

"You hardly need the formal title to put a name to what the rest of us already know, Princess Sophia. You are everything that is regal and fine."

"Ah, yes. Spoken like the 'elder brother' that you are. One could accuse you of partiality."

"One could. But one would be wrong. Come, I'll introduce you to Mr. Darzi."

The prince turned at Anthony's greeting and smiled as Sophia was formally presented to him. "A pleasure, Miss Elliot! And I must add that your costume for the ball this evening is most original." He gestured to himself and two companions. "I fear we are not nearly so. We wear the region's traditional dress—much more intricate than our usual attire—yet I have been contemplating something more exciting for Lady Pilkington's next costume ball."

Sophia smiled. "And will you share your ideas, sir?"

"Ah, but I mustn't." He glanced conspiratorially to one side. "I should hate to be overheard and find my costume duplicated." He paused, and then offered a sheepish grin. "Truthfully, I cannot conjure a single original idea."

Sophia laughed. "Might I suggest Lady Pilkington's costume collection? It is vast and exceedingly clever."

Major Stuart quietly approached Anthony and apologized for interrupting, then pulled him aside.

The prince turned at a nudge from one of the men standing at his side. "Miss Elliot, allow me to introduce my two companions, Dhruve Sai and Eshan Verma. They shadow me endlessly, rarely allow me a moment's peace."

The men chuckled, and Sophia curtseyed, offering her hand to both men.

"He is the cousin of a prince and seeks constantly to distract his friends who would protect him." Mr. Sai was both taller and heavier than Mr. Darzi by a significant amount, and he eyed Mr. Darzi with what seemed to be good humor. There was an easy familiarity about the three men that spoke of comfortable friendship, although Mr. Sai and Mr. Verma were clearly tasked with the prince's safety.

Mr. Verma was the shortest of the three, but there was a lean stockiness to his build that suggested he knew his way around the business end of a scuffle. She spied a slight irregularity at the men's waistbands beneath their lavish silk tunics. Guns, most likely. At least a sharp knife or two.

Sophia chatted with the trio a moment longer, fascinated at the men's excellent English and polished skills. Given the attitudes of many British women she'd met thus far, she'd expected their behavior and manners would be lacking. The theory prevalent among the Europeans seemed to suggest that Indians were rather childlike in their intellectual capabilities, and as non-Christians, certainly lacking in knowledge of a proper deity and the social mores that accompanied it. And yet Sophia realized quickly that Taj Darzi could hold his own in any ballroom or dining room or gentlemen's club in London.

The crowded ballroom seemed to have a life of its own, breathing with the swell of people and growing stuffier by the minute. Sophia considered shocking the attendees all the more by removing the heavy jacket she wore and simply walking about in her shirtsleeves. She was prepared to make a polite escape onto the verandah when she noticed Mr. Darzi's attention fixed on somebody else in the room. Curious, she followed his gaze but could see only throngs of people dressed as sheep, circus animals, Greek gods, and clergy. Try as she might, she was unable to discern the person or group that held his attention so steadfastly.

A man wearing a Bengal tiger mask approached Mr. Darzi and patted his shoulder with a large paw, asking after his cousin, the prince.

"If you'll excuse me," Sophia murmured to Mr. Sai and Mr. Verma, who both nodded with a bow, their attention focused on the man in the tiger costume. By Sophia's best guess, the tiger had already helped himself to a fair amount of the Pilkington's champagne, and the prince's two protectors shifted subtly, more aware and alert.

As the musicians started up again, she made her way to the wide double doors that led onto the verandah. The air was significantly cooler there, and while many people took advantage of the space, their numbers paled in comparison to the crush inside.

Sophia wandered to the edge of the verandah, which was in essence a balcony screened to keep out bugs and pests. She looked through the netting and took a deep breath, daring to unbutton her topmost button on the uniform jacket. The breeze was light, and cool against her neck. She closed her eyes and took a deep breath, inhaling myriad scents that blended together—flowers and foliage, spices from the kitchens—and notably absent were the combined scents of overpowering perfume and body odor that invariably found their way into any public gathering within an enclosed space.

She found the breeches extremely comfortable and wished for all she was worth that women's fashion would change overnight so that, come morning, she could don the ensemble again without raising so much as an eyebrow. The ease of movement when not encumbered by yards of material was astounding. When she had seen the outfit in Lady Pilkington's costume room, she had grabbed it but wondered if her sponsor might take issue with her choice. On the contrary, Lady Pilkington clapped her hands in delight and helped her locate boots and a small shirtwaist.

Someone joined her at the railing, and she turned to see Rachael Scarsdale in her Joan of Arc ensemble. "Do you also require a breath of fresh air?" Sophia asked her friend with a smile.

"Do I ever! Mercy, but it grows warm in there. I just danced with Dylan and wondered if I might faint before the thing was through."

Sophia laughed. "Your cousin is a good man. He is very kind."

Rachael eyed her speculatively. "Do I detect a note of interest? I do not mind admitting that I would be thrilled if such were the case. While cousins do often marry, Dylan and I have ever been as siblings, nothing more."

Sophia released a light sigh and looked through the screen netting at the dark world beyond the verandah. "I would love nothing more than to admit such is the case, but I find my heart still in a state of befuddlement."

Rachael patted her hand. "Fret not, my friend. The befuddlement will come to an end before you realize it and your heart will be unencumbered."

Sophia looked at her dubiously. "I should think you must be very much mistaken, but I know you are nothing if not practical and intelligent. I will believe it because you say it."

"Do you feel sufficiently refreshed to jump back into the fray?" Rachael motioned to the ballroom behind them.

Sophia smiled. "Indeed. And if I should faint from excessive heat, perhaps someone wonderful will sweep me off my feet."

"Literally, if you've fainted!" Rachael laughed, and Sophia couldn't help but join in. Rachael did not speak in great detail about her life in England, but her sense of optimism and amusement with society made for pleasant, diverting company.

Once back in the throng, Sophia and Rachael were besieged by a horde of gentlemen who wished most ardently to quench their thirst with drinks or to secure a dance. Strains of a waltz drifted through the room, and Rachael allowed herself to be escorted to the dance floor. Just as Sophia had decided to do the same, Anthony appeared at her side.

"If I might have the honor?" He held out his hand.

Chapter 8

"Hey, now," a gentleman interrupted. "The lady was set to dance with me!"

Anthony looked the man—who was dressed as Humpty Dumpty—up and down before turning back to Sophia with one brow raised.

"I would love to dance the *next* set with you, Mr. Dumpty." Sophia smiled at him, and he nodded somewhat irritably. Anthony didn't spare the other man a glance as he grasped Sophia's fingers and escorted her to the edge of the dancing couples. He placed his hand high on her back as she stepped into his arms.

He swept her into the swirling mass of couples, and she suppressed a sigh of contentment. He maintained a very respectable distance between the two of them, which was in marked contrast to the last time they had danced the waltz together nearly two years ago. He had held her much more closely, then, more familiarly.

"You disappeared. I was beginning to wonder if you'd left the party for the night."

"I needed some fresh air." She paused. "Are you looking for someone?"

Anthony's eyes were scanning the ballroom just beyond her head, but at her question, he snapped his attention to her face. "No. Well, yes."

"Oh?"

"There is a sea captain who frequents the Residency when he is in town, and I must extend felicitations from a former colleague. Major Stuart told me he saw the seaman not twenty minutes ago, though I cannot seem to locate him."

Sophia wrinkled her brow. "These must be crucial felicitations indeed, if you are so determined to find him."

"Yes, I . . . yes."

Sophia cocked her head as he turned them smartly away from another spinning couple. Something in his demeanor was off. "You're flustered."

He glanced at her in surprise. "I am not."

"Why must you find this man? Truthfully, this time."

"Too perceptive by half," he muttered.

"Perhaps you seek to avoid him? Does he have a sister who is an opera singer or actress, by chance?"

His eyelids lowered, and he shot her a flat look. "You should not believe everything you hear, Miss Elliot, and no, I am not avoiding him. I am not at liberty to explain, but it is important I locate him."

"Secrets, hmm? Very well, tell me what costume he wears, and I will help you look."

"Stuart tells me Captain Miller is dressed as a court jester. And the man is not small in stature. He ought to be spotted easily enough."

"A court jester . . ." Sophia looked at the groups of people standing against the walls and in the corners as Anthony continued to guide them smoothly around the room, but she couldn't find much interest in locating a court jester when she was finally dancing with Anthony Blake again. She was aware of everything about him and could focus on little else. That he was distracted and searching for a random stranger began to grate on her nerves.

Movement at the ballroom's double doors caught Sophia's eye, and she nodded toward Major Stuart, who clearly sought Anthony's attention. "I believe your friend needs you."

Anthony turned her so he faced the doors. She felt him tense and miss his footing ever so slightly, and that small error, while not noticeable to most, told Sophia all she needed to know. Anthony was extremely invested in finding the sea-captain-turned-court-jester, and she wondered if he would be so gauche as to leave her in the middle of the waltz. Surely not. It would be a stain upon her character, rather like delivering her the cut direct.

To his credit and her relief, he finished the last two minutes of the dance, and while he tried to redirect the conversation, he was clearly distracted. Once the music came to an end, he led her from the floor, bowed, begged her to excuse him, and left the room with Dylan Stuart.

Sophia stared at the doors, baffled beyond words and too curious by that point to be insulted. Mr. Humpty Dumpty approached her for the next dance, but she claimed a sudden headache, managed to make an apology, and beat a hasty path to the door before she could be besieged by any other well-meaning gentlemen. The hallway outside the ballroom was frustratingly full of people. If nothing else came from the evening, Lady Pilkington had solidified her role as the Most Successful Hostess in the Entire British Empire.

Sophia moved further down the hallway, peering through open doors into rooms that were available for guests to mingle. Anthony was not in the library, the billiard room, or the lounge where gentlemen enjoyed a glass of spirits and conversation about their impressive selves.

She made her way to the front foyer and large atrium that boasted a high domed ceiling, a multitude of plant life, and several benches for conversation. Where on earth could he have gone? She knew by now that he sought to reclaim her good opinion of him, though dancing with her in such an abrupt and distracted manner would not further his cause. Something about the mysterious sea captain must be of greater importance to Anthony than he'd admitted.

She frowned and put her hands on her hips, deep in thought as she wandered from the atrium to the front hall. She crossed the hall to the wing of rooms on the other side of the ballroom. A few doors were open, but most were closed, and she didn't see a highwayman or a handsome prince anywhere.

She traveled the length of a darkened hallway—the sconces had been extinguished—her attention drawn to a pool of light that spilled from a room several doors down. As she neared the room, she heard agitated exclamations that were quickly shushed. She reached the room but hid just outside and peeked around the doorframe, hoping the occupants wouldn't notice her.

The room was a study, classically and definitively masculine in décor. A large mahogany desk acted as the room's focal point, with a comfortable seating arrangement next to an impressive marble hearth. A large window overlooked the darkened exterior of the side yard. Bookcases lined one wall, and the whole of it was anchored with a thick Turkish rug that was a light tan in color.

Stately though the space was, there was clear evidence of a disturbance. A large lamp had fallen to the floor, broken, and spilled its kerosene. An errant match would see the room in flames instantly. Several small pieces of statuary littered the hearth, as though someone had come along and swept aside the mantel's adornments. A painting hung crookedly on the wall above the mantel, exposing a safe that stood wide open with several objects inside. One of the chairs in the seating arrangement had been overturned, and there was no mistaking a large, garishly dark stain on the rug near the desk—evidence of significant blood loss.

Lady Pilkington stood near her husband, wringing her hands, her face ashen. Anthony placed a hand at her elbow. "My lady, allow Major Stuart and me to search out details concerning this. You've a house bursting at the seams with guests, and we should hate for your costume ball to be remembered with sensational gossip."

Lady Pilkington put a hand to her midsection and nodded. She glanced at her husband, who was as white as the fabric of his costume. He stared at the dark stain on the rug, one hand at the back of his neck, clearly dazed.

"George," Lady Pilkington said, "I believe you should accompany me. It won't do to have such scandal attached to our name or the Residency."

"Quite so," he mumbled.

"Sir," Stuart said to Pilkington, "I shall notify my superiors immediately that we have a situation likely involving foul play. Many officers in the unit are currently involved in diplomatic affairs with the prince; I suspect they may instruct me to lead an investigation into this matter. I shall, of course, be discreet."

"Yes, I do appreciate that."

"Before you return to your guests, can you tell me if you note anything missing?"

Pilkington ran a hand through his thinning hair. "The safe is open, of course, though Captain Miller's packet of papers seems to be the only thing missing. My other valuables are all accounted for."

As Pilkington closed the safe and spun the combination feature, Sophia leaned closer to hear Anthony's quiet question. "Could Miller have simply retrieved the packet of papers? Did he know the combination to the safe?"

Pilkington shook his head. "I am the only one who knows the combination. But more to the point—where is Miller?"

"I saw him arrive roughly an hour ago," Dylan said. "Before I knew it, he had slipped through the crowd and I lost sight of him. That was when I pulled Lord Wilshire from the ballroom, and then, of course, Lady Pilkington directed us here to you."

Lord Pilkington's eyes were clouded with confusion. "Miller told me he had a party interested in some documents, asked if I'd meet him here to open the safe. I was delayed by several minutes, and when I finally arrived, the safe was wide open, the furniture knocked askew, and there was *that.*" He gestured to the stain on the rug.

Anthony nodded. "The fact that only his packet is missing suggests either he took it himself or he met someone here, and that person now has it. Whether or not the meeting began cordially is of no consequence, given that there are clear signs of a struggle."

Lady Pilkington shuddered. She produced a handkerchief and dabbed at her eyes. "Please, Major," she implored, looking at Stuart, "you mustn't allow news of this unpleasantness to become common knowledge. Lord Pilkington's reputation must remain above reproach. He . . . we . . ." Her voice trembled.

"I shall be the soul of discretion," Major Stuart said. "But, my lady, clearly someone was badly wounded in this room tonight, perhaps even murdered. I shall do all in my power to keep the Residency from being cast in an unfavorable light, but we must consider the fact that either someone attending the party had issue with Captain Miller and wanted the documents he possessed, or Miller himself was the perpetrator and fought someone, ending the altercation with what looks to be an enormous amount of blood loss." Stuart glanced at Anthony. "We must locate Miller."

Anthony nodded, his expression tight.

"You would help Major Stuart investigate?" Lady Pilkington looked at Anthony as if she were a lost child. "You're a good sort, Lord Wilshire, and I do feel infinitely reassured by that."

His face softened, and he again took the lady by the elbow. "We shall solve this mystery, never you fear."

Lord and Lady Pilkington headed for the door, and Sophia flattened herself against the wall, hoping she might go unnoticed in the dark hallway, that the dark blue of her uniform costume would blend in. The Pilkingtons walked past her, unseeing, and Sophia held her breath until they turned the corner and disappeared from her view.

"You may as well come out now, Sophia," came the dry comment from the doorway.

She turned to see Anthony watching her with a half-smile.

"When did you see me?" She was rather disgruntled; she thought she'd been very stealthy.

"The moment you spied around the corner." He gestured toward the room with his head, and she followed him into the study.

Stuart's expression registered surprise. "Miss Elliot?" He looked at Anthony in question.

Sophia waved a hand at them. "You needn't worry—I shan't tell tales of your espionage. I simply wondered why Anthony was so preoccupied while we danced, so I tracked him here."

Stuart squatted to examine the Turkish rug; he touched his finger to the edge of the garishly dark red stain. "Drying around the edges," he said. "This probably happened just after I spotted Miller the first time and then lost him."

Anthony frowned. "Given the time frame, I'm not certain I remember who was in the ballroom."

"The crowds are in constant flux," Sophia said. "People are shifting between the ballroom and the verandah, and I also saw several people in the library and lounge."

Anthony nodded. "And we do not even know for certain that whomever scuffled in here were official party attendees. It could have been someone else Miller knew, someone who had nothing to do with the party."

Stuart stood. "We must assume that one of the people was Captain Miller. It is his packet of documents that is missing from the safe, and now the man himself has disappeared."

"We also might assume that if Miller wasn't the victim here, whomever bled on this rug will have family or associates who will soon report him missing."

"Or her," Sophia put in. "It could have been a woman who fought with him."

The two men nodded, Stuart with apparent respect. "Very foolhardy of me to not have considered the things a woman would notice."

"She is observant—sometimes uncomfortably so." Anthony smiled, rueful.

"Gentlemen," Sophia said, clasping her hands. "My curiosity knows no bounds. If I may, what is the nature of this business with Captain Miller?"

The two men exchanged a glance, and Stuart circled the desk near the blood puddle, examining the floor as he walked. As evasions went, it was well-executed. Sophia turned her attention to Anthony.

"He is Jack's former sea captain, Sophia. His ship was the *Firefly*."

Sophia blinked. She didn't remember Jack sailing on any ship by that name. What was Anthony not telling her? "So you were passing along Jack's well wishes?" she asked carefully.

Anthony gave the barest hesitation, then nodded, his eyes and expression giving nothing away.

"You certainly are devoted. Given your distracted manner earlier in the ballroom, it seemed that your intent in locating the man involved more than a mere exchange of felicitations on behalf of a former first mate."

Anthony ran a hand through his hair and briefly closed his eyes. "Sophia, I—"

She held up her hand. "Clearly there is more at work here than you wish to discuss with me. Do remember, however," she said, looking at Major Stuart, who regarded her with the same calm, careful manner as Anthony, "that there are places a woman can access that a man cannot. Should you find yourself in need of an additional pair of eyes, I am at your disposal."

Sophia looked at the bloodstain and suppressed a shudder. "How on earth did someone move a body without leaving a blood trail, I wonder? Wrap something about the wound, then . . . drag the person to either the window or door? But venturing into the hallway would run the risk of witnesses. . . . There should be some sort of dragging pattern somewhere, wouldn't you think?"

Anthony and Dylan both looked down at the floor, and Anthony's mouth turned upward as he glanced back at her. "The rug here is matted along the edge." He pointed to the spot and then followed it to the large window that opened onto the Residency's side yard. The window slid open easily, and he looked over the edge.

After a moment, he closed the window with a chuckle. "I do believe you are right, Miss Elliot. Bind the wound to avoid leaving an even larger blood trail that might be followed, drag the unconscious person to the window, and dump him out. It appears that the orchids growing alongside the house have been crushed."

Dylan shook his head, his smile wry. "We have not been here long enough to assess the scene, you know, Miss Elliot. Our first priority was getting the Pilkingtons out of the room. We would have discovered this evidence eventually." He clearly teased her, and she laughed.

"Of course you would. Well, gentlemen, I shall leave you to it." Sophia left the room, determined to stick close to her sponsor's side for the rest of the evening. At one time or another, the woman would likely speak to everyone in attendance, even if only to wish them farewell at the evening's close. Someone in the big house knew *something.*

Chapter 9

Sophia returned to the ballroom, this time looking over the crowd of guests and servants with an eye attuned to discomfort. Nobody in the throng seemed to have witnessed a scuffle in Lord Pilkington's study, if demeanor and aspect were indicators. The ball was still in full swing, and its attendees were joyous and loud as ever. She spied Major Stuart once he reentered the room. He scanned the crowd, made his way to Lord Pilkington, whispered something in his ear, received an answer with a nod, and then disappeared again.

Sophia crossed the room to Lady Pilkington, who was still pale but had regained a large portion of her former composure. "My lady," she said and placed her hand on her arm. "I can only imagine you must be weary after preparing for such a grand event."

Lady Pilkington looked at Sophia with eyes wide, and nodded. "I . . ." Her voice cracked, and she cleared her throat. "I am quite exhausted, I must admit. But, dear girl, you mustn't fuss over me—I shall be fine. You should dance and enjoy yourself with the other young guests."

"I confess to being a trifle fatigued myself, my lady, and I have quite enjoyed the party thus far, I assure you. I doubt I could convince my feet to dance any more this evening." Sophia smiled. "I thought to make a trip past the refreshment table. May I bring you juice or champagne, perhaps?"

The woman nodded. "Champagne," she murmured, and when Sophia turned, she grabbed hold of her arm. "Miss Elliot, I—" She dabbed at her forehead with a handkerchief. "I thank you for your concern. I haven't a daughter—I mentioned to you before—but I should have had. And she would have been of an age with you, had she lived."

Sophia swallowed, emotion gathering in her throat.

Lady Pilkington squeezed Sophia's arm. "I appreciate your compassion."

Sophia nodded, feeling slightly guilty that her purpose in approaching the woman had been twofold. Indeed, Lady Pilkington's face was alarmingly pale and cause for concern, but Sophia also hoped she would take her into her confidence. There may be something the woman knew, something she didn't even realize she knew, that might shed light on the night's events.

Sophia surveyed the ballroom one more time. It was as she suspected—a few people were offering Lady Pilkington their good-byes as they left, and rather than miss the chance to observe the guests more closely, Sophia raced as gracefully and unobtrusively as possible to the refreshment table to grab a glass of champagne. Mistress Manners would have taken issue with Sophia's rush, but she was dressed as a man, after all. Surely she could be afforded a bit of leniency.

As she left the refreshment table, she saw Rachael

Scarsdale dancing with a professor who was dressed as William Shakespeare. Sophia didn't have the heart to interrupt her with news of murder and mayhem in the lord's study, and she wasn't altogether certain she should mention it to anyone at all. It was just as well Rachael was occupied. Sophia might have been tempted to divulge what she knew.

For her own part, Sophia politely refused offers to dance and instead lingered near Lady Pilkington until the wee morning hours when the ball began to wind down. She felt oddly protective of her sponsor. The lady swayed on her feet, while Lord Pilkington behaved as though nothing untoward had occurred in his study hours before. It was to their credit that none of the guests seemed any the wiser. Beneath the surface, however, his distraction was evident. He made eye contact with his wife frequently and once clasped her fingers in a tender grip.

Eventually the last of the guests trickled either upstairs to their rooms, outside for their carriages, or for a short stroll back to their various residential compounds. Nobody seemed out of character to Sophia, but then she didn't really know very many people at the party, and she was hardly a professional investigator. She felt a stab of frustration at her limitations, but shoved it aside for Lady Pilkington, who still hadn't admitted her knowledge of a huge puddle of blood in her husband's study.

"What a smashing success." Sophia offered her arm to the woman. The lady hadn't succumbed to a fit of vapors or excused herself early. She had stayed on her feet to the bitter end, knowing full well that someone might have been murdered in her home. Regrettably, her concern for the reputation of the Residency was not exaggerated. Sophia knew that the wrong snippet of gossip whispered in the right ear could mean upheaval and disgrace.

Lady Pilkington smiled at Sophia but her eyes were tired and her thoughts clearly elsewhere. "Thank you, dear. It was quite the crush, was it not?"

"The most splendid of crushes. In all of my time out in London society, I have never seen an event so well lauded or attended."

The compliment had its desired effect, and Lady Pilkington's eyes brightened.

"May I escort you to your room and hand you over to your maid, my lady? You have been running ragged all day and must be exhausted."

Lady Pilkington's brow creased. "I had wanted a word with George," she said absently. "But he is likely speaking with . . . some of the gentlemen. I'll have my maid deliver him a message to see me before he retires." She managed a smile. "Yes, I would dearly love to retire to my chambers, and I feel positively spoiled with your kind attention."

Sophia left her sponsor in the capable hands of her maid. She then returned to her own room, deep in thought and rather exhausted. "Briggs," she asked her maid, "were you with the other servants at all this evening?"

"Yes, miss." Briggs covered a yawn and moved to help Sophia disrobe. "I spent some time in the kitchens, but truthfully, it makes me rather uncomfortable. They prepare our food sitting on the floor, did you know? Very nice, they are, the local servants, but very much different. I returned to the sitting room upstairs in the servants' quarters and played card games for a time."

"Did anybody mention something strange? Goings on that may be out of the ordinary?"

Briggs frowned as she shook out the costume jacket and laid it over one of the chairs by the hearth. "No, nothing of note. Just that this costume ball drew in even more people than the last one. I suspect Himmat or Abdullah might be better informed if anything peculiar happened. They were likely on the main level for all of it. Not to mention the kitchen staff. They were running back and forth like mad."

Sophia stripped out of the rest of the costume and sighed with relief at the simple nightgown Briggs draped over her head. "You go to bed, Briggs. I am going to wash up and then sleep until next week."

Briggs smiled and curtseyed. "Pleasant dreams, miss." She left the room, closing the door quietly behind her.

Sophia washed with the cool water in the basin at the dry sink. She barely remembered to clean her teeth before falling into the soft bed and pulling the mosquito netting around it. Her claim to Briggs may not have been exaggerated. She'd been months aboard ship, finally arrived in India, met again the man she'd loved who had stolen—and broken—her heart, and was now searching for answers about a possible murder. One week of sleep might not be enough.

She closed her eyes and settled in against the cool, crisp white sheets and sighed. Bliss.

Asleep nearly immediately, she woke to a quiet but insistent knock on her door. Using a shaft of moonlight from the window, she consulted the pocket watch she kept at the bedside. She'd been asleep for only two hours—not enough time even for dawn to break.

Before she could summon the wherewithal to answer the door, it opened a crack and Rachael's head appeared.

"Sophia!" The whisper was more of a loud hiss.

"Rachael, what on earth?" Sophia pushed herself upright and opened the netting around her bed.

Rachael entered and crawled up on the bed with Sophia. She pulled the netting shut behind her and grasped her hand. "Something is horribly amiss."

Sophia's fog began to clear, and her heart stuttered. "What do you mean?"

"I've been unable to sleep, and I heard my maid speaking with a servant in the hallway. There was some sort of upheaval in the nursery. The ayahs are upset, and something is wrong with Charlie. I went up to see for myself."

Fear gathered thick in Sophia's stomach as she thought of the bloodstained Turkish rug in the downstairs study. "And?"

"Amala Ayah is beside herself, but if I understood what she was trying to articulate, Charlie may have been witness to a serious crime." Rachael paused. "I need to find Dylan, but I don't know where. I cannot very well go down the hallway, looking in each guest room."

Sophia swept the mosquito netting aside and found her outer wrap, feeling horribly tired but painfully alert. "Let us see if we can get the whole story. In a few hours, when the house begins the day, we can question a servant about the location of your cousin's room, should there be cause."

Rachael nodded and led the way through the darkened house to the nursery suite on the third floor. Muffled crying sounded from within, and Sophia didn't bother knocking. She followed the sound through the playroom and into one of the bedrooms, where she found Amala Ayah sitting on her bed, cradling Charlie.

"What is it?" Sophia sat down next to the weeping woman and touched her arm. "What has happened, Amala?"

"Oh, miss," the older woman sniffled. "I do not know what to do. Lord Pilkington's valet will not give him a message, and Lady Pilkington has taken laudanum for a head pain and is deeply asleep."

"Let me help you." Sophia rested her hand atop Charlie's head. The little boy hiccoughed as though at the end of an exhausting bout of emotion. He clutched his wooden toy horse to his chest, tears still pooling in his eyes. "What happened?"

Rachael gave Amala Ayah a handkerchief, which the nanny used to wipe her eyes and nose.

"Master Charlie was in bed for the evening. I had gone to the servants' sitting room with the others. When I returned, Charlie was gone." Tears rolled afresh, and Sophia resisted the urge to pull the poor woman close.

"I looked everywhere, but there were so many people. Finally, I found him in his father's study."

Sophia's heartbeat increased. "Was he alone?"

Amala Ayah nodded. "Yes. But he had been in there for some time, hiding under his papa's desk." She rubbed the boy's curly hair. "Earlier in the evening he had heard the other children say that Captain Miller had brought special treasures for this visit, and he hoped to take a peek at them."

Sophia looked at Charlie's earnest little face. "Why did

you go to the study, Charlie? Did you know the captain would be there?"

"Maybe," Charlie said, his breath catching. "He visits Papa in the study for a drink that Mama doesn't like."

Amala Ayah smoothed his hair again. "They meet there for whiskey," she murmured over his head to Sophia. "Lady Pilkington does not approve."

Sophia thought back to the desk in the study. It was large, and the back panel was slatted, not solid. A young child could easily fit beneath it and still see the room. "Charlie, will you tell me what you saw?"

His eyes grew even larger, and he turned his face toward Amala, whose face crumpled and she rocked him like an infant.

"Has he told you what he saw?" Sophia asked Amala Ayah.

She nodded. "Partly." She covered Charlie's exposed ear with her hand, sniffing back her own tears. Leaning forward, she whispered, "Captain Miller was in there with a man who opened his father's safe. They took something out, argued, and then the other man hit Captain Miller in the head many times with something Charlie couldn't see."

Sophia closed her eyes. "Then did this man drag Captain Miller to the window and shove him out?"

Amala Ayah's eyes widened. "Yes! After Charlie told me what had happened, I took him to find his parents, but they were somewhere in the crowd. I eventually found Himmat, who said Lord Pilkington was in his study and had requested his wife attend him. Himmat left to find her, so I returned to the study with Charlie. His lordship was so distraught and frantic when he saw me there with his son. He ordered me to take Charlie away, to put him safely in his bed. He wouldn't hear me." Amala Ayah fell silent, still rocking the boy.

Sophia looked up at Rachael, who stared at her.

"How did you know about any of this?" Rachael asked.

Sophia shook her head. "I have much to tell you. But first, we must determine which room belongs to your cousin." Her heart ached as she looked at Charlie, who was miserable, afraid, and confused. She put one last question to the nanny. "Does he know the man who did this?"

Amala shook her head. "He says he does not," she whispered. "But when I asked, he was very quick to answer 'no.'"

Sophia bent forward and touched Charlie's knee. "Charlie, will you help us? Do you know the man who hurt Captain Miller? We must find him so he cannot harm anyone else."

Charlie turned his face toward Amala Ayah, saying nothing. He shuddered, his small shoulders shaking with the force of his sobs.

Sophia's eyes burned. She turned the conversation to innocuous topics, attempting to quiet the tone of the discussions and help Charlie feel a sense of calm. She and Amala spoke for ten minutes, fifteen, and finally Amala murmured to Charlie, asking if he'd like a drink of steamed milk. He shook his head, and she frowned.

"Are you certain? It's your favorite; it helps you sleep."

Charlie's cheek nestled against Amala's shoulder and he stared straight ahead, not bothering to shake his head again. He remained silent, except for the occasional halting breath that followed his endless tears.

"Would you like for me to summon your mother or father?" Amala tried again.

Still he stared, quiet, unmoving.

"Charlie, I am so sorry," Sophia murmured. "We'll not bother you more about it tonight. If you remember anything else, will you tell Amala Ayah?"

The little boy shook his head, so subtly Sophia thought she'd imagined it. He blinked slowly, evidence of his fatigue. She stood and exhaled quietly. It was a conundrum she'd never before faced. How did one go about convincing a terrified child to give voice to his worst fears?

She chewed on her lip in thought, then turned to Rachael. "We must locate Major Stuart."

Chapter 10

Anthony awoke to an insistent knocking on his bedroom door. He glanced at the window to see dawn was only just breaking—early enough that his valet, Pierre, was still abed. Anthony's heart pounded with familiar urgency. An early morning meeting rarely boded well. He batted aside the mosquito netting and rose, grabbing the house coat Pierre had placed neatly over the back of a chair the night before.

He opened the door a crack, shoving his arm into the sleeve. "Dylan? What is it?"

His friend stood in the hallway fully clothed, his face grim. "We have a witness to the crime."

The carriage traveled the distance from the Residency to the *Firefly* slowly, with several interruptions. Anthony sat across from Dylan, each lost in thought, each processing the information at hand. According to the only—and very young—eyewitness, Captain Miller had indeed been the victim in Pilkington's study the night before.

Since Sophia had known Dylan was the "official" investigator, and as such was the man to notify, she and Rachael had gone straight to Major Stuart, though Anthony found himself irritated by the fact.

He preferred to take charge, but since his cover was to simply be a visiting member of London's peerage, a lord from home who traveled the world at his leisure, too many direct questions from him about a missing sea captain or private documents taken from a safe would have aroused unwanted attention. Major Stuart was the face of the investigation; Anthony would have to play second fiddle.

He'd learned to play his role well, had always dealt with the frustrations of eking out information while not seeming to care one way or the other about anything, but with so much at stake and his focus alarmingly diverted by the presence of the one woman in the world he wanted, he found himself on edge. In a position to make mistakes.

Nobody aside from Dylan Stuart knew it was *his* job, ultimately, to locate Miller and the packet of papers, one of which Anthony was sure was the Janus Document. It grated, though, that Sophia believed him to be useless.

He shoved back his pride as the carriage came to yet another stop, this time behind two slow-moving bullock carts and an elephant with a monkey riding on its head.

They eventually reached the slip where Miller's ship sat docked. It was eerily quiet. There was little movement; Anthony noted three sailors on deck as he and Stuart made their way up the gangplank. Stuart was in full uniform, and he introduced himself and their purpose—to investigate the disappearance of their captain.

The three sailors blinked, the surprised expressions appearing genuine, but Anthony knew better than anyone how easily people could be deceived.

"Where are the rest of the crew?" Stuart asked the eldest of the three, a grizzled man named Smith who served as the ship's cook and had likely spent the majority of his life at sea.

"In the city, they are, sir." The man spoke around a mouthful of tobacco. "We got three more days afore settin' sail again. We take turns keepin' watch, but ye'll not see most of 'em afore we have to leave."

Dylan nodded. "We have orders to search Captain Miller's cabin, Mr. Smith. You are the keeper of the keys, I see?"

The other two sailors returned to their watch, wandering the deck in the morning sun and likely bored to tears. Anthony and Dylan followed Mr. Smith across the deck, down a short flight of stairs, and to a heavy oak door, which Smith opened with the ring of keys attached to a rope that served as his belt. With a nod, he stepped aside, but cleared his throat.

Anthony paused at the threshold. "Yes?"

"Sirs, the men will be needin' to know, o'course, where the cap'n is, what's happened. Ye'll keep us informed?"

Stuart nodded, withdrawing a small notebook from his pocket. "I will need the name of the captain's first mate, if you please."

Anthony stepped into the cabin, which was large in comparison to many and well-appointed. A solid berth, desk, two chairs, and a small wardrobe filled the space. The furniture was of good quality and craftsmanship. Miller was—had been—a very successful merchant, and it showed.

Stuart finished with the cook and closed the door behind him. Anthony began pulling open drawers in Miller's desk, giving the contents of each a cursory glance. Then he came across a drawer that was locked.

"Shall I request Mr. Smith back?" Dylan asked, his mouth turned up at the corner.

"Not necessary." Anthony smiled and withdrew a small packet from his pocket. Using the tools inside it, he picked the lock and had the drawer opened in short order. Inside was a large, leather-bound volume that proved to be the ship's log. Anthony handed it to Stuart.

Further examination of the drawer produced what Anthony had hoped to find—a false bottom that hid a smaller book, a personal diary. "Here we are," he breathed and motioned to Stuart.

Dylan, still perusing the official log, moved to Anthony's side and looked over his shoulder at the diary. Anthony flipped pages until he found the dates he needed. He had only read a few entries before he realized that his assessment of the thief, Harold Miller, may have been made in haste.

"What does it say?" Stuart asked.

Anthony frowned. "Apparently Harold Miller, the man who stole the Janus Document, found his uncle, Captain Miller, in France. Harold was frantic. He told him, 'I must leave the country at once. I am in possession of a packet vital to England's security.' Miller says his nephew had taken the packet into his own hands to keep it from another unnamed party or parties who wished to use it for financial gain."

Dylan softly read aloud the next passage from the captain's diary. "'I told Harold I wasn't bound for home yet, that the cargo is full and my course set for delivery before returning to England. He was relieved, said that the voyage would give him not only distance from his enemy but time to consider the best course of action.'"

Anthony looked at Dylan, his thoughts spinning. "If Harold had encountered trouble while trying to sell the document to his contact in France, it would make sense for him to paint himself in a hero's light to his uncle so he could escape from the Continent. If he were truly innocent, why not return immediately to London and seek asylum with a trusted source in the War Department?"

"He was Braxton's subordinate, you say?" Dylan asked.

Anthony nodded. There was another possibility that hovered in Anthony's thoughts that he couldn't share with Dylan, however, and it concerned Braxton himself. It wouldn't be the first time the man had not told Anthony the entire truth of a matter. Anthony had completed at least two missions during his war years that Braxton later admitted had been a diversion to protect someone higher on the ladder than himself. There were often deeper layers of intrigue to these puzzles that necessitated a stretching of the facts.

In short, Braxton may well be protecting someone again, and Harold Miller may have been the scapegoat. Supposing Harold had gone to France with a companion, perhaps a trusted colleague from the War Department, he may have been an unwitting accomplice to an act of which he was ignorant until the transaction was nearly upon them. If that were the case, Anthony admired the man's courage to act. He had taken something worth millions and run with it, likely knowing the consequences would be dire if he were caught.

Anthony flipped another page and read another entry. "'I placed Harold's packet of papers in my personal safe. I asked him about the contents, but he insisted nobody should know, that it represented danger for a large number of people.'" He paused, reading further, and then said to Dylan, "As the ship skirted South Africa, an illness swept through the crew, killing three before they made land. Several were sick but recovered. Harold succumbed and died after one day in port. Miller had him buried there."

Dylan nodded, looking at the official log. "He says the same thing here."

Anthony turned to the last few pages of the personal diary. He shook his head, his smile grim and without humor. "It seems Captain Miller looked at the papers once Harold was dead. The pages were all written in some kind of code." He looked up at Dylan.

"The Janus Document," Stuart said.

Anthony nodded. "I suppose I can't blame him—curiosity might have gotten the better of me, also. What he doesn't say here, though, is what he planned to do with the packet, if he intended to hand it over to government officials or find someone else to buy it."

Dylan raised a brow. "Wise to not incriminate himself in his own diary." He paused. "So after Harold's death, Captain Miller had the Janus Document locked in Lord Pilkington's safe."

"It appears so."

"And then, during the ball, the safe was opened, and Captain Miller was killed by an unknown assailant—who, we suspect, then stole the document."

"A fair summation." Anthony sighed. He had been so close to retrieving the blasted document.

"How is it you never met the man once you arrived? You were both at the Residency for several overlapping days."

Anthony shook his head, frustrated. "I could never pin him down. Each time I talked to someone who knew where he was planning to be, I followed up only to just miss him. I wonder if he was perhaps looking for a contact who could help him either sell the document or decipher the code."

Dylan frowned. "Would that be easily accomplished? Who has access to the code?"

Anthony shrugged. "War Department officials. Braxton." Anthony himself had memorized the code and knew where the key was found. All correspondence between agents and the Home Office was communicated via that code. Each of the agents he worked with knew it as well, but it was something none of them ever admitted—to do so meant to risk one's life. That Braxton had created a sensitive roster of information using such a familiar system had frustrated Anthony ever since the night Braxton had shown up in his library.

Dylan consulted his timepiece. "I'm needed back at the post for an hour. Do you join me or return to the Residency?"

Anthony reached for the official log, which Dylan handed him. He placed it back in the drawer but put the smaller diary in his coat pocket. "I believe I'll chat with the three sailors up on deck. See if I can learn anything useful."

Regrettably, nothing useful came to light. Anthony spent the better part of the afternoon tracking down sailors in Bombay's multitudinous bars, gaming holes, and brothels and introducing himself as a "friend helping Major Stuart with an investigation." The few men he spoke to had no idea where Captain Miller had spent his days following the ship's arrival, or with whom he might have spoken. The one assumption each of them made, however, was that he had gone to the Residency—a fact Anthony already had established.

When he finished learning absolutely nothing of value, he returned to the Residency hot, tired, and dusty, the scent of Bombay's squalor still heavy in his nose. He bathed, took tea in his chambers, and allowed his valet, Pierre, to fuss over the condition of his sweat-stained clothing.

He put a hand to the back of his neck and rolled his head to release tension. He was tired. He hadn't slowed down since leaving London and desired a vacation far away. Preferably with a bride named Sophia. "What has been the tenor of the gossip below stairs today, Pierre?"

"I wouldn't know, sir, as I never gossip." Pierre sniffed. He had served Anthony in Paris during the war and had willingly accepted the post again when Anthony had found him two years ago. Anthony's London valet, Faring, was aging and not the sort to go off on an adventure. Pierre was middle aged, proper, enjoyed travel well enough, and took an inordinate amount of satisfaction in trying to transform Anthony into a respectable peer of the realm. Although Pierre himself was a Frenchman, his mother had been English, and he regarded duties of nobility in any country as a serious responsibility.

Anthony smiled. "Let us assume, for the sake of discussion, that you did gossip. Or listen with an attentive ear. Which I happen to know you have. What might you have overheard today?"

"I suppose I may have heard one of Lady Pilkington's

maids conversing with a cook, a Hindu woman with three sons and two daughters, all of whom are employed here at the Residency."

"Mmm. And the Hindu cook and the maid spoke in English, yes? Unless you are trilingual and have hidden it from me."

"They spoke in English." Pierre held up Anthony's suit coat and slapped at a smudge of dirt on one of the sleeves. "Apparently Lady Pilkington's young son is quite distraught about the missing sea captain. Lady Pilkington does not know what to make of the child's sudden reluctance to speak to anyone, and she seems to believe his ayah must be mistaken about the child's actual knowledge of events. Certainly he would share such details, if he had them."

Anthony frowned. "The lady doesn't believe her son witnessed something distressing?"

Pierre lifted a shoulder and examined the other sleeve of the jacket. "It is my opinion, sir, that the lady is easily overwrought and prone to avoiding unpleasantries over which she has no control."

"And the inciting matter itself? What does the household have to say about that?"

"Chatter in the servants' third-floor sitting room, of which I take no part, indicates a popular belief that the sea captain is not merely missing, but most definitely dead. There was a particularly distasteful cleaning task awaiting the staff in Lord Pilkington's study." Pierre disappeared into the adjoining dressing room with the offending suit coat and returned with fresh dinner attire.

Anthony glanced at the waistcoat, cravat, and coat that

Pierre placed neatly over the arm of a chair. He had lived his entire life as a member of the aristocracy, so piling on the clothing was second nature to him. There were times, though, when he dearly would have loved to flout convention and show up to dinner in just trousers and a shirt.

Fighting back a sigh, he put on the uncomfortable garments, Pierre rolling his eyes the entire time and muttering about an Englishman's constitution being inferior to the French. Pierre dusted off Anthony's shoulders, tugged the coat into smooth perfection, nary a wrinkle in sight, and made quick work of his neck cloth. He stepped back, examining his handiwork as would a proud parent or a Bond Street *modiste*, and pronounced Anthony fit for dinner.

Anthony made his way to the drawing room where many of the guests gathered before the evening meal and heard snippets of conversation about a missing sea captain. Missing, not dead. Stuart had promised the Pilkingtons that he would keep the details of the crime as vague as possible for as long as possible, but Anthony wondered how long it would take for the gossip to spread from below stairs to the guests' chambers.

He noted Dylan, who stood half a head taller than anyone else save himself, and crossed the room to see Rachael and Sophia conversing with him. To his irritation, Mr. Gerald, the forward-minded, educated-women-adoring professor also approached the trio, and Anthony ground his teeth in frustration. Dinner the night before had been an exercise in agony as he'd watched Sophia turn the full blast of her charm on the other man.

" . . . hope you've enjoyed your second day in India," Gerald was saying as Anthony reached them.

"We have indeed." Sophia smiled at the man and extended the pleasantry to Anthony. "And so good to see you again, Lord Wilshire. Major Stuart tells us you've gone into Bombay today."

"We did, although we saw only a fraction of the city. I understand there's more to experience here than one can comfortably manage in a week. And although I've been in Bombay that long already, my time has mostly been spent here at the Residency or at the military compound nearby."

"As I've spent the last decade at home here in India, I must rely on visitors from England to keep abreast of news," Mr. Gerald said. "Major Stuart mentioned your military time in France—was it a lengthy engagement?"

Why did the man have to be so blasted affable? Handsome with pleasant manners, charming and humorous in conversation, sincere in the most basic of exchanges. For once Anthony wished Sophia was a snob and wouldn't deign to socialize with a mere academic. Feeling peevish and petty, Anthony fought to keep himself from scowling.

"Three years," he told Gerald. "Some of it pleasant enough, much of it not nearly so, most of it tedious." How he wished it were true. His entire tour in France had been fraught with secrets and lies, the danger of discovery hidden in every exchange.

"But he made so many acquaintances." Sophia spoke to Gerald, not bothering to glance at Anthony. "Lovely, accomplished people he still communes with to this day. His sojourn in France must not have been nearly so tedious as he implies." She turned to Anthony with a smile that certainly seemed sincere enough on the surface. He knew her, though. The smile did not reach her eyes. His heart sank. He'd thought they were making progress. She was clearly still bitter, and his distracted behavior the night before hadn't aided his cause.

Dylan cleared his throat and saved Anthony from having to fashion a response. "I believe we're being summoned to the dining room." He motioned his head toward the door where Himmat was indeed informing the group that mealtime was at hand. They followed the crowd, and Dylan murmured in Anthony's ear, "Sorry, old man."

Anthony shrugged. He didn't want sympathy. He didn't want anyone else knowing Sophia's barb stung. She was not a mean woman, or cruel, but he had intentionally led her to a place of ignorance and the level of hurt she clearly felt at his desertion was hardly the boon he might have imagined it would be. He'd wanted to know she still cared for him, to know that she would have welcomed his suit. Realizing he'd truly caused her pain, though, dampened the thrill.

Chapter 11

Sophia placed her fingers on Anthony's sleeve and fought back a pang of guilt. He hadn't smiled, hadn't tried to deflect her earlier jab, but his expression was sad. Resigned. For a moment he seemed to carry the weight of the world on his shoulders. She tried to dredge up the familiar resentment to assuage her guilt. He'd been the one who left—and then all those rumors floated back to London in his absence. If he didn't want people thinking he was a wastrel, then he ought not behave like one.

Still, something was off. They walked into the dining room, but he didn't meet her gaze, didn't try to engage her in even the lightest of exchanges. It was the first time—probably ever—that he'd been quiet. Truly quiet, the kind that went beyond companionable silence or a comfortable lull in conversation. He had nothing to say, and it was disconcerting. Guilt, then? His conscience catching up with him? She tried to find satisfaction in it, but whatever the reason, it saddened her, and she didn't like it.

"Did you see anything in Bombay to recommend it?" she finally asked once they were seated at the table.

He looked at her in some surprise but found his footing quickly enough. "Much, but as I mentioned earlier, it requires more time to explore. I expect the other guests will make an excursion into the city before long. Perhaps we might join them."

She nodded, her throat suddenly tight. His face was so familiar, so dear. She wanted to lay her palm against his cheek and place a kiss on his forehead. Or maybe his lips. She swallowed back a sigh. She didn't know how to properly kiss a man, and he clearly wasn't interested in pursuing such activity with a woman he viewed as his little sister, so that was that.

Sophia made a decision as the rest of the guests settled in and the first course was served. No harm would come from reestablishing her former rapport with Anthony, and she needed to commit, if not for his feelings, then for the sake of her sanity. Either she would be nice to him or she wouldn't, and it was time to stop waffling from one to the other.

Although Anthony had shown mild signs of irritation the night before when she'd paid attention to Professor Gerald, she could reasonably attribute that to his protective feelings for her well-being, not unlike those that Jack might experience. Since Anthony clearly wasn't interested in a romantic relationship with her, she could prevent her feelings from developing along that vein, and they could hopefully enjoy the easy communion they'd had before.

"So. Tell me about these people." She glanced at him as she picked up her soup spoon.

He met her gaze and her breath caught.

I can be his friend. I can be his friend without dreaming of more.

"What would you like to know? And about whom?"

She gestured toward the room at large. "Anything. About anyone. Come, Anthony, you've been here for more than a week. Surely you've observed some amusing things. This is what we do, *n'est-ce pas*?"

"*Mais oui.*" His lips quirked, and he raised a brow, casting a glance down the table. "Seated near the head of the table is Taj Darzi; you met him last night at the ball."

"Ah, yes. Didn't you say that his cousin, Prince Ekavir, is ill?"

"Very near death, as we understand it. He seeks to subject his wife to *sati* on his funeral pyre."

Sophia paused and lowered her voice. "Cremate his body and her along with it?"

He nodded. "Most of the princely states have done away with the practice, if for no other reason than to keep peace with England. But there are those who still remain committed to the tradition. It can be a delicate balance. Lord Pilkington's purpose as a Resident—and indeed the role of the Bombay Army itself—is to function as a support for local rulers and royalty, as this is a princely state."

"I was told this area is under the wing of the Bombay presidency."

"It is. And although we recognize local princes, British might often rises to the fore and 'support' frequently becomes 'control.' Lord Pilkington, to his credit, seems to respect the Residency and his role in it. His relationship with Mr. Darzi and the prince is one of partnership. He seems to view

Mr. Darzi as a man of integrity and optimism." He lowered his voice. "I often suspect Lady Pilkington to be the true diplomat of the pair, however. She seems to have an astute grasp of local politics. Lord Pilkington often seems a happy bystander."

"And how do you know all of this?"

He winked at her. "Ah, my dear, I listen very, very attentively."

She nearly sighed like a ridiculous debutante. *This* was how it had been between them. The easy familiarity, the humor—only before he might have also trailed a fingertip lightly along the back of her arm. Discreetly, of course. And not during dinner. It would have been at the side of a ballroom while conversing with mutual associates, or perhaps trying to catch her attention in a drawing room over a hand of cards.

She felt warm at the memory and fought the urge to fan herself with her napkin. Thoughts, impressions, conversations suddenly tripped through her mind as would tumblers in a lock. And suddenly, the pieces all lined up neatly and clicked into place. She narrowed her eyes, knit her brows in a frown, and looked at him surreptitiously from the side, her head tilted as she thought. And thought. And remembered. So many little things, flirtatious things, loving gestures, whispers about nothing of consequence but meant for her ears alone . . .

Older brother, my giddy aunt.

Unless he was indeed a very sick man, there was no possibility that he had ever viewed her as he would a sister. She knew it as well as she knew her own name, and the realization quite took her breath away. But truly, she'd known it all along.

Why, then?

Why had he run? Had he been afraid? She knew he'd never felt enough affection for any woman in the past to warrant a proposal of marriage, and he'd never needed to hunt for a bride to fill the family coffers. Had his close association with her engendered emotions that were unfamiliar and unsettling? Had he fled because he viewed her as anything *but* a sibling?

Sophia pursed her lips and tapped her spoon lightly against the bowl. He turned his head and caught her scrutiny.

"What are you thinking in that clever brain of yours?" he murmured, his expression guarded.

The corner of her mouth lifted in a smile. "I am thinking I have been quite vexed with you for leaving London."

He swallowed, the guard slipping. "I . . . Sophia . . ." He cleared his throat. "We can discuss the matter later this evening, perhaps? I . . . It's as I told you in my letter—"

"Oh, I am well aware of what you said in your letter."

He blinked, and the mask was back in place as though it had never faltered. "Splendid!" he declared with a smile. "Nothing more to discuss at all, then." He gave her elbow a friendly nudge.

She narrowed her eyes. What would he do next? Slap her on the back and call her a good old chap? Invite her to Tattersalls to peruse horseflesh? This would never do. He *would* admit to her, like an adult, why he had run away from England. She may not like the truth; it may, in fact, put her in a mind to dismiss him permanently. A woman could hardly depend on a fulfilling relationship if the man grew frightened of it and left on a whim with no warning whatsoever. But if he couldn't find the courage on his own to explain himself, she would play his game and beat him at it. One way or another, she would have her answers. Once equipped with them, she could then make an informed decision.

Feeling strangely empowered for the first time in a long time, she elbowed him back and winked. "Nothing to discuss at all," she echoed. "And I suppose I forgive you for leaving in the midst of the Season when there were so many people still to analyze."

He blinked again. "You do?"

"I do. A true friend finds it in her heart to forgive all but the grossest of insults. Besides which, it really is past time I search in earnest for a husband. Now that we are together again, you can advise me. Jack is too busy these days. Put him in the same room with Ivy and Catherine and he's utterly useless." She fought the urge to slap Anthony's back and give him a huge, affable grin—camaraderie between friends, after all—but there was no sense in overplaying her hand. She glanced at his face, satisfied to see his mouth momentarily slacken before he recovered himself.

"Help you find a husband?"

"Yes." She nodded and continued eating her Korma Kashmiri, which was chicken in a sweet and creamy curry sauce with pineapple and cashews, a dish she was finding particularly to her liking. "When I failed to settle on a suitor for whom I felt even a modicum of affection, I had quite resigned myself to searching elsewhere. The Fleet seemed an excellent option. And, of course you know how tiresome London can be." It was an effort to speak with sincerity, to avoid ruining her performance by sounding trite or forced. Anthony was not stupid, and his ability to read people was exceptional. He would know if she were putting on a show.

And a show it was. The last thing she wanted was for Anthony Blake to find her someone else to marry. Whether or not he felt the same remained to be seen, but before they left India, she would know.

She leaned back slightly when the footman cleared her plate and replaced it with a dish of fresh squid and prawns spiced with curry and fresh coconut. She fought a grimace and glanced at Anthony. "Some of this region's wonderful food is wasted on me," she whispered. "I do not care for seafood."

Anthony smiled. "I remember. I suppose you shall resort to the time-honored method of moving the food about on the plate to appear as though you're enjoying it?"

"One does what one must," she grumbled. "Distract me with tales, if you please. Surely you've made observations on more than simply Mr. Darzi, the prince's cousin."

Anthony speared a bite of his squid and nodded at her as he closed his lips around the fork and chewed. She gagged in the back of her throat, and her eyes watered. She quickly put her napkin to her mouth and looked away from him with a cough. She heard his answering laugh and wondered how badly it would embarrass her sponsor if she were to dump her plate of seafood in Anthony's lap and storm out in a dramatic huff.

"Very well," Anthony said, his voice merry. "Seated at the other table is Clergyman Denney, Mrs. Denney, and their two daughters. He leads the flock each Sabbath with verses from the Old Testament and is less concerned with growing the flock than he is filling those who already attend with fire and brimstone. His wife is very gentle, very kind, and very likely trampled beneath her husband's formidable personality. Their daughters return to London soon to enjoy the Season—their second and first, respectively, I'm told—and Mr. Denney is quite determined that one, or preferably both, daughters will make a splendid match. There is soon to be a dowry at play which could serve both daughters very well."

Sophia studied the family as she absently stirred her food about on her plate. "The younger of the two is the prettier, is she not?"

Anthony's answering smile was wry. "I had arrived at the same conclusion myself. I anticipate exactly what you're about to say."

"I fear that unless the elder is gregarious, she may find herself eclipsed." Sophia paused. "Although, she does seem to have captured the attention of the soldier seated to her right. Of course, he seems to be doing the majority of the conversing."

Anthony leaned toward Sophia to look at the couple in question. "Ah, yes. That is Corporal Mailor. He was the shepherdess at the costume party, if you'll recall." He lowered his voice. "He fancies himself a bit of a charmer. I do hope Miss Denney has a good head on her shoulders and will not be deceived by a few flowery compliments."

Sophia scowled at the young soldier. "Does he mean her ill, do you suppose?"

"I certainly have no basis to suspect it, but in the short time I have been here, Corporal Mailor has attempted to endear himself to no fewer than seven women, and he leads three other like-minded corporals about like the Pied Piper."

"Ah. The sheep."

"Yes. Such short-lived attention for any one woman is hardly rare here, of course, but he seems to me to be an opportunist." He drew his brows together and paused, thinking. "He is rather more shiftless than most. His ambitions far exceed his potential, in my opinion, but he will reach upward, nonetheless."

"Hmm." Sophia frowned. "One hopes her father might spot a ne'er-do-well and offer her some useful counsel. And you say both girls have been in Indian society for a time?"

He nodded.

"Perhaps they are more discerning than some. From what I've experienced in these scant two days, Major Stuart had the right of it. The Fishing Fleet ladies are often met fresh off the boat with multiple proposals. That the Denney daughters have lived here in this society and remain unattached speaks to their perspicacity, perhaps."

"Multiple proposals have been your experience? Was this what you were hoping for when you sought to join the Fleet?"

Sophia snorted lightly. "Certainly not." She then cursed herself for answering too quickly. She had wanted him to believe she was here to find a husband.

He glanced at her but left the comment alone. Mercifully, he turned the discussion back to the Denney girls. "Whatever their reasons for remaining unattached, the daughters must be impressive indeed to defend such a stance against their father. Mr. Denney does not strike me as a parent who is concerned if his daughters marry for love or affection."

"A pity." Sophia set her fork down on her plate. "My parents married for love and, true, it cost them dearly. But to this day my mother insists she would not change history even if she could." She smiled, but it felt bittersweet, and she lowered her voice. "We used to sit in our flat, with barely enough to eat, Mama sicker and more frail by the day, and she would tell me stories of my handsome and wonderful father who would have so loved to see his beautiful children grow. He would be so proud of Jack, working hard at sea even as a child, all to help provide for his mother and little sister."

She glanced up at him and blinked away telltale moisture. "She always insisted that if a man and woman have love and affection, a desire to put each other above all else, that life is livable under any circumstances." She cleared her throat. It wouldn't do to cry her way through the meal, even if she didn't like the squid. "And as I now have opportunities that she never dreamed of, I intend to take advantage. I'll not marry simply for the sake of being married."

"Very progressive thinking, Miss Elliot." His smile was gentle.

Sophia nodded. "Yes. I shall marry someone I love, or not at all. So you see, my lord, your task is a challenging one. You must find me a husband I can adore." She glanced at him from the corner of her eye, and her mouth dipped in a smile. "If I am relegated forever to the proverbial shelf, it shall be entirely your fault."

His jaw clenched before he shoved another bite of food in his mouth. Could it be the man was feeling uncomfortable?

Sophia smiled. *Good.*

Chapter 12

The mansion sat in the midst of lush vegetation and green lawn that sloped gently down to a river just deep and wide enough to allow for light boat traffic. There wasn't much movement this time of night, but torches spaced evenly along the bank gave an air of civilization to the otherwise untamed, colorful land. Anthony strolled with Dylan, Rachael Scarsdale, and Sophia, her hand resting in the crook of his arm.

His frustration knew no bounds. Apparently Sophia was now fully resigned, even comfortable, with the notion that he wanted nothing from her beyond friendship. She had asked him to help her find a blasted husband!

Another man. A man who was not him. For the love of heaven.

His only hope was that he would be able to find fault with all potential suitors, of which there were legion in British India, and that she would assume his excessive criticism was due to his protective nature as a surrogate brother. It was laughable.

He cursed Braxton again, as had become his habit of

late, and made an effort to rein in his thoughts when Dylan stopped and glanced around. The four of them had wandered to a secluded spot by the river; likely the bulk of the other guests and visitors had opted to remain closer to the house. Even in the cooler season, snakes and a host of crawling creatures ventured toward human habitation, and Anthony kept one eye on the ground as they stopped.

"Now then," Dylan said, "once more—what exactly did Charlie and Amala say when you went to the nursery?"

The women told of a young boy who had most assuredly witnessed a violent altercation but was too traumatized to speak of it. Indeed, he was now saying nothing at all to anyone, not even to his beloved ayah. Clearly, the victim had been the sea captain, after he and his attacker had fought over something removed from the safe. The attacker had dragged the captain to the window, thrown him out, and then disappeared.

Anthony turned their revelations over again in his mind and wondered how on earth to proceed. The only witness to the captain's likely demise was a young child too terrified to speak. How to remedy that? Anthony was well versed in manipulating adults, but children?

Anthony sighed. "Very well. We are agreed that this information stays amongst us, yes? The fewer people with knowledge of the finer details, the better. I spoke with the Pilkingtons, and they both agreed, readily, to keep quiet while we continue investigating."

Sophia briefly looked at him, eyes narrowed, but she nodded. If she wondered why he sounded as though he were the point man for the investigation, she kept it to herself.

"Suppose we return to the house," Anthony suggested. "The torches are not bright enough to illuminate everything that might wish to crawl up and say hello."

Rachael's eyes widened. "I should hate to find bugs or worse in my skirts."

"Long gone are the days when we searched for frogs then, cousin." Dylan smiled at Rachael, and she laughed.

They made their way slowly back up to the mansion, Rachael and Dylan walking just ahead and reminiscing. Anthony felt Sophia's attention and glanced at her. "What is it?"

Sophia narrowed her eyes. "You're hiding something. And so is that one." She motioned toward Dylan.

Anthony frowned. "I have no idea why you would suggest such a thing. What on earth would we have to hide? Well," he amended, "other than the fact that we are investigating a murder in secret."

Sophia studied him still. "Yes. *You* are investigating."

He laughed. "I see no issue with seeking to aid a friend."

She raised a single brow, but remained silent, and for one brief moment, he wondered if she would see straight through his attempted subterfuge. He wasn't prepared to explain everything to her, not yet. If he were to tell her exactly what they faced, she might behave differently, say something to the wrong person entirely in innocence . . . It simply wasn't worth the risk. Before long, he hoped, the matter would be solved and settled. Perhaps then he might stand a chance of winning Sophia's heart. If she hadn't coerced him into finding her a different man to adore by then.

Chapter 13

Sophia awoke the next morning with the sun and felt surprisingly refreshed. After the discomfort of the long voyage, her first day in India had been frenetic from the moment she'd stepped from the carriage. She'd been tired upon arrival, the costume ball had been eventful, and then she and Rachael had hardly slept that night. Yesterday she'd found herself constantly moving to avoid falling asleep.

Feeling much more herself, she looked forward to the day. She and Rachael had spoken briefly the night before upon their return from the river and decided to spend as much time as possible with Amala Ayah and Charlie. The answers to their questions lay somewhere within the child, and any hope of finding them was predicated on earning Charlie's trust.

Breakfast was a casual affair, much as at home, with food placed on sideboards as a buffet. Sophia finished eating before Rachael made her way down. She left the dining room and went onto the wide verandah that spanned the length of the mansion on the back side. The large space functioned as another room all its own, and from what Lady Pilkington had said, was often the only place to find even a modicum of relief when the hot weather settled in. The Pilkingtons and their attending servants traveled north into the hills to wait out the worst of the summer months, but until that time, the verandah became a gathering place.

It was screened to keep out bugs and snakes, and there were two large fans suspended from the high ceiling. The fans were attached to ropes that servants pulled on to provide comfort from the heat. Sophia had stopped counting the number of times she was forced to hold her tongue. She couldn't help but feel compassion for the servants who worked in the heat to provide comfort for their employers. They were paid, it was true, but not well. The arrogance Sophia heard from more than one quarter reminded her painfully of her own time spent serving her "betters." She didn't suppose her feelings would ever quite go away, and she wasn't certain she wished them to. Heaven help her if she ever treated another person the way she had been treated herself.

She settled comfortably in a chair on the verandah, waiting for Rachael and the children with their nannies and ayahs. They were bound for adventure to a site of ancient temple ruins a short one-mile distance from the Residency. She picked up one of the local English gossip sheets placed on the coffee table and scanned it, smiling in spite of herself. The paper described the same sorts of things she read about in London: clothing, courtships, balls, parties, and more about clothing.

She glanced up at movement in her periphery to see Rachael and the two Misses Denney, the younger of whom was speaking earnestly. "I have told Papa repeatedly that neither Beatrice nor I wish to return to England again, but he refuses to hear it."

Sophia stood and smiled at the threesome. "Won't you join me here, ladies?" With some luck, perhaps one of the sisters would remember something about Captain Miller from the costume party.

The two sisters exchanged pleasantries with Sophia and sat in a small wicker sofa. Rachael sat next to Sophia.

"I met Miss Denney and Miss Charity Denney yesterday afternoon," Rachael said to Sophia. "Miss Denney is quite accomplished in watercolors."

"You're too kind," Beatrice, the elder sister, murmured.

Rachael smiled. "I beg to differ, in that I am most certainly not offering platitudes about your artwork. It is extraordinary."

Beatrice Denney blushed and tucked a stray curl behind her ear. She smiled, though, and that was something to celebrate. Sophia had developed a soft spot in her heart for the girl, perhaps because she knew Beatrice didn't live up to her father's expectations. She wasn't comfortable in large groups of people and seemed anxious around gentlemen. If Beatrice couldn't land herself a good husband, Mr. Denney was not likely to be pleasant about it, and Sophia was defensive on the girl's behalf.

"She is very talented, but also modest." Charity gave her sister's hand a squeeze, an act that raised Sophia's estimation of her. Charity was vivacious and pretty, and she had an easy manner with people. Sophia liked her better knowing she loved her sister enough to act as an intermediary.

"I should love to see your work," Sophia told Beatrice. "If you would be comfortable sharing, of course."

Rachael smiled. "She didn't have much choice with me, I'm afraid. I spied her as she worked under the shade tree outside my bedchamber window. I opened it to feel the fresh air, and there she was."

Beatrice blushed yet again, and Sophia's heart ached a little more for her. The world was not always a kind place to the gentle. "Beatrice, have you ever painted the temple ruins close by? Rachael and I are accompanying some of the children on a picnic today. Is it as spectacular as I've been told?"

A sparkle lit Beatrice's eyes. "Mama used to take us to the ruins at least once a week when we were small. It was there I began painting true-life scenes."

"Beatrice's portfolio is full of beautiful paintings of the ruins," Charity added enthusiastically. "The orchids are an absolute explosion of color—they are everywhere! There are so many things to see there, and I daresay through the years we've combed every inch. There is one large building still mostly intact, but trees have grown up and around and through it so they appear to be part of the building itself. It is very dark inside, and creatures of all sorts roam through its halls, or so we've been told."

"It sounds remarkable," Sophia said.

Charity's energy dimmed slightly. "Papa put a stop to our adventures when Beatrice turned fifteen. He said we were too old for romping around." She lifted her shoulder. "I would never admit it to anyone else, but I would still dearly love to go romping around the ruins and gather a bouquet of orchids for our mother—she likes the bright yellow and orange ones the best." She gave a small laugh. "All this talk of running about like a child—it is quite gauche of me, I know."

Sophia laughed. "Not at all, Miss Charity. A lady should never be too old to enjoy such a worthy pastime. In fact, you should join us today."

"Thank you for the invitation," Beatrice said. "My sister and I would love to join you. I hope you don't mind if Charity appoints herself your tour guide for the day."

"Indeed, Miss Elliot," Charity said. "India has much to recommend it, especially this time of year. And the gentlemen are so very attentive. The two of you shall make the most splendid of matches! Did you know that there are multiple Englishmen for every Englishwoman in British India? You'll forgive me for making reference to gambling, but the odds for women are ever so much better here than in England."

Sophia wondered how she could ask Charity why she and her sister weren't married yet, given such excellent odds. In the end, she didn't have to.

"As I was telling Miss Scarsdale before we found you here, Miss Sophia, I beg Papa continually to allow Beatrice and me to remain here. We spent a few years in England for school, but it was his home, not ours. We missed everyone here dreadfully, most especially Mama and our ayah. After we returned home from our last holiday, we prevailed upon him to allow us to remain here rather than go back to England. Even Mama aided our cause. He relented, but he still insisted we have a Season last year, and he intends to send us off again this year. We've been home for such a short time! We have spent more time aboard ship than on solid land over the last two years."

Beatrice grimaced. "Traveling by ship is wretched. We both get so very ill. I believe Papa's agreement to suspend schooling in England came in part because of our condition when we returned last. I'm afraid we looked and felt quite pathetic. Risking life and limb for a successful Season, however, he sees as another matter entirely."

Sophia nodded in sympathy. The ocean crossing was indeed wretched, and she'd had the best benefits money could buy. Her ship was large, the accommodations plentiful, including enough fresh water for both bathing and laundering clothes, which was nearly unheard of. Most Fishing Fleet voyages were a veritable hell on earth. A fairly small ship to carry hundreds of people, inadequate bathing accommodations, no fresh water available to launder clothing, live animals to be slaughtered for food, rotting food as the journey continued, which prompted stomach ailments . . . Include the pitching and rolling of the ship on stormy seas and she knew that many people questioned their own sanity for embarking into such madness.

"Yet now he wishes for us to return." Charity frowned. "I am quite prepared to run away."

Beatrice glanced at her sister with irritated affection. "You shall not run away, Charity. Where would you go?"

Charity grinned. "I shall run to the jungle and live with the animals."

Beatrice laughed, then, and the sound was delightful. It quite transformed her, and Sophia watched the young woman with a smile of her own. "You do not like the animals at all; they frighten you witless. A silly sight you would be, trying to live among the tigers and snakes and screaming each time you encounter one."

Charity laughed with her sister, but sobered gradually. "Would it be so much worse than having to brave the Bay of Biscay again?"

Sophia shuddered at that notion and shook her head in agreement.

Rachael viewed the other young women with sympathy in her clear, blue eyes. "Perhaps your father will yet change his mind. After all, if he wishes you to wed, surely this is a good place to accomplish it."

Beatrice shrugged and answered quietly, "Truthfully, we both could have been married here several times over. Papa has always regretted the necessity of leaving England, and he wants the two of us to find gentlemen who are not destined to remain here with their careers for a lifetime. He does not care for India at all, but we—" She glanced at Charity. "Mama loves it, and we were born and raised here. It is very much home to us. England feels foreign and cold."

"And wet," Charity added. "Monsoon season here is intolerable, yes, but it eventually ends. England is gray and dreary all the time."

Beatrice glanced at her sister with a wry smile and nudged her arm. "Not all the time. It just isn't . . . home. Not to us. We certainly mean no offense."

Rachael shook her head. "I am certainly not offended." She spread her hands. "I am here, after all."

Sophia heard children chattering and turned to see Rachael's young friends, the twin girls, bounding down the stairs. Several more children followed from the nearby residential compound with their ayahs, and finally, she saw Charlie and Amala Ayah.

"Good morning!" Amala Ayah called. "I hope you've not been waiting long."

The women stood as the others approached, and Sophia smiled at the ayah's resilient tone. Amala was determined to make things better for Charlie.

"Amala, I have invited the Denney sisters to join us today. I trust no one will object," Sophia said.

Charity Denney bounced on the balls of her feet, and the sparkle was back in Beatrice's eye.

"Have you a picnic basket made?" Charity burst out as though unable to hold it back any longer.

Amala laughed at the girl's enthusiasm. "It is being assembled as we speak, and will be brought to us in two hours. Shall I instruct the kitchen to send more?"

"We should hate to be a bother," Beatrice said, her light blush staining her cheeks.

"No bother at all," Amala said. She turned to one of the other ayahs. "Please notify the kitchen. The carriages will be brought round in five minutes; you can meet us out front."

Sophia walked with the entourage, listening with half an ear as Charity requested a servant inform Mr. and Mrs. Denney of their whereabouts. Beatrice's brow creased lightly, and she hesitated for the briefest of moments before stating she needed her travel paints. She dashed off to grab them from their bungalow, which was in a compound of homes adjacent the Residency.

Amidst some jostling, hustle and bustle, much chatter and several giggles, the group finally found themselves situated in carriages and headed for the temple ruins. Sophia missed her niece, Catherine, dreadfully, and when one of the toddlers, Ruth, if Sophia recalled her name correctly, lunged impulsively out of her caretaker's arms and into Sophia's lap, she laughed and righted the child. She bounced Ruth on her knee, singing silly songs. She had intentionally maneuvered to sit across from Amala and Charlie, and the young boy watched her antics with the baby. He didn't laugh, but he also didn't duck his head or hide behind his ayah's sleeve. And she might have been mistaken, but Sophia could have sworn she saw the tiniest curve at the corner of his mouth when she lifted the toddler and pretended to gobble the little girl's tummy.

It was a small thing, but it was a start. She held it close to her heart, because a pall had been cast over this exotic land of beauty, and Sophia felt it. It was not lost on her, although she hadn't verbalized it to anyone, that if Charlie could identify Captain Miller's attacker, the young child may be in danger.

Chapter 14

Anthony and Dylan had just returned from another trip to the *Firefly,* having observed the reassignment of Miller's sailors and questioning any who had spent significant time with the captain. Their efforts yielded nothing new, and Anthony massaged the back of his neck, which was knotted with stress.

They had retired to the library to make notes on the morning when a laugh outside the door drew their attention to the hallway as a handful of young soldiers passed the room.

Dylan huffed in irritation. "That sounds like Mailor, regrettably."

Anthony's ears perked up. "You do not care for Corporal Mailor?"

"My personal opinion of him is that he's rather an idiot. My professional assessment is that he is a lackluster soldier. Does only the barest he can manage."

"Have you reason to distrust him?"

"Why do you ask?"

"I've observed him on one or two occasions myself, and

came to much the same assumptions you've voiced. Did he know Captain Miller?"

Dylan shrugged. "I am not aware of an association between them, but the thought of Mailor being anywhere near Pilkington's study on the night in question seems unlikely. He would have been easily noticed. Was he not dressed as a shepherdess that night?"

"The dress and wig could be removed easily enough, I expect."

Dylan nodded. "So we keep watch on him."

More laughter echoed in the hallway, and Dylan went to the door. "What are they doing here this time of day, even if it is their free time? Nobody is about—even the children are out." He paused, looking down the hallway. "They are loading up with baskets of . . . food and picnic supplies."

"Did you say Rachael and Sophia were going to the ruins this morning with young master Charles and his ayah?" Anthony came to his feet.

"Indeed." Dylan continued to look out into the hallway with narrowed eyes.

Anthony joined him at the door and eyed the activity thoughtfully. "If the gentlemen are delivering luncheon to the party at the ruins, we should accompany them. They may require help carrying all of it."

Additional voices joined the throng, and Anthony walked to the front hall to see Mailor and his sheep friends joined by Mr. Denney and his wife. Anthony angled nearer the pair while keeping his eyes on the young men shuffling the picnic baskets, gathering collapsible tables and chairs, and shouting orders for carriages to be brought around.

"You must rein them in, or I shall," Mr. Denney snapped at his wife. "I've allowed you too much leeway with their discipline. I've told them repeatedly they must behave appropriately."

"They are attending a picnic with the sister of an earl. I doubt they are behaving inappropriately," came the quiet reply.

"Beatrice retrieved her paints, and you didn't stop her! And you know as well as I do that Charity runs like a hoyden if she is let loose in any space larger than the back gardens. At the ruins, she is practically uncontrollable!" Mr. Denney pushed his way into the thick of the throng. "Did I hear someone mention delivering baskets to the ruins?"

"Why, yes, indeed, Clergyman Denney," Corporal Mailor said. "You will join us, of course? I heard your daughters also joined in on the fun!"

Denney's answering smile was strained. "Yes, that is correct."

"Oh, that's excellent! And I understand Mr. Darzi is headed to the ruins as well with several of his cousin's court. A pity the prince himself cannot join in, but he has been so ill of late."

"Mr. Darzi is there?" Mr. Denney's features stilled. "I see. We will most certainly be joining you."

Anthony exchanged a look with Dylan. "We are most definitely accompanying the picnic baskets to the ruins."

"My goodness, I do believe that cloud right there looks like Chestnut!" Sophia pointed at the sky and leaned closer to Charlie. They sat together on a blanket in the center of an ancient stone structure that was void of a ceiling and whose walls had crumbled to waist-height in some places. There was one wall, however, that still maintained a good portion of its original structure and contained a wide stone archway framed with vines and large orange, yellow, and purple orchids that were so lush and thick they appeared to be imitation.

Sophia repeated, "Do you see the horse?"

Charlie had yet to utter a word, but he did at least communicate with Amala Ayah by nodding or shaking his head. Now, he looked up at the sky where Sophia indicated and gave her a small nod.

"I wonder if he gallops as quickly as Chestnut does. Do you think he might?"

A tiny smile flickered on the child's face, and he shook his head.

"Of course, you must be correct. Clouds do not move with nearly as much speed as do horses. Even toy horses, I daresay." She smiled at the boy, and her heart thumped. He was adorable and so little and sad. She completely understood Amala Ayah's tendency to pull him close. The boy was six, but, Amala had quietly explained, when he reached age eight, he would be sent to England to attend school. The thought of sending this frightened young child across the ocean to a home he'd never known made Sophia feel slightly ill. To make matters worse, if he were not speaking by then, he would be branded slow, or an idiot. It boded no good.

Little Ruth crawled across the blanket from her English nanny, who was chatting with an ayah her own age, and scooted to Sophia. She plopped her hands on Sophia's leg.

Sophia picked up the baby and asked what she thought about clouds outrunning toy horses. A glance at Charlie's face told her he thought, clearly, that a baby wouldn't know one way or another.

The temple ruins were extensive, and covered an area larger than even the Residency. In fact, Sophia imagined the ancient place had once been its own compound. The whole of it had been comprised of several buildings, only one of which was still largely intact with a roof and all exterior walls—the one Charity had mentioned. It was enormous, and Amala Ayah and the Denney sisters cautioned the group to avoid entering, as it was dark inside and home to all manner of snakes, insects, and other things that Sophia was certain she wanted to avoid meeting closely. She could see the building—picturesque and deliciously spooky—from where the party had gathered to wait for lunch. It was visible through the trees and the other, smaller buildings that were reduced to a portion of their original glory.

There was something hauntingly romantic about the old site, and Sophia adored it. Elaborate stonework jutted toward the sky and was framed against a brilliant blue backdrop. The jungle had done its best to overtake the area but had been beaten back, to some success, by local British families who had lived in Bombay for two generations and held the old place in affection. The vegetation was tenacious, however, and clung to crumbling walls and arched doorways, decorating the whole of it with glorious abandon.

True to Charity's word, the orchids were indeed an explosion of color. They gathered at the bases of crumbling walls and entangled themselves in lush green vines that climbed up arches and stretched alongside broken stones, lending the battered architecture a renewed sense of life. In a multitude of colors, the majestic flowers scattered themselves throughout each individual building and along paths that had been trampled and established by hundreds of feet throughout hundreds of years. Sophia saw easily why Charity would choose yellow and orange orchids as a bouquet for her mother; they were bright and joyful, the very embodiment of Charity's disposition.

The area in which most of the group now sat was referred to as "the courtyard," and contained a carpet of grass and flowers that seemed innocuous. The adults, however, were on constant watch for insects that might climb onto blankets and leave a lethal bite. The Residency staff would be sending chairs and makeshift tables with the picnic, and Sophia wondered if she sought to distract Charlie or herself from the prospect of spiders and snakes in the meantime. Rachael sat on an adjacent blanket with her little twin friends and occasionally smacked the ground with a grimace.

Word had spread when they departed the mansion and the interim had produced another dozen ladies from the area who now gathered with the Denney girls or wandered around the site or in the courtyard. They were a lovely collection of women, colorful in dress, but always very British. The weather was warm—not dreadfully so—but quite humid. Sophia looked at Amala Ayah's sari with a fair amount of wistful envy. It was beautiful, the fabric was delightfully designed and bright, and at most the ensemble amounted to two layers of cloth in some areas, and that was only because the fabric wrapped around itself.

More children and nannies had also joined the group—Lady Pilkington had sent notice around to some of the other families the day before—and Amala Ayah pointed out several of Charlie's friends. He elected to stay close to her side while the rest played in the relative confines of the courtyard, and the ayah's brow creased in clear concern.

"I believe I hear carts, Charlie," Amala Ayah said, speaking in English to the child for Sophia's understanding. She patted the boy's back. "The food is arriving!"

Sophia wondered for a moment if she should go in search of Beatrice Denney, who had left the courtyard to paint a short distance away and was out of sight. She then realized the young woman would surely hear the noise. It grew until Sophia was convinced the entire city approached the ruins. Delighted laughter and surprised cries filtered through the air as multiple carts and carriages approached the ruins and came to a stop.

"Will there be enough to go round, do you suppose?" Sophia asked Amala Ayah. The small gathering had greatly multiplied in size.

"Oh, yes," the woman answered. "Especially for the children and nannies. They will have their own accommodations. The mothers here do not trust the other households to properly boil milk for tea, so we always supply our own refreshments when we gather."

Sophia frowned. "Properly boil the milk?"

"Yes, miss. Illness is so common, you see, and the young ones are at increased risk. If the milk is improperly prepared, ailments often follow." She smiled, one brow raised. "Why one family would be equipped to prepare the tea properly over another I can't imagine. We all care for the children."

Sophia grinned. It was the closest she had ever heard Amala come to criticizing her employers or their peers. A friendly shout at the courtyard archway drew her attention, and she stared in surprise as approximately thirty more people, mostly men, joined the group and began mingling. Indian servants carried in tables and chairs, complete with starched white linens.

Those seated on the ground stood and gathered blankets, supplies, and reticules as the space was inundated with happy chatter and the smells of fresh food. Sophia held Ruth close, indicating to her nanny that she would keep her for a bit, and stepped out of the way, looking in amusement at the children's-outing-turned-adult-social-gathering. She caught sight of Dylan Stuart, and just behind him, Anthony. He made eye contact, and for a moment her heart stopped. She hadn't expected to see him, and the rush of pleasure she felt at his presence quite overwhelmed her.

His eyes held hers, and his smile slowly spread. It was as though he knew what she was thinking, and she wondered if she were so transparent, if her thoughts were written so clearly on her face.

A little gasp pulled her from the silent exchange and drew her attention to Amala, who had knelt down at Charlie's side. The child was pale and trembling, much as he'd been when Ruth had bloodied her nose in the nursery, and a trickle of urine trailed down his leg. His eyes were huge, focused on the crowd, and then he hid himself against Amala's shoulder with a shuddering sigh.

Sophia's heart thumped as a sense of foreboding crept up her spine, and she suddenly felt cold. She looked in the direction Charlie's eyes had been locked but saw only the thick crowd of people. Nobody appeared to be injured, there was no blood, and certainly no acts of violence or fighting had broken out. What had triggered the little boy's terror? Enough that he would have an accident?

She crouched down next to Amala and rubbed her hand gently on Charlie's back. "What is it, Charlie? Did you see something that frightened you?"

He sobbed, then, and his legs buckled. He collapsed fully against Amala, whose own eyes were bright with unshed tears.

"What happened?" Sophia murmured.

Amala shrugged miserably. "I haven't the least idea."

"Did he see something . . . someone . . ." Sophia stood quickly, holding Ruth close, and scanned the crowd again. There were several faces she recognized, but more she did not. She looked down at Amala again, who held the little boy close and gathered his bag of toys with the other hand. "Has this ever happened before?"

Amala shook her head, looking as bewildered as Sophia felt. She scooped up Charlie and held him against her, heedless of the risk of dirtying her own beautiful silk sari. Sophia's already good estimation of the ayah's character shot into the sky.

"I must take him back home," Amala whispered as Charlie buried his face in her neck. "Please make our excuses should someone notice our absence."

"Of course. And I shall visit the nursery when we return."

Sophia unconsciously clutched Ruth tighter as she

watched Amala leave with Charlie, and Ruth squirmed with a disgruntled screech. Sophia's eyes found Anthony again, who seemed to take in the entire scene at a glance. He looked at Amala and angled his way forward into the crowd, which by now flowed around Sophia and Ruth like a river.

There were so many faces, so many strangers. She locked onto those she recognized: the prince's cousin—Taj Darzi—and a few others with him dressed in fine native apparel; several women she recognized from the Fishing Fleet; Corporal Mailor and his three sheep; Professor Gerald; Clergyman and Mrs. Denney.

Mr. Denney approached Sophia, looking especially fierce. "Have you seen my daughters?" he asked without delay.

Sophia fought the urge to step back. "Just over there. Painting, I believe." She pointed to the last place she had seen Beatrice, just outside the courtyard. She had no idea of Charity's whereabouts and felt a stab of guilt. Should she have been paying closer attention to the girl?

The clergyman muttered something to his wife and tugged her away.

Anthony finally reached her side. "What is it?" he asked, breathless. "What's happened?"

"Oh, Anthony." Sophia winced. "Charlie is so terrified. I think he might have seen the person who hurt Captain Miller. I should go to him; I must find a way for him to trust me. He cannot live out his life in fear—" She felt her own eyes burn with unshed tears.

Anthony placed his hand on the back of her neck. He nudged her gently away from the chaos of the crowds and toward the nearest crumbling wall. He led her toward a portion of it that stood only shin-high and helped her step over the rocks, still clutching Ruth, who chattered and smacked Sophia's face.

He took the baby from her and ducked his head to meet her eyes. "Breathe for a moment," he told Sophia while he bounced Ruth and babbled nonsense to her.

Sophia inhaled and blew the air out slowly, closing her eyes. "He is terrified. And so little. And his awful parents are sending him away to school in two years."

She opened her eyes to see Anthony smiling at her. "My parents sent me away to school when I was young."

"And they were awful."

"You're not wrong."

Sophia knew she was being dramatic and overwrought. The Pilkingtons were perhaps absent regarding their son, but not truly *awful.* Her heart still hurt for Charlie. "Why would a mother send her child away at such a young age to be harassed by cruel peers and smacked about by harsh professors?"

"If it's any consolation, I've heard many parents here intentionally maintain distance from their children because they know they will be sending them away in a few short years. It is very difficult, especially on the mother." He smiled at her. "It is the way things are done. Makes men out of boys."

She snorted and muttered something very unladylike. It made Anthony laugh, and she looked at him holding the little girl. He was so handsome it hurt. The only thing to improve upon the scene would have been a puppy in his other arm. Perhaps a kitten.

"What do you think Charlie saw just now?" he asked her quietly. "The person who killed the captain?"

She shrugged, uncertain why she was feeling so ridiculously teary. Perhaps because Charlie was so small and utterly without defenses. He was not a rough-and-tumble boy; he was the sort who could be a target of ridicule. And his automatic physical response to his fear today was something that would see him mocked mercilessly by other children should it repeat itself in a different setting. She wanted to hide him from the world, from anyone who would be cruel.

"Why do you think he was so afraid?"

"He . . ." Her lip trembled and she forced the whisper. "He wet himself, Anthony. And he was pale and nearly fainted."

Anthony's brow knit. "Could he possibly be ill?"

She shook her head. "He was fine earlier, nearly smiling. And then the crowd arrived, and everyone poured into the courtyard. He stared at someone, but I couldn't tell who." She took another breath and blew it out, pulling herself together. "Amala took him immediately to one of the carriages. I told her I shall visit the nursery later."

Anthony nodded. "I am going to circle the crowd, make note of everyone here. Young Master Charlie may have just seen the person who killed the captain." He handed Ruth back to Sophia. "You find Miss Scarsdale. I am going to reconnoiter."

Chapter 15

The group returned from the ruins dusty and tired, but for the most part in good spirits. Anthony found Sophia in the Residency foyer and was about to offer to accompany her to the nursery to check on Charlie when Himmat approached and placed his hands together with a bow.

"Miss Elliot, you have a caller. Memsahib instructed me to place him in the front parlor."

Sophia blinked. "A caller? Who would call on me?"

"The gentleman said he met you at the costume ball." The old man's lips twitched. "He was dressed as a gladiator."

"Ah." Sophia nodded. "Mr. Belving, the Darjeeling expert." She turned to Anthony, trying to shake what he knew was a worried mood. She found her smile, even if her eyes still held concern. "He runs a plantation left to him by his father and desperately needs an heir."

Anthony felt his eyes narrow slightly. There was only one reason for a gentleman to call on a lady in India, especially one so recently arrived. "Well, then," he said tightly, "perhaps my task shall be finished before it's begun."

"Your task?"

"Of finding you a suitable husband."

"Ah." She smiled. "Suitable. But I must also adore him."

"You do not adore the gladiator?"

She tipped her head to the side. "It is difficult to judge my level of adoration after spending such a short amount of time with a person. I suppose I must rectify that before I make a proper decision. Himmat," she continued, turning to the butler, "please inform Mr. Belving that I shall be with him momentarily. I must freshen up."

Anthony ground his teeth together and offered what he hoped resembled a smile. "I must meet with Major Stuart. I hope to see you at dinner?"

She curtseyed very prettily and smiled. "Of course. Until then."

He watched her cross the foyer, turn when her name was called by an acquaintance, and then make her way up the stairs, chatting easily with the young woman. Her laughter floated back down toward him, and he took a deep breath. He glanced at Himmat, who looked at him with something akin to sympathy.

"Yes?" he asked the good-natured old man, whose wrinkled face settled into a smile.

Himmat shrugged. "When Miss Elliot returns, I must inform her that another caller also awaits her in the second-floor sitting room."

Anthony glared at the butler, as though it was his fault Sophia would likely be on the receiving end of two proposals before dinnertime. He pinched the bridge of his nose as Himmat laughed softly. He had to find Dylan as soon as possible to avoid making a fool of himself by interrogating the gladiator in the front parlor.

"Who is the man in the second-floor sitting room?" he asked Himmat, not bothering to affect a casual air, which the butler would undoubtedly see as false.

"Sir Larkin, the Baron from Swansea. He has an interest in Indian railroad development. Quite successful, I hear."

"Of course he is." Anthony paused. "And he is well advanced in years?" He heard the pathetically hopeful note in his own voice.

Himmat smiled widely. "Not so many years beyond yours, my lord." The butler placed his palms together and bowed to Anthony, whose nostrils flared at the man's retreating back.

He needed a distraction, and badly. Anthony found Dylan without delay, and the two men retired to Anthony's chambers to compare notes on the picnic. Anthony scribbled a list of everyone he remembered seeing at the ruins. "There. Have I missed anyone?"

Dylan nodded when he reached the end and held his hand out for Anthony's pencil. "There are a few other women I recognized, plus three additional men from my unit." He jotted on the paper and added, "We can assume the other nannies and their charges are exempt. Miss Sophia indicated the boy was fine until all of us arrived later."

Anthony nodded and rubbed his forehead. He sat back in his chair with a sigh and tugged at his cravat, his coat having been already divested. Entering the ruins and seeing Sophia standing there, holding a baby, had been quite the most alluring sight he had ever seen in his life. It reaffirmed everything he knew he'd always wanted with her, and he felt slightly guilty thinking about it while her brother was one of his best friends.

"What's got hold of your thoughts, old man?" Dylan crossed his legs at the ankles, leaned back in his chair, and closed his eyes.

I am in love with my friend's sister and desperately want her to be the mother of my children. "Nothing. Tired, I suppose." He took the paper back from Dylan and reviewed it. "How do you plan to move forward?"

Dylan's eyes remained closed. Anthony knew he was tired. Between his duties with the First Cavalry Light Brigade and now this investigation, his friend was spread thin. "I believe we might try a two-pronged approach. I shall make it known to Pilkington and a few others here who are prone to gossip that I am officially investigating Captain Miller's disappearance. Those with nothing to hide may be forthcoming with details yet undiscovered. Others, however, may be more inclined to let something slip to a less-threatening party. You, for instance."

Anthony nodded. "I shall be the charming aristocrat with nothing better to do but . . . be charming."

"Good. I believe I shall beg continued hospitality of our hosts and remain here at the mansion."

"Although Pilkington outwardly supports the notion, I am under the impression he isn't thrilled about people officially poking around in this thing. I wish you good luck," Anthony said.

Dylan smiled. "He owes me a favor. Or two."

Anthony gave him a salute. "'Tis a smart man who collects favors."

"And I am nothing if not a smart man."

The drawing room that evening was abuzz with chatter as groups of young people played hands of whist or vingt-et-un, without gambling, of course. Women took turns at the pianoforte with eager gentlemen offering to turn pages. The verandah doors were wide open, hosting excess socializers as the drawing room eventually proved too confining, and it was there that Sophia found the Denney sisters.

She hadn't seen the girls since the outing at the ruins. Their father had spirited them away, and Sophia hadn't been seated near them at dinner. Charity beckoned from a spot near the wall of netting that allowed access to the cool outside breeze. Sophia approached, and Charity grasped her hands.

"You must forgive us for disappearing so suddenly!"

"Not at all, I worried that my invitation to join us at the ruins caused contention with your parents." Sophia looked at Beatrice, whose face was characteristically impassive. The girl frowned, and something in her eyes gave Sophia pause.

"I grow weary of it," Beatrice said quietly. "It is a very small thing to enjoy a day with friends and paint with watercolor. In point of fact, it is what we are raised to do."

Sophia bit her lip, noting the light tension in the air and wondered if she was witnessing the seeds of an oncoming rebellion. "That is certainly true," she ventured, uncertain whether to discourage or encourage it.

"Your mother, Miss Sophia—what is her nature?" Beatrice said.

Sophia blinked. It was the most forward question she'd heard the young woman ask anyone. "My mother? She is very gentle. Our circumstances were . . . That is, we have not always enjoyed the status we do now. My mother worked as a seamstress, and I was a lady's maid. My mother was ill more often than not, and I worried constantly."

Beatrice's eyes softened with sympathy, and Charity's were round with curiosity. "Gentle," Beatrice murmured. "She sounds much like our mother. And your father?"

"'Tis a long story best saved for another time, but my father had been disinherited by his father. It does not happen often. But my grandfather was a very powerful man with an enormous amount of influence. My brother came into the title at my grandfather's behest and everything changed for the three of us."

"Ah," Charity breathed. "That is the reason you are addressed as 'Miss Elliot' rather than 'Lady Elliot.'"

Sophia inclined her head. "But why do you ask me this, Beatrice?"

Beatrice shifted her gaze to the netting on the window, which she suddenly seemed to find very interesting. "I find myself at a crossroads."

"Oh?"

"I have attracted the interest of a man, and I suspect my father will either heartily approve or vehemently forbid his suit."

"My goodness, such extremes." Sophia wished Rachael were part of the discussion, but she was in the drawing room with Anthony and Dylan Stuart. Rachael had been reared as a woman of gentility. She would know how to guide Beatrice. Sophia's inclination was to tell the girl to follow her heart. She glanced at Charity, who was uncharacteristically silent. The younger girl pursed her lips as though trying to keep her mouth closed.

Silence stretched, and Sophia cast about for something to say that might be of use. She could not bring herself to tell Beatrice to listen to her father. From the little she'd observed, and according to Anthony's impressions, the man was heavy-handed and immovable, which was never a good combination. Beatrice and Charity both were looking at a lifetime spent in a place they didn't like because their father had been dissatisfied with the choices he'd made for himself.

Charity bounced, the movement barely discernible, until she finally grabbed Sophia's arm and hissed, "It is the prince's cousin!"

Sophia's mouth rounded in surprise, and she looked at Beatrice, who stared at her sister with murder in her eyes.

"Charity!" Beatrice ground out.

"I'm sorry!" Charity slapped both hands over her mouth and looked at Beatrice in horror. "But if anyone might understand, certainly it's a woman who used to be a lady's maid!"

Sophia squinted at her, unable to follow the logic. She turned her attention back to Beatrice and put a hand on her arm. "Shall we stroll outside for a moment?"

"Perhaps in the atrium? That way we shall avoid the insects."

Sophia nodded, and Charity blurted, "May I come also?"

Beatrice made a sound resembling a snarl, but Sophia

nodded, more concerned about keeping the younger sister quiet than desiring to involve her further into Beatrice's admittedly *not* dull *affaire de coeur*.

Sophia led the way through the verandah, into the drawing room, past the two gentlemen whose proposals she had gently declined, and out to the front foyer. They turned a corner that led to the atrium, which was blessedly empty of people, and chose a bench at a bay window that overlooked the back gardens. There were a few sconces lit, but most of the light came from the bright moon outside and the torches placed evenly outside the windows.

Sophia turned to Charity first. "I know you love your sister, and you do care for her splendidly. I heartily approve of the way you champion her."

Charity nodded.

"I need you, however, to just listen for a moment. Beatrice is going to talk, and should she require a response, it will come from me."

Charity blinked, but nodded again.

"Beatrice." Sophia turned to the other sister and clasped the girl's hands, which were ice-cold despite the comfortable temperature inside. "Have you been corresponding with Taj Darzi?"

Beatrice sighed. "Yes, for four weeks. I noticed him when we returned home after last Season, but he took notice of me only recently and asked if we could exchange letters. He is here often as a representative of the prince, of course, and I feel I have come to know him quite well. He is attentive, very charming even when we cannot remain long in each other's company, and he writes beautiful things in his letters. We share many similar interests."

Sophia took a breath and tried to be fair despite her proclivity for jaded assumptions. It may well be that the man had seen in Beatrice the same potential Sophia saw, but it might be wishful thinking. Taj Darzi was a man who moved in his cousin's political circles, and while his reputation was sound, there was no way to determine whether or not he acted in his own interests.

"Admittedly, I do not know him well, but I would exercise caution."

Beatrice's features tightened.

"I do not suggest you should not encourage his suit, but as with any courtship or potential marriage, a woman must be very, very sure of both herself and the gentleman in question." Sophia paused. "Do you understand? When I was a lady's maid, I was propositioned *most* improperly by men who were supposedly above reproach in behavior and station. They were appalling, but to outward appearances, they seemed everything a gentleman should be."

"What did you *do*?" Charity interjected.

Sophia held up a finger to the girl and kept her attention focused on Beatrice. "Mr. Darzi has enormous wealth, enormous influence. I suppose what I mean to say is if you decide you would like to pursue a life with him, be absolutely certain. Much as any woman should be when choosing a husband. But when a man has power such as Mr. Darzi has at his command, your options, should matters not . . . go well, would be extremely limited. Even more limited than those which a woman usually finds in a marriage."

Beatrice nodded and gave Sophia's hand a squeeze. "I do understand what you're saying. And I have not made any rash decisions. I've not made any decisions at all, in fact." She sighed and a frown creased her forehead. "I do not know what to do." She paused. "He is kind. And I quite adore him."

"Has he suggested furthering your association?"

She lifted a shoulder. "He would like to. The prince is ill, and he fears his health will only grow worse. Mr. Darzi is his heir."

"He would like to secure his bride before then?"

"I believe so, yes."

"Certainly, marriage to a British woman of good reputation is a wise political decision," Sophia said gently. "Caste considerations aside."

Beatrice nodded. "I harbor no illusions that he is captivated by my beauty or charm. Frankly, however, I do have the most sterling of reputations for the area—especially with the Fleet continually arriving." She grimaced apologetically. "There are those girls from England who behave with a certain amount of scandal and bog down the reputation for the rest, I'm afraid."

Sophia nodded and pursed her lips in thought. If Darzi were indeed in search of an impeccable reputation, he could do no better than Beatrice Denney. Sophia didn't know if the man's motives were pure, but was he really worse than any of the young men who surrounded them? So many of the Englishmen in India were desperate enough for wives that they proposed multiple times per Season. And dalliances on the side with native women or Eurasians—offspring of

European and Indian—were common. It wasn't as though marriage to a British citizen guaranteed love and fidelity.

Sophia drew a breath. "As your friend, Beatrice, and one who finds you enormously talented and gracious, I would suggest you take the matter as slowly as you are able. I realize you feel an untoward amount of pressure from your father and the fact that he plans to send you back to London again soon. Be certain, though, that Mr. Darzi has *your* best interests at heart, as well as his own, before you commit to him."

Charity clapped her hands. "That is beautiful, and exactly what I would have said. Had I thought of it."

Sophia and Beatrice both glanced at the younger girl, and Sophia fought to keep her expression neutral. Charity was flighty, perhaps, but she was genuine. And she loved her sister.

Beatrice smiled at Sophia. "I thank you for your advice and your friendship. I do not have many friends—"

"—*any* friends," Charity murmured.

"But," Beatrice continued with a glare at her sister, "I am so grateful to know you. I do hope your visit will extend at least until the warm weather is upon us." She laughed. "'Warm' understates it, of course."

"I do hope so as well." Sophia smiled and wondered if Beatrice would care for a hug. Sophia didn't give them out freely—Ivy was truly the only friend she embraced—and with anyone other than family, she always found it awkward.

Beatrice leaned forward slightly and pulled back, as did Sophia, and in the end they simply squeezed hands again. "You will keep me abreast of your comings and goings with this?" Sophia hoped desperately that Mr. Darzi was a man of integrity, for he could do no better than Beatrice Denney.

Beatrice nodded and smiled, a little lift to her shoulders betraying her excitement.

"Miss Sophia?" Charity said. "I have heard that Major Stuart is officially investigating Captain Miller's disappearance. Is it true? I *wish* I had information to share. He is incredibly handsome."

Sophia laughed. "That he is."

"But perhaps you will be able to help Charlie, Miss Sophia," Charity said, head tipped to the side. "Himmat told Abdullah, who told our butler, Ashmel, that Charlie has been most distraught since the captain's disappearance. He seemed to enjoy your company yesterday at the ruins, though. He seemed very comfortable with you. I must say, it is singular a lady of your consequence would take an interest in children. It isn't done, you know."

Sophia smiled wryly. "I know. Much of what I do 'isn't done.'"

"Oh, but it is so refreshing! You encourage me to imagine I might be myself and not feel ashamed that I enjoy dancing in the ruins." Charity stood and pulled her sister's hand. "We should find Papa so he doesn't think we're being inappropriate somewhere. Will you join us again on the verandah, Sophia?"

"Yes, absolutely. I believe I shall sit here and admire the stars for a moment and then I shall rejoin you."

The young women left, and Sophia turned her gaze to the shimmering world of silver beyond the window, feeling heavy-hearted. She leaned her shoulder against the glass, touching her head to it, and closed her eyes. Little, adorable

Charlie was frightened, literally beyond words, by *something;* gentle, wonderful Amala Ayah was worried sick about him; Beatrice Denney was being pursued by a powerful man who may or may not care for her; Charity Denney would likely find herself shuttled back to England with or without Beatrice; Sophia herself was beginning to doubt whether they would ever know what had happened to Captain Miller; and she didn't know if the man she loved would ever admit he wanted more from her than sisterly affection.

"Now that is the picture of a very weary woman." The voice was soft, low, and came from the shadows. She recognized it instantly and wondered how long Anthony had been standing there.

"How much did you overhear?" She remained leaning against the window, eyes still closed.

"All of it. I was here when you arrived."

"And you didn't think to make your presence known? Not gentlemanly of you at all, my lord."

"I am accustomed to fading into the shadows."

She opened her eyes and slowly straightened. "That sounds not only cryptic, but melodramatic."

He made his way toward her, hands in his pockets. "Sound advice you gave to Miss Denney just now."

Sophia shook her head. "I do not trust her suitor."

"I believe she would be safe with him. I believe he is genuine."

"Do you know more than you've implied?"

He smiled. "I always know more than I've implied."

"Except what fate befell Captain Miller."

He acknowledged that with a quirk of his head and a raised brow. "Except that."

"I must continue to work with Charlie. The world will eat that little boy alive, Anthony."

"Not if he has you for a champion."

He looked at her for a long time, and she suddenly felt very warm. He hadn't moved closer, hadn't moved an inch at all, but he was suddenly very much more *there.*

She stood. "My reputation will be in shreds if I am found alone with you."

"With anyone, or just with me?"

"Cryptic *and* brooding." She meant to sound light, but the end result was rather more breathless.

He nodded toward the atrium entrance. "Go. I shall follow at an appropriate distance."

She walked toward the entrance, forced herself to keep moving forward. What would he do if she went to him, stood before him, wrapped her arms around him, and simply held him? Would he take his hands from his pockets and hold her close? Would he finally kiss her? Or would he set her firmly away from him and tell her what a good friend she was?

Would she be ruined?

Only if discovered . . .

She gave a light shake of her head and kept moving forward. As she made her way through the front hall and back toward the drawing room and verandah, she tried to console herself with the fact that she hadn't thrown herself at him. Perhaps, she hadn't bolted at the first sound of his voice as a proper lady would have done, but she wasn't there with him now, when she had never in her life wanted something more desperately.

She massaged her temple with her fingers and stood just outside the drawing room. Inside were dear friends, a well-meaning sponsor, and several lovely new acquaintances. It was a group in which she knew her presence was warmly welcomed, and yet she couldn't bring herself to go back in.

Instead, she turned and wound her way to the back of the mansion to the servants' staircase and headed up to the third floor. She hovered outside the nursery, wanting to enter and kiss Ruth's soft cheeks, wanting to sit next to Charlie's little bed and hold his hand and tell him everything would be fine. In the end, she did neither, knowing waking the children would serve only her interests, not theirs. She turned and made her way back down to the second floor and entered her bedchamber. Her lady's maid sat reading near the unlit hearth, a lamp at her elbow.

Briggs looked up with a start. "Miss Sophia, I wasn't expecting you!"

"Briggs, you look tired, and I am exhausted. Help me out of this dress and then you go to bed, too. I'm finished for the evening."

"Are you well, miss?"

Sophia nodded and sat at the vanity, pulling jewelry from her fingers and wrists and unfastening a strand of pearls from her neck. Briggs began dismantling her coiffure and released multiple pins, allowing the curls to fall down her back. Sophia ran her hands through the heavy mass with a sigh, massaging her scalp.

Briggs met her eye in the mirror and frowned. "You're certain you're well?"

"Briggs, are you happy?"

"Miss?"

"Do you have heavy problems? Anything worrisome on your mind?"

"Nothing aside from life's usual worries, I suppose, miss. You're so good to me, and I've never been happier in a post in my life. I am here in a different land, I get on well with the other servants, and I am even learning some Hindi." The young woman smiled. "Nothing so worrisome I lose sleep at night."

Sophia's shoulders sagged. "That is indeed a relief. I am glad to hear it."

"Miss Sophia, 'tis certainly not my place, but you are not quite yourself this evening."

"Many good people bear heavy burdens, Briggs, and I suppose I want to shoulder them all. Or rather, that I feel I should. Or could." She shook her head at the nonsense. "I am merely tired. You go to bed, and we shall arise fresh tomorrow."

"Tomorrow evening is the ball at the Club. Do we have something special planned for the day?"

"A trip to the bazaar, I believe, where I plan to purchase a special toy for a special little boy, whose burdens are much too heavy for his small shoulders."

Chapter 16

Downtown Bombay was a cacophony of sights, sounds, and smells that overwhelmed and delighted Sophia. There were textiles, flowers, and spices spilling out of enormous bags propped just outside shop doorways and underneath awnings ranging in color from red, orange, blue, purple, and yellow. Enormous fruits and vegetables warred with trinkets for vendor space down crowded streets and alleyways.

And people! There were more people than she'd ever seen in one place at one time together. Women in saris of the richest blues, greens, reds, oranges, and yellows shopped and worked alongside the men, who wore the more understated attire of a white tunic shirt and loose-fitting white linen trousers. Men wore turbans, and women wore beautiful veils and head scarves—some translucent, others opaque silk edged in intricate beadwork.

Hands were beautifully decorated with henna, certain symbols on foreheads signified one's caste, religion, or the god one worshipped. Music played on strange-sounding flutes, and a woman danced with beautifully flowing veils.

Children laughed and darted from one stall to the next, some well-dressed, others in rags. Big, brown eyes, dark hair, white teeth, most laughing—the children were like children anywhere. They wanted to be happy and fed. They instinctively sought out joy.

Sophia stood at one of the many tents in the bazaar and ran her hand along several colorful stacks of fabric and wished she might have a sari made from each one. She would wear the light clothing, and sandals like the natives wore, and she would adorn her wrists with multiple bangles that would clink lightly together with each movement of her arm, just like Amala's.

Theirs was a rather large group. Much like the day before at the ruins, word had spread that a party was forming to make a foray into the city for shopping and sightseeing, and three conveyances quickly became four, and then five. Sophia and Rachael had sent word to the Denneys' bungalow, and the girls were permitted to accept the invitation. Several other members of the Fleet joined the group, as did a few local bachelors who owned tea and dye plantations nearby and never missed an opportunity to spend time with unattached women. Sophia wasn't as familiar with them, but they seemed amiable enough. Professor Gerald had wished to join the group but had other obligations at the university. Sophia took note that Rachael seemed disappointed by that news.

The gentlemen present became makeshift mules until packages could be handed off to accompanying servants who shuttled purchases back to the carriages. They were good-natured about the whole business, and even Anthony carried a few items Sophia had picked up along the way.

"Thank you ever so much," she said to Anthony with a smile as she handed over another length of fabric for him to hold. This bundle contained three yards of red cotton with rows of appliqued elephants along the edges. "Abdullah will return momentarily, I'm certain."

Abdullah was a boy in his later teens and a servant in the Pilkington household. His uncle was Himmat, and his aunt worked in the kitchens. He smiled and laughed often, and Sophia suspected he worked very hard to contain his gregarious nature. His eyes often twinkled, and she could easily imagine him executing a very effective wink. Quiet, humble servitude simply did not seem to sit well on his shoulders. The more time she spent in his presence, the better she liked him. He would rise in the ranks of British servitude, if he chose that path, but she imagined his sights were set upon bigger things.

"What are your plans for this cloth?" Anthony asked.

"I've no idea yet, but it's certain to be spectacular."

He dropped his voice to a murmur. "How fares our young friend today?"

Sophia glanced down the crowded street at Amala Ayah, who held Charlie's hand firmly as she pointed at something on one of the tables. She knelt next to him with a smile and spoke to him, but as Charlie's back was to her, Sophia didn't see his response.

"No worse than before, thankfully. Amala did tell me that Charlie cried out in his sleep last night and mumbled something that she couldn't quite decipher. I see the strain in Amala's face and feel quite helpless. It seems there is so little to be done."

Anthony nodded. "We may have to accept the fact that he won't ever discuss it."

Sophia's brow wrinkled, and she moved forward to a large yellow awning that covered a table full of carved toys. "I've considered writing Jack a request to continue his acquaintance with the Pilkingtons so that when it comes time for Charlie to attend school, if he is still struggling with this"—she waved her hand, encompassing the area around them—"they might be amenable to allowing us to sponsor him. He could live at one of the estates with Amala, if she cared to join him, and we could hire a tutor."

She felt his gaze and looked up at him, silently daring him to find fault with her plan. Sophia could be stubborn, and on this issue she was not prepared to give an inch.

"Supposing the Pilkingtons do not agree?"

She felt her shoulders sag despite her resolve. "That will be the one hurdle, I suppose. However," she said, shifting closer to Anthony and lowering her voice, "when faced with the option that he will be labeled mentally unstable, would they not rather have him with us than institutionalized?"

He inclined his head as though ceding the point. "One can hope." He lifted the corner of his mouth in a smile. "You have a remarkably generous heart." He cupped her arm, his fingers trailing softly along her skin where her lightweight shawl draped away in a scoop.

She swallowed and stepped back. "Lord Wilshire, friends do not take such intimate liberties."

Frustration crossed his features, and for the first time, he didn't bother to mask it or quickly shrug it off. It was quite possibly the most real emotion, the most authentic reaction he'd made and sustained, since her arrival. A muscle moved in his jaw. He looked at her but said nothing. She was rooted to the spot, felt pinned there, and she waited for him to speak, to admit he was playing a ridiculous game that she didn't understand. She refused to be the first to break the silence; she willed him to respond.

He took a breath and looked away, running his free hand through his hair. He closed his eyes briefly and muttered something she didn't hear. She wanted to cross the distance between them and grasp his lapels. She wanted to shake him and yell and tell him how much his desertion had devastated her. How she had missed him so much it was a physical ache in her chest.

"Look at me," she said quietly, and was fairly surprised when he did. "I do not understand what you are about."

He inhaled and exhaled slowly. "That would make two of us."

"Miss Sophia!" Charity entered the space under the awning and arrived at Sophia's side, her usual ebullient spring in her step. "Have you found a toy, then?"

Sophia blinked. A toy?

"My favorite fruit vendor, Mr. Ahmahd, says this is the best toy shop of them all."

Sophia placed a hand on her midsection and drew a deep breath, trying to pull herself from the befuddled haze Anthony seemed to have wrapped them in. "Yes, I am just now reviewing this selection of toys." She managed a smile at Charity. "What do you think?"

Charity clasped her hands together as she perused the table before them. "Oh, there are so many! And look!" She lifted a carved elephant that had been painted in bright colors. It had a *howdah* on its back, mirroring the enormous saddles that were used to transport people and cargo. Within the howdah were six carved figurines: five humans and one little monkey. The figurines contained articulated arms and legs that could move, bend, and sit on the tiny benches within the saddle.

Charity grinned and carefully lifted one of the ladies from the elephant's back. "They are likely off on an adventure in the jungle, wouldn't you say?"

Sophia smiled. "I would say so, yes. And I think you have found the perfect toy for Charlie. I shall also purchase one for my niece, Catherine."

Charity beamed. "Charlie will adore it. Perhaps it will help him find his voice again."

Sophia gave Charity's hand a squeeze. "Perhaps it will." Sophia took two of the elaborate toys and made the purchase, watching as the shopkeeper wrapped the pieces in tissue paper. His face was wreathed in wrinkles that were pronounced when he extended the package to Sophia with a smile. His gnarled hands had seen years of work. She placed her palms together and touched her thumbs to her forehead with a light bow and, when she took the bundle from him, he responded in kind.

She turned to leave, altogether too aware of Anthony, who still stood nearby, watching her but saying nothing. He kept pace with her as she stepped away from the awning and extended his hand for the package. She thought of being churlish and retaining it, but decided that would be silly and she'd had enough game-playing to last a lifetime. The worst part was that she did not know what game she was supposed to play.

The large group from the Residency spent the next two hours perusing stalls and meandering the streets around the bazaar. Sophia intentionally stayed near Rachael and Dylan, finding it easier to hide her impatience with Anthony while they were in a crowd.

As they strayed farther from the bazaar, she began to notice signs of poverty unlike anything she'd ever seen before. The tall buildings—tenement housing—were stacked adjacent to one another and whole rows looked ready to fall in a stiff breeze. The stench of filth encroached upon the vibrant dream of the bazaar, and just as at home in London, the line between wealth and poverty was staggering in its harsh division. Children in tatters and rags begged for coins, and an elderly woman dressed in dingy white sat in a doorway, her head bowed in her hands.

"She is a widow," Beatrice murmured to Sophia and Rachael as they passed her on their way back to the carriages. "The color system among castes defines a person's station. Red is the color brides and married women wear, and if a married woman dies before her husband, she is dressed in red. A woman who is widowed, however, must wear white and is considered bad luck. She is often shunned by her family and then buried in white, as well."

Sophia's mouth dropped open. "That is . . . that is . . ." She heard herself sputtering and closed her mouth. She pictured her mother, draped in dishonorable white and sitting unloved in a filthy doorway. There was a time when she herself had lived in abject poverty with her mother, but even that had been a far cry from the scene before her. Her eyes stung, and she shook her head lightly to pull away from the image. "That is one of the most awful things I have ever heard."

Beatrice nodded in sympathy.

Sophia stopped walking, and Rachael paused with her, her eyes a mirror of Sophia's own distress. "Can we do something? Do we have anything to give her?" She thought of all the beautiful fabric she'd had carted back to the carriage and wondered if something there might be of use to the old woman.

Rachael cleared her throat and reached into her reticule. "I have a small piece of bread left from luncheon that I thought to feed to the birds back at the Residency with the twins." She shrugged. "Do you suppose?"

"I don't know that she can accept it from us," Dylan said gently as he joined them, clearly having overheard the conversation. "Remember how strict the rules are among the servants at the Residency? Certain sects and castes are not allowed to share food with foreigners. We are lower on the rung than Untouchables."

Sophia glanced around. "Perhaps Abdullah can take it to her?"

By now, some of the rest of their group had gathered, wondering aloud about the delay. Rachael explained Sophia's request, and one of the plantation owners, Mr. Griffen, a quiet man who had lived in India for twenty years, looked on with sympathy. "There is so much poverty here, feeding one woman is but a drop in a bucket riddled with holes."

Sophia straightened. "For a short time, it will mean something for that one woman." She motioned to Abdullah and explained her errand. He glanced at the widow and hesitated.

Sophia wondered if he were concerned about the old woman's bad luck spreading to him. She fought back instinctive impatience and tried not to marvel at the fact that they had stopped in the middle of a street to debate how best to show kindness to a starving old woman.

"Abdullah," she said, "if you should feel unclean from contact with the woman, from communicating with her, is there a ritual you can perform later to remedy the problem?"

He looked as though he would dissemble for a moment but finally nodded. "Yes, miss." His face was a study in genuine distress that was such a dramatic departure from his usual affect that Sophia felt a stab of compassion for the young man.

"Perhaps you will consent to do this thing, then," she said gently. She reached into her reticule and pulled out a handful of coins, which she then knotted into a handkerchief and handed to him. "Please give her this also."

He nodded, and Rachael handed him the wrapped remainder of her lunch. He took both offerings to the old woman, crouching down next to her and speaking a few words in a tongue she must have understood. He set the food and coins next to her on the step and left her alone.

Sophia was lost in thought as the group traveled back to the Residency, largely sober. She nodded rather absently when they reached the mansion and Anthony helped her from the carriage, telling her he'd have her packages sent to her room.

He caught her arm as she moved away. "Sophia, are you not feeling well?"

She shrugged and looked at the huge mansion that glistened in the waning sun. "Does it not seem rather futile, at times? Mr. Griffen is correct: one small gesture of kindness cannot fix things."

His thumb rubbed slowly against her arm, and she finally looked at him. "A gesture of kindness is never wasted. Ever."

She nodded, consumed with her thoughts and unable chastise him for again being too familiar. The poor widow deserved dignity, respect, a warm bed, and a full stomach. How many more were there like her in the city? In the country? In the world? It was too much, and she was overwhelmed.

"I shall meet you in the foyer before we depart for the Club," Anthony said.

She exhaled a sigh, feeling foolish and ridiculously like a woman of privilege. "What is it, exactly?" They moved aside as more people exited the carriages.

"There are British clubs all over the country called, originally enough, 'The Club.' It is simply a gathering place to game, dance, dine together—just what you might imagine a place with that name to be."

Sophia nodded and turned when Rachael appeared at her side. She told Anthony she would meet him in the foyer and then walked with Rachael to their rooms inside the house. Rachael seemed as preoccupied as she was, likely still thinking about the widow.

Briggs bounced in front of Sophia as she entered her bedroom and thrust a plain box at her. "Miss Sophia, a gift arrived for you earlier!"

Sophia's brow knit. "Who sent me a gift?"

"I do not know, only that it was sitting outside the door and it bears your name. See just here?"

Sophia opened the plain seal on a folded piece of paper and held it up to read.

Leave the boy alone.

Sophia's heart thudded once, hard, and then began to race.

"What on earth?" Briggs took the strange note from Sophia.

Sophia pried open the gift box with fingers that trembled, and she stared, horrified, at a little wooden horse that had been cut cleanly in two.

"Oh!" she cried and sank into a chair. Her stomach clenched, and she felt decidedly ill. "Who would do this to Charlie's favorite toy? Does he even know it is missing?"

Briggs stared at the toy with wide eyes, then her gaze darted to Sophia. "Is the boy in danger, miss? Are you?"

"He cannot see the horse like this. I must tell Amala to distract him until I know what to do." Sophia placed shaking fingers on her forehead. They were cold. "We will fix it. It is a clean enough cut. Somehow we will repair it."

She stood and took the note from Briggs' hand.

"Are you still going out, miss?"

Sophia nodded, feeling a surge of anger and welcoming it. "This is unacceptable." She slapped the lid back on the box and took it, with the note, to Rachael's room.

"I will not be cowed, and I will not hide," she said as soon as Rachael answered her knock.

"Sophia?"

Sophia thrust the box at her friend as she entered the room. "Do a favor for me, will you, and deliver this to your cousin? I cannot go knocking on his bedchamber door without causing a ruckus."

Rachael stared at her and then opened the box and read the note, a horrified gasp following. "I shall take it to him immediately. The Pilkingtons must be made aware. Perhaps Dylan can assign a pair of his men to guard the nursery." She paused. "What of your safety? Should we remain here this evening?"

Sophia's nostrils flared. "I do not answer to cowards who prey on children."

Rachael closed the letter inside the box. She stepped around Sophia to the door. "I'll deliver this to Dylan now, and ask that he tell Lord Wilshire. Surely he will want to be advised."

"Thank you." Sophia fumed as she returned to her room, and her heart beat a steady thrum she knew was a testament to the undercurrent of fear that threaded beneath her anger. If it guaranteed Charlie's safety, she would stay away from the nursery for the moment. Her determination to resolve the matter, to solve the mystery of Charlie's fear, however, had leaped to the forefront with a vengeance.

Chapter 17

Pierre straightened Anthony's cravat with a nod of satisfaction. "*C'est magnifique.*"

Anthony rotated his head to one side and the other, bumping up against the stiff points of his collar and causing Pierre to emit sounds of distress. "I am wound up like a spring, Pierre. I do not wish to smile and talk and laugh and serve young ladies punch from the refreshment table."

"What do you want to do, then? There was a time when you would have given anything for such to be the entirety of your tasks."

What do I want to do? He knew very well the answer to that question. He also knew he couldn't do it. A knock on the door saved him from a perfunctory response and Pierre's all-knowing, all-seeing eye. "Likely Himmat, informing us that the carriages are ready."

Pierre shot him a glance that suggested he recognized Anthony's prevarication for what it was, but answered the door. "Major Stuart?"

Anthony turned to see Dylan at the door, his face like a thundercloud. "What is it?"

Dylan entered and thrust a piece of paper at him.

Leave the boy alone.

Anthony looked up. "When did you receive this?"

"I did not receive it. Sophia did. With this." In his other hand, Dylan held a box containing a small wooden horse that had been severed in two.

An angry heat started deep in Anthony's gut and rose until he felt he would choke on it. "When?"

Dylan paced back to the door. "Just now. It was packaged and in her room waiting for her. She told Rachael, who found me." He paused. "Anthony, I do not like her or Rachael remaining in the dark any longer. Forewarned is forearmed, and they may need to defend themselves. They must be vigilant. I do not mean to force your hand, but that"—he pointed at the broken toy and letter—"is a thinly veiled threat. Sophia is beside herself over how Charlie will react to the destruction of his favorite toy, but you and I both know that this will be the least of her problems if she continues to interfere. Not to mention the fact that there is much more to this mess than one missing sea captain. Whoever is behind this has much to lose."

Anthony exhaled. "What Sophia knows, I would not ask her to keep from Rachael. I hope you're prepared for questions."

"Questions are fine." Dylan opened the door. "Wondering

how they'll respond when I tell them I think they should go back to England immediately has me worried."

The door closed behind Dylan, and Anthony's heart sank at the thought of Sophia leaving India. The present danger to her would likely dissipate if she left, would it not? The person who wanted her to stop seeking answers from Charlie was presumably the same person who killed Miller and stole the Janus Document. If Sophia were no longer in India, the person who threatened her would have no further reason to continue.

It was a sound plan, and he resigned himself to the notion that she needed to go home, and likely Rachael, as well. Dylan's concern was justified; Rachael was embroiled in the drama as much as Sophia was. And hovering at the back of his mind was the suspicion he'd been harboring that someone at the War Department had been behind the theft in the first place—that person wasn't Harold Miller. Which meant that if Anthony couldn't get his hands on the document, everyone was still in danger, even at home. Perhaps it was time to enlist Dylan in a more direct capacity and search each room in the mansion. He had frustratingly few other leads or options.

Pierre shot Anthony a look of uncharacteristic sympathy as Anthony exited the room and made his way through the mansion toward the front door. He forced himself to relax, unclenching his jaw before it could show signs of stress. Several of the guests, the Pilkingtons included, gathered in the atrium and for a fleeting moment, he imagined taking Lord Pilkington by the cravat and shoving him up against the nearest wall until he told him whatever he knew about Miller's disappearance. There must have been something the man had missed, *something* he knew. Who would have been in a position to discover the combination to the lock on his safe? Who had Miller been seen talking to in the days before his death?

Dylan was already among the gathered guests, and he subtly inched closer to the Pilkingtons until he was upon them and they couldn't scuttle away. Anthony smiled in spite of his foul mood. Dylan was clever.

Lady Pilkington spied Anthony, and her face lit up. He swallowed a groan when she motioned to him. She was overcompensating for the fact that her nerves were raw and the household was strangely off-kilter. Events surrounding them were beyond her control, and she was twice as ardent in every emotion as before. Stuart was keeping Lord Pilkington occupied with conversation that had the man looking slightly ill, but he wasn't able to keep the wife corralled, so Anthony followed the summons dutifully.

"Lord Wilshire, three of my closest friends arrived from their yearlong tour of Europe and Asia earlier this week and they are going to the Club with us! I think you may know them!" She reached behind herself and pulled on an arm that was attached to a woman Anthony did indeed recognize. She was Maria Vale, Lady Seadon, and the younger sister of a friend of his late mother's.

And of course, he mused as Lady Seadon motioned across the room, she had brought her daughter and niece.

He felt cold all over and tightened his lips at the conundrum his life had become. Alissandra Vale—Lissa—had pursued him more after his immediate return from the war than he would have imagined any one person could. She'd tried on multiple occasions to be accidently "caught" alone with him, which would have forced his hand and landed her the role of Countess Wilshire. He had never encouraged her, had never even offered a whisper of a suggestion he was interested either in an association with her or in finding a wife in general. His cover "reputation" as a rake, however, had preceded him home, and since his father had been on his deathbed and Anthony's ascension to the title imminent, tongues wagged that he must soon find a mother for his future heirs.

And now here she was—and wonderful!—here *Sophia* was, entering the atrium with Rachael and the Denney sisters.

"Anthony." Lissa smiled, and the sight brought to Anthony's mind the image of a cunning feline. She had black hair and enormous blue eyes. Perfect in face and form, she was well aware of her assets and used them to full advantage. He felt not a stirring of interest for her, but rather a sense of worry that Sophia might witness something she would misunderstand.

"Lord Wilshire," he corrected quietly and bowed over her gloved hand, intentionally withholding a perfunctory kiss.

Her brows drew together in a tiny frown that she quickly smoothed over. "Of course you remember my cousin, Miss Adeline Vale?"

Cousin Adeline was a nice girl, but cast forever in the shadow of her intense relative. Adeline was "obliged to live on the family's charity," Lissa had informed him once with a sad but kindly smile.

Adeline smiled, self-consciously tucking a stray lock of auburn hair behind her ear. She really was lovely, with curls any girl would envy and vivid green eyes, and Anthony felt a stab of pity that her circumstances placed her in such an unpleasant and vulnerable position. Lissa's tongue was vicious, and she ruthlessly flayed anything she viewed as competition. He imagined Adeline had been firmly shoved into place from the moment she found herself living on her family's charity.

He smiled at Adeline and bowed over her hand as well, deliberately placing a light kiss on her gloved fingers.

Lady Pilkington gestured to Sophia and the other women, and when they approached, Anthony smiled at Sophia and moved closer to her until his sleeve brushed hers. Lissa glanced at them, and he caught the fractional narrowing of her eyes. His fingers itched to grasp Sophia's shoulders and pull her from the room. Lissa would most definitely see the beautiful Sophia as her fiercest competition yet. He realized too late he'd have done Sophia a favor had he stayed away from her.

"Miss Sophia Elliot, sister to the current Earl Stansworth." Lady Pilkington introduced Sophia grandly with evident pride.

Lissa smiled and curtseyed, as did Sophia, and Anthony felt a sinking sensation in his gut when Lissa eyed Sophia with one arched brow.

"Of course! We were never properly introduced in London. Lady Pilkington, I vow, is it not beyond imagining to look at Miss Elliot now and realize she was once a maid?"

The air around them stiffened, and Anthony wanted to throttle the girl. Before anyone could form a response, she opened her blue eyes wide and feigned innocence. "Oh, I certainly mean no disrespect! Dear me, I do tend to say the wrong thing at times."

"It might be well worth your consideration, then, to give some thought to your words before you open your mouth." Sophia's lips twitched at the corners, offering the barest of smiles that was little more than an insult.

"Oh, indeed! You are privy to advice on all things polite and proper. I forget, your sister-in-law is the famed Mistress Manners. What a delightful and refreshing *vocation*. That she *worked* for a publication and was *paid* to do it—why she quite nearly set the *ton* on its ear when her identity became known."

Anthony took a deep breath and braced himself as Sophia straightened slightly.

Lady Pilkington laughed loudly and shrilly, cutting off any further exchange between the two. "So delightful it is to meet acquaintances when one least expects it. Ah, excellent—the carriages have arrived out front." She shot a guarded glance at Lissa, who had fixed her eyes on Anthony.

He turned and reached for Sophia's hand. She glanced at him in surprise, likely shocked at the presumption, but he was taking no unnecessary risks. He would keep her glued to his side until they saw the last of Lady Lissa. He didn't trust her any more than he would a viper.

He lifted Sophia's hand and tucked it into the crook of his arm and placed his other hand atop it. When she pulled slightly back, he muttered, "Stay with me."

"Ah. You need a friend to waylay unwanted attention?" She focused straight ahead as they walked through the foyer and out the large double doors to the waiting carriages.

"Stop, Sophia," he hissed. He was aggravated, worried,

and finally at his snapping point. "You know very well I never meant a word of that letter."

He registered her startled gaze as he eyed the long line of carriages. At the back of the line were three large elephants equipped with howdahs. He pulled her quickly to them and chose the last one, which held the smallest of the elephant saddles. It carried only two people, but Sophia's reputation was safe. After all, what sort of ruination could happen to a young woman when she was seated atop an elephant for all the world to see?

The attendant touched the elephant's knee, and the giant animal lowered itself so Anthony and Sophia could climb aboard. She sat back, breathless, and when the elephant lumbered upward she clutched Anthony's arm with a muted shriek.

"What on earth . . ." she wheezed and stared down with her eyes opened wide. She swallowed. "Anthony, I don't care for high spaces, I—"

He pulled her hand under his arm and linked their fingers together. "Shh," he said. "You're perfectly safe. The elephant moves very slowly."

"What are you *doing*? Why are we not in a carriage with Major Stuart and Rachael?"

"Because I must speak to you alone. About several things."

"Such as the Lady Seadon?"

There was something in her tone that gave him pause.

"I remember now," Sophia said. "She had quite set her cap for you before you left."

Ah. The questions raised about her tone were answered.

"Regrettably, yes. But I never encouraged it, never desired her attention."

She glanced at him and then looked straight ahead as the large party filed into the carriages and onto the other two elephants. "What is a woman to think, do you suppose, when a man comes home from war with a reputation like yours? She knows she is pretty, she knows you adore pretty women—"

"Sophia." His jaw was starting to ache again. "Please, for the love of Heaven, let me explain. Once we start moving and there is some distance from the rest of the group, I have things I must say to you."

She didn't look at him, but he felt the tremor in her fingers. He wasn't certain if she was still afraid of the high perch on the elephant's back or if her anger and frustration with him were at a breaking point. He couldn't blame her. As far as she knew, he had a woman in every port. More than one. And although she hadn't seemed to believe it before, Braxton had circulated the gossip again so effectively over the last two years that he could only imagine what she must have heard. He massaged his eyes with his fingers and wondered how to extricate himself—all of them—from the mess.

Once the last of the guests finally settled in, the carriages began rolling forward. The procession was a long one, and it took some time before their attendant issued the command for their elephant to walk.

Sophia tensed again, squeezing his fingers tightly, though she was probably unaware of it.

"See," he said, seeking to soothe her. "It's rather rhythmic, like rocking in a chair or a cradle."

"Only not nearly so smoothly," she breathed and closed her eyes.

Soothing her clearly was not going to work. He opted for distraction and the bluntness of the truth and dropped his voice to a near whisper. "Sophia, I am a spy for Britain's War Department."

Her eyes shot open, and she slowly turned her head toward his. Her mouth grew slack, and she stared, unblinking. He wished she would say something. Anything.

"I am certain this must come as a shock to you, but I have been on assignment these past two years and have not been at liberty to disclose the truth of it to you or anyone. My reputation as a rogue—it is nothing more than a sham, a cover story to divert suspicion away from my true activities."

Still, she stared.

"I wanted to tell you the truth. I have wanted to so many times." He ran a hand through his hair, agitated and knowing he was blabbering like a fool and not giving her even a moment to process his admission. "I was compelled to write you that letter because your safety came first—it still does—but there are things now that you must know—"

"A spy," she interrupted, blinking once.

"Yes." He was winded, as though he had run a long distance without stopping.

"That is your story? You're a *spy*?"

He felt his own mouth slacken this time. "Well, yes, I—"

Her eyes narrowed, and she pulled against his fingers but he held tight to her hand. "If you do not wish an association with me, Anthony Blake, I certainly do not care for one with you! You needn't create outlandish tales, *ridiculous* tales, merely to put me off. I have never begged for your affection, have never made demands on your time or friendship! And now because you see a woman from your past who you wish to keep at bay, you concoct this . . . this . . . bizarre scheme so that I will stay by your side and make it appear as though you are spoken for? Ha!"

"Sophia, shh—"

"I should march straight up to Lady Seadon and say, 'Here! Take him, please, because he is a *philanderer* and a *liar* and you are welcome to him because I want none of it!'"

He clapped a hand over her mouth and smiled at the four people on the elephant ahead of them who had craned their necks around at her outburst. "Sophia," he said through his teeth.

He felt the sharp sting of a bite and yanked his hand away.

"Do *not* attempt to placate me or hush me," she hissed, and he was grateful she had lowered her voice. "I am not a child! I am a woman of marriageable age and when I think of the gentlemen I have brushed aside because I was convinced I could never feel deeply for anyone again, I am ill! I might have fallen in love with someone else, might have had a chance at happiness! I have wasted my youth, and for what? A *liar*!"

At that, he laughed. "Sophia, you have not wasted your youth—"

"Do *not* laugh at me! Do not even look at me. I want to get down from this elephant."

He had never seen her so furious. And cad that he was, he couldn't help but think she'd never looked more beautiful. "You cannot get down from a moving elephant."

"Then tell him I want to stop."

"Tell the elephant?"

She ground her teeth. "Tell the attendant who is driving the elephant that I want to get down."

"No. And stop moving around so, you'll frighten the beast."

She stopped moving immediately, and he felt guilty for using her fear against her. "Now, before we arrive at the Club, please tell me the details of the package you received."

She glared at him. "Giving up your pretense already, are you? I suspect you realized it for the pathetic scheme that it was."

"It is not a scheme; it is the truth. Every word. We can discuss it later, but I would like to know about the broken toy and note that Major Stuart brought to me."

She deflated, then, her shoulders dropping. She closed her eyes and rubbed her forehead with fingers that shook. He pressed the hand he still held between his two and rubbed his thumb lightly across her knuckles.

"Someone sliced Chestnut completely in half, and I do not know how to explain it to Charlie. I do not know who did it, or why, and the note makes no sense to me at all. I can only assume someone seeks to keep me from discovering his identity through Charlie, but now I am afraid that the boy's life is in danger more than I fear the danger to my own life. I am horrified that someone would be so cruel as to destroy his favorite toy, his security." Her voice trembled.

"We can fix the toy," he said and continued his slow massage of her hand. "It will not be exactly as new, but perhaps we can explain that it was hurt but it has been mended. We can even affix a bandage to it and tell him the wound was sustained whilst Chestnut was doing something heroic."

She narrowed her eyes. "Something like spying for God and country?"

He couldn't help but smile, but he did his best to hide it. She didn't sigh, or faint, or meekly accept whatever he might say. She came at him head-on as would a hissing cat, and he much preferred that. Now he knew the state of her heart for certainty. At least the state in which he'd left it. Reclaiming it might prove to be more of a challenge than he'd imagined.

"We shall fix the toy," he repeated, "and I think it best if you keep away from Charlie for a time. In fact, I believe Dylan may suggest to you and Rachael both that you should consider returning home."

She shot her attention back to his face. "Did he tell you that?"

He nodded. "I hate to say I agree with him. Captain Miller is most certainly dead, and I believe you are in danger."

"Major Stuart is delusional—*you* are delusional—if you believe I am leaving until the matter is settled with that boy. Rachael can return home if she wishes, but I am not going."

He ought to have expected it and didn't know why he was surprised. "Dearest—"

She flared her nostrils at him, and he held his hand up in supplication.

"Sophia, you know Jack is your guardian. I must write to him, and ultimately he will decide whether you remain here or go home."

She cocked a brow and looked him squarely in the eye. "I shall marry someone here, then. I have already received half a dozen proposals from men I could tolerate well enough, and I have only been here a week. I will remain here and continue to help Charlie and the Denney sisters."

He frowned. "Who have you met that you could tolerate? And *half a dozen*? I thought there were two!"

"I don't see how that is any of your business. You are not my *brother*, after all." She laughed but there was no humor in it.

He winced. "It makes absolutely no sense for you to tie your fate to a man you feel you might 'tolerate well enough,' merely to remain with people who have, until a few days ago, been complete strangers to you."

"The man tells me he's a spy and then dares reference *my* ill use of common sense." She stared straight ahead, again tugging on her hand.

Still he held it tight, knowing she had her wits about her enough to realize she couldn't fight him without causing a ruckus other people would see. It was brutish of him, but desperate times called for brutish measures. He had her captive on the back of an elephant, they had the rare liberty of conversing alone without ruining her reputation, and he would hold her hand as though it were the last opportunity he might ever have. Which may well be the case, because the odds of success at maneuvering her alone onto an elephant again were slim.

Chapter 18

Sophia couldn't get off of the elephant quickly enough. Once her feet hit solid ground, she left Anthony without a backward glance and dashed along the side of the dusty road, looking in each carriage for Rachael. She finally found her descending from the second vehicle in the long line, glaring at her cousin. Rachael stepped onto the ground, and Sophia flew at her.

"I am livid," she said, as she linked arms with Rachael and pulled her toward the doors of the social club. "I do not believe I have ever been angrier. I have much to tell you, but later. First, I must think. And that one," she said, motioning her head behind them at Major Stuart, "thinks to make us go home immediately."

"I am aware of his plan," Rachael told her, grim.

"I am not going home yet."

"Nor I."

They eyed each other for a moment and then nodded. They approached the front of the building, which resembled a large bungalow, not as large as the Residency mansion, but still impressive in size and structure. Once inside, Sophia noted a mixture of traditional British and Indian décor, with a few hunting trophies stuffed and posed ferociously in the corners.

One large social room fed into two additional chambers, one of which was used as a drawing room for card games while the other was a ballroom that led out onto an enormous verandah that swept around the building on two sides. Music played in the ballroom, glasses clinked as guests enjoyed champagne, and conversation floated on the air punctuated with feminine laughter and the chortle of male amusement.

Sophia scowled, her mood foul. "Just as any other gathering at home."

Rachael nodded. "Of course it is. East India Company has merely recreated what everybody left behind. If they miss England so much, perhaps they should return."

"Hear, hear." Sophia put a hand on her hip and tried to assemble her swirling thoughts. Anthony was truly stupid if he thought for one moment she would believe his ridiculous tale. She needed time to think, and she certainly couldn't do it while near him. She glanced over her shoulder and spied his dark, handsome, infuriating head as he ascended the front stairs with Major Stuart. She wondered if Anthony had tried to pass his lies off onto him.

"I shall be in the ballroom," she told Rachael. "You'll find me dancing with all and sundry." And in truth, she wasn't more than two feet into the ballroom when she found herself besieged by tea planters, indigo plantation owners, three military men, and a clerk from a local countinghouse. It never hurt a girl to have options, and she was afraid if she couldn't hang on to her righteous anger and indignation, she would dissolve into a puddle of pathetic tears.

She was in the middle of a quadrille with the clerk when she spied Anthony standing near the wall in conversation with Major Stuart. She turned her head smartly when Anthony looked at her, and, as she came around again, she focused on Major Stuart instead. Perhaps she could fall in love with him. He likely didn't suffer from compulsive lying or womanizing.

In fact, he was single, smart, had a good career, provided a comfortable living for himself, and perhaps he might be interested in her dowry. It was a good enough beginning.

She made every effort to keep her attention from drifting back to the dark-haired earl at Major Stuart's side when a fluff of pink tulle in that direction pulled her eyes to him anyway. Lissa Seadon had found him and smiled up at him as though he were a breakfast pastry.

Sophia rolled her eyes and huffed a noise of disgust before she realized she was hand-to-hand again with her partner, the poor clerk who probably wondered what he might have done to earn her disdain. She forced herself to smile at the man, truly repentant when he stammered his hopes that she was enjoying her evening before the steps of the dance took her away from him again.

The set seemed interminably long; she felt as though she would keep spinning in the same monotonous circles for eternity, each full spin bringing Anthony and that wretched, clinging woman into her vision again. The quadrille eventually came to its end, and she curtseyed to her baffled partner, who likely was reconsidering furthering an association with her.

Strains of a waltz began next, and couples flooded to the floor in delight. Anthony was saying something to Lissa Vale, and Sophia felt her nostrils flare. Perhaps he was trying to convince the young woman he was an international man of espionage. And what would Lissa care? All she wanted was his title and money.

"By some miracle sent from heaven, are you unclaimed for this dance, Miss Elliot?" Professor Gerald stood at her elbow, and she turned to him with a smile.

"I am indeed unclaimed."

He bowed very nicely and led her back to the floor. They settled into a comfortable rhythm. He was smooth on his feet and sure in his movements. She smiled at him and cast about for a conversation opener. She could always remark on the weather, or the differences in climate between India and England.

"He looks at you constantly, you know."

She blinked. "I'm sorry?"

"Wilshire. I am an observant study of character, and when you are in the room, he has eyes only for you."

She shook her head and looked at a spot beyond his shoulder as he spun her effortlessly around the room. "Mr. Gerald, you are entirely too sympathetic. I fear you will have me in tears when I should much rather remain indifferent."

He smiled and she looked at him. He really was rather handsome with those haunting blue eyes fringed by thick black lashes, black hair, and olive-toned skin. What was wrong with her? She didn't feel anything special when she looked at him, even with one hand holding hers and his other at her waist. His firm shoulder beneath her hand told her he had no need to fill out his suit coat with padding. Should things progress between the professor and Rachael, her friend would be a fortunate woman indeed. Physical attributes aside, he was a good man.

"You have a past with him, of course?"

She sighed. "We were close once. I had assumed more than I should. Then he left England and I was quite bereft. I do not desire to return to that emotional place." She smiled. "So now you know my secrets, and I apologize for pouring them out onto you."

"Not at all. I asked. I consider myself your new friend, and I believe you could certainly do worse than encourage the earl."

She laughed.

"He is a good man."

Her laughter faded, and she tried to hold on to her smile. "I believe he is. But I also believe he will never be content with the company of just one . . ." She flushed. It was beyond the pale to even broach such an indelicate subject with a gentleman.

"Just one woman?" he finished gently.

She nodded miserably, feeling a sting in her eyes, the prelude to a torrent of tears if she couldn't hold herself together.

"And what would lead you to assume such a thing?"

She blinked, incredulous. "His reputation has followed him even here, to India. He is a rake. A scoundrel. He is seen constantly with opera divas and women who tread the boards."

One corner of his mouth shifted in a smile. "Miss Elliot, you ought not believe everything you hear. One thing I have learned as a person of two races and cultures—and neither one truly knowing what to do with me—people say all manner of things when they do not understand the truth."

She frowned. "But it is such common knowledge—"

"You said you were close. Was his behavior suspect then? The least bit worrying?"

Her brows drew together. "No. I never could . . ." She paused. "I never could reconcile the rumors with what I knew to be true of the man."

"Might I suggest you follow your own instincts in the matter?"

She laughed, but it sounded hollow even to her ears. "I no longer trust my instincts. They are all befuddled."

The waltz came to a close, and they slowed their movements. "Well," he said, "I shall leave you to puzzle it through. I will say, however, when I find myself confused, I try to focus on only the matter before me and block out all other noise. And there will always be a plentiful amount of exterior noise."

He smiled and bowed. She dipped into a curtsey, perplexed, and watched his back as he disappeared into the crowd. A hand on her elbow pulled her attention away, and she looked over her shoulder to see Anthony's glowering face.

"Would you like me to offer felicitations now?" he asked. "I suppose he is someone you might find tolerable enough to marry?"

Chapter 19

Sophia gaped at him for a moment before recovering herself. "He is one of a few, yes," she said truthfully. "I do not believe, however, that he has an interest in me."

He shot her a flat look, as though she was ridiculous. "Of course he has an interest in you. Why wouldn't he?"

"He appears to fancy Miss Scarsdale." She pulled her elbow away from Anthony's grasp. "He sang your praises highly enough. Did you send him to me in order to convince me you are—"

"Might I accompany you for a stroll on the verandah?" he interrupted with a light bow and a gesture toward the doors. She was aware, then, of the thick crowd and close press of people. They had no privacy, certainly, and irritated as she was, she didn't care for an audience.

She led him out, aware that he was signaling someone behind her. She turned to see both Major Stuart and Rachael making their way toward them, and when they all reached the relative cool of the outdoor space, she took a deep breath. There were far fewer people outside than she might have imagined, given the crush inside. The air was heavy with the exotic scent that she was coming to identify as uniquely India, and she wished for a moment she might run by herself into the dark of night and do nothing but breathe.

"I do not know what he has told you," Sophia said to Major Stuart in an undertone, "but—"

"Sophia, it is true. All of it."

"Major." She shook her head. "I know you are friends, but his tale is ludicrous!"

"That may be, but it is no less than the truth." He paused. "I have seen the verification of it with my own eyes. Captain Miller left behind a private journal that verifies the things Anthony has told me."

Rachael also stared at Major Stuart. "Did you never think to mention this to us?"

Stuart glanced uneasily at Anthony, whose gaze Sophia had felt heavily upon her since the moment they'd stepped outside. He'd refrained from speaking, and she wondered if he'd say something, anything, that would extricate his friend from the hole he was neatly digging for himself.

"I must speak to Sophia for a moment," Anthony finally said. "I would prefer it be alone, and if you would remain in the vicinity, it could be accomplished without stain on her reputation."

Silence met his request, after which Rachael nodded. "I have been wanting a walk along the river after the stuffiness inside. The four of us can take a stroll, and you may have your conversation in relative privacy."

Major Stuart led the way to a door leading from the verandah out onto the grounds. Torches similar to those at the

Residency lit a nearby pathway, and before long the gentle sounds of a river were apparent. Other party guests were also enjoying the scenery along the river and throughout the grounds, and Sophia mused that it really could not have been a more pleasant setting. The air was heavy with humidity but not unpleasantly hot, they were far enough from Bombay proper that the slightly unpleasant waft of filth and sewage that occasionally blew over the land was absent.

The river wound its way through ever-thickening trees and flowers, their brilliant colors muted in the dark. "Rachael and I shall stop here, and you may walk a bit further with Sophia," Stuart told Anthony. "Stay within earshot. I will notify you if we receive company."

"Thank you." Anthony gave Sophia his elbow, and she took a deep breath, blowing it out slowly as they began walking further down the path. He strolled with her until a bend led them from sight, after which he dropped his arm and grabbed her hand. He pulled her a few steps off the path and into the thick of the trees. His face was still visible from a nearby torch but the small space was entirely more secluded than propriety probably would have preferred.

He retained possession of her hand, but now that they were finally alone, he seemed at a loss for words.

"It is true, then?" She was pleased her voice didn't waver when so many emotions swirled in her chest she was nearly overwhelmed. Perhaps the worst of all was a sense of pain. Betrayal.

He nodded. "I am infinitely sorry for leaving so abruptly, for being unable to explain."

"You could explain it to me now." Her voice was still steady.

He ran a hand through his hair, a sure sign of agitation. "I was assigned an information-gathering position during my time in France. During the war. I was compelled to create a story for myself, a persona, that would allow me access to circles where I might learn secrets."

He paused. She remained silent, and he continued.

"When my brother died, and I was called home as the next heir to inherit, I was happy to be finished with the whole of it. I did not enjoy the ruse, the lies, the secrets. I lived in constant worry for my safety and the safety of those who worked with me. I met Jack shortly afterward, and then you." He swallowed and looked solemn. "Then my father died, I became the earl, and I quite fell in love with my new best friend's sister."

Drat. Tears formed unbidden in her eyes, and she turned her head.

"On the night I intended to ask Jack for permission to court you formally, I had a visitor—my former employer. He told me of a sensitive document that had been stolen and explained I had no other choice but to resume my former role and retrieve it."

She shook her head. "Why did you not just tell me, Anthony?" She looked at him, her vision blurred. "I am not a vapid, silly woman. I would have kept your confidence, as I have kept every personal and private thing you ever shared with me. I could have borne the rumors then, knowing that it was all untrue, that you were not simply leaving—" Her voice hitched, and he closed his eyes. "Leaving me."

A tear fell from her eye, and he thumbed it away. "Sophia, my dearest," he murmured, "how I wanted to. That blasted stolen document contains information that puts you at risk. You, Jack and Ivy, Catherine, and hundreds of others who are close to operatives for the crown, who have much to hide and much to fear from our enemies should anyone else obtain the document."

"Explain to me how we are at risk."

His thumb continued to trace small circles on her cheek, and she hurt so much she felt her heart would break.

"There is information about all of you," he whispered. "Information about each operative's loved ones and friends. Intelligence that could be used as leverage by the French or by any government or entity that wishes to extort something. You were all safer not knowing. Even Jack."

She felt the shock of the pronouncement begin in her chest and spread to her extremities, a tingling sensation that made her feel faint. Suddenly it all made sense. Anthony's unusually keen interest in the captain's fate; his suggestions—guidance, really—to Major Stuart on whom to question about that fateful night. Anthony clearly could not investigate on his own and maintain his innocuous identity.

"So the captain was a thief, then."

Anthony nodded. "He was a temporary custodian of the document I seek. He had decided to sell it; instead, he was killed for it. My theory is that whomever he had decided to partner with was greedy in the end and wanted the whole of it for himself."

"And presumably, the killer wants his identity kept

hidden, and if Charlie witnessed the crime . . ." She looked up at him. "He is in more danger than I even supposed."

"There is much at stake. And the more people who are aware of the particulars, the more risk we all find ourselves facing. It was never a matter of not trusting you, Sophia. You, Jack, Ivy—there is safety in ignorance. Innocent comments do not accidently slip. A glance, a gesture—those who are trained to look for the smallest of nuances will be aware of the extent of your knowledge. I could not take the chance with your life, especially at the outset when I knew precious little about what I faced. But now you are in the thick of it, and I am terrified for you and dare not allow you to remain in the dark." He paused. "Aside from that, I grow weary of other men proposing to you."

She laughed, just a bit, unable to help it. And then she thought of the time that had passed, of how miserable she'd been, and the tears formed again. She was angry and frustrated, but not *at* him anymore.

"It hurt so badly," she confessed on a whisper. "I loved you with all of my soul. And then I heard about your dalliances across France, your further travels through Europe, South Africa, for heaven's sake . . ."

He shook his head. "It was never true. I have been faithful to my love for you—body, mind, and heart."

"You never even kissed me! I had no desire to be publically ruined, but gentlemen steal kisses from ladies quite frequently. I hear all sorts of gossip in the retiring rooms. Do you have any idea how long I was waiting for you to snatch a moment at a party, perhaps two seconds in the shadows on a balcony—"

He tilted her face up with both hands and cut off her sentence. For all that his hands were gentle, the kiss was not. His lips moved over hers with an urgency, a demand, an explosion of emotion that matched hers to the last degree. He cupped her head, his fingers threading under her hair, caressing the back of her neck. He traced his thumbs along her jawline, pausing the kiss only long enough to rub his thumb lightly along her lower lip, as though unable to believe she was really there.

He continued the kiss, and she thought she would die from the pleasure of it. His attention, his ardor, was so much more intense than anything she had ever expected, ever imagined. When he finally lifted his lips from hers, his breathing was as unsteady and labored as her own.

He touched his forehead to hers and whispered, "The only truth in my letter to you was that you had indeed become my very dearest friend and confidante. I told you things I would never—*have* never—told another soul. Do not ever think that I have not wanted you every moment of every day since I first laid eyes on you."

Her eyes filled again with tears, and she reached up to place her palms against his chest, over his heart. "I worried you would never be able to love only one woman, truly build a life of fidelity."

He shook his head, a sound of protest on his lips.

"And I thought I was not enough," she continued, determined to have it all spoken. "That because my station in life was once so far below yours, that—"

He pulled back and met her eyes, his own widening in disbelief. "How could you ever believe such a thing? I don't give a fig for my title, and when did I ever suggest or imply that would be a cause for concern, an issue? Sophia! I would love you if you were still a lady's maid!"

She smiled sadly. "And then all we would ever be is the master of the house catching the servant girl on the back stairs."

He placed his hands on her shoulders and shook her gently. "Never." His voice was fierce and gave her pause. She had confided in him, had told him of the times as a maid when others had attempted to take advantage of her vulnerability. That he remembered warmed the cold places in her heart. "Never would I be that man. Sophia, I love you. I have always loved only you."

Sophia closed her eyes as the bombardment of his revelations, of the truths behind the subterfuge, mingled with the grief she'd felt for years. She hardly knew what to think, how to feel. The only thing she knew for a certainty was that she loved him. She was worried for his safety and her own, terrified for her family, Catherine, little Charlie, but the thought of running away was not an option. Trouble would surely find them all if the problem at hand was not resolved, and the thought of running away from *him* was more than she could bear.

"I actually believe you." She smiled and sniffed.

He cupped her face in his hands again, his brow creased. "Can you love me again?"

Another tear escaped and rolled down her cheek and onto his finger. "I never stopped," she whispered.

A whistle sounded—Major Stuart's warning. Anthony stole one more quick, decisive kiss, and she pulled back and wiped her cheeks, managing a shaky laugh. She felt rather self-conscious, suddenly, and looked up at him through her spiky, wet lashes. He was tall and strong and beloved. His expression was wary, tentative, as though he expected her to change her mind about believing he'd told the truth.

"Anthony." She bit her lip and found another smile. Impulsively, she reached for him, wound her arms around his neck. He pulled her close, crushing her, lifting her up against him until she was certain she felt the beating of his heart against her chest. She twisted her fingers through his hair and uttered a very dramatic sigh worthy of poetry.

"Finally," he murmured in her ear, and she couldn't agree more.

Chapter 20

Anthony entered the dining room early the next morning and considered the state of his affairs as he made his way to the sidebar where food sat in warming dishes. He had finally told Sophia the truth of his life, but they still were not engaged to be married. The timing was wrong, he knew it. There were still too many things at stake, too much unfinished business to rectify.

Of all the rotten luck.

He was grateful beyond words that he no longer was forced to hide anything from her. He supposed she might be wary, at first. He felt as though he must earn her trust again, and he was more than willing to do so. He would prove his fidelity to her every day, forever.

But for now he was forced to still pretend that his heart was unattached. If he allowed himself to examine his baser emotions, he knew full well that he wanted his ring on her finger as a primitive and overt way of staking his claim. She was a vibrant individual, someone who should never be dictated to or subjugated. The laws of the land favored the husband, but he didn't, wouldn't, own her. Even still, he couldn't help but stew as he piled food on his plate and thought of the throngs of men always surrounding her. She was *his*.

He turned at movement in his periphery to see Sophia also looking over the food. She glanced at him askance with her lips quirked, and his heart tripped.

Mine.

He couldn't halt the smug, self-satisfied grin that spread across his face as she curtseyed to him and bid him good morning. He strolled beside her as she added rice pudding and a small piece of naan to her plate, and then he held a chair for her at the table where they sat together and pretended not to be in love.

"You're wearing lavender," she murmured and touched a fingertip to the small sprig on his lapel.

"Do you remember what it means?"

She blushed. In all the time he'd known her, she'd never blushed at him. Because of him. "You're thinking of me." She bit her lip, her smile a combination of innocence and confidence.

He fought another wave of lovesickness as he realized they were finally continuing on the trajectory they should have been following two years earlier. She had always been straightforward, honest to a fault, and deadly accurate in her summation of people even after only a few moments observation. She had a sympathetic listening ear, a quick wit, and a broad knowledge base as a result of her rather unconventional upbringing and tendency to read or study whatever interested her. He had returned from the war with his faith in mankind jaded, but something about being with her had made him feel whole again—perhaps because her life had not been an easy one, yet she still radiated positive strength.

All of those things were reasons he had been attracted to her from the start. But this girl who now blushed, who glanced at him with a mixture of coy and shy, who looked at him as though they shared a secret—which they did—he felt himself falling harder still. He almost wished he didn't know how wonderful it felt to finally kiss her, to feel her physical response and know it matched his own. To know that in truth he would propose and in a short time—a very short time—they would belong to each other, morally and legally allowed to know each other as well as two people ever would.

The dining room soon gathered more guests, and Rachael and the Denney family joined their table. Anthony made appropriate small talk, acknowledged Professor Gerald with a polite nod, and refrained from rolling his eyes when Sergeant Mailor and his three sheep friends joined the fray.

Clergyman Denney sat rather stiffly at the table next to Sophia, though he remained aloof to her attempts at conversation. She fell silent, and he eventually invited her to services the next Sunday. She politely accepted, and Anthony groaned inwardly. That meant that he and her other friends likely would attend also because Sophia would insist she not be the only one to suffer.

Mrs. Denney sat on her husband's other side and quietly watched the people around her. Her gaze rested fondly on her own daughters, benignly enough on the Fishing Fleet ladies, and skipped her husband altogether. She seemed to shrink into herself when he spoke, as though his personality overpowered and devoured hers. The only person with whom she ever seemed to converse with any sense of ease was Lady Pilkington. Perhaps a conversation with the lady of the manor might shed further insight on Mrs. Denney's friends and guests. Heaven knew he was running shy of options.

It was a weekend, which explained the influx of guests at the first meal of the day. The Residency was the social hub of the region, and Lady Pilkington outdid herself in her efforts to be certain the mansion was always in a condition to receive and feed guests. The woman herself entered before long to oversee proceedings, and with her trailed the Seadon women.

Sophia straightened fractionally, and he thought he detected a muttered "Ugh" from her quarter, but she recovered herself quickly enough and returned her attention to Beatrice Denney, who spoke softly and infrequently. Sophia laughed when Charity told an amusing anecdote about a monkey named Badmash who lived in Calcutta, but as the conversation around them shifted and flowed, he noted Sophia's attention remained speculatively on Beatrice.

Dylan joined the meal and settled next to Lissa Vale, likely unaware of what he was in for. Or maybe he was aware. He was clever and quick, and didn't miss much. He saw Dylan also glance at Mailor and the other soldiers and then he offered a quick nod at Anthony.

Anthony was to accompany Stuart back to the barracks for a quick, unobtrusive toss of the soldiers' belongings to see if one of them, by chance, might be harboring a particular stolen document. Find the document, find the murderer. The reverse was also true.

Whenever possible, Stuart was also formally questioning

each guest who had reportedly been seen the night of the costume ball, but the list was long and to date he had turned up nothing new. Thus Anthony and Dylan would begin at the barracks and systematically work their way down the list.

Late the night before, he had spoken briefly with Dylan about their next plan of attack, and they realized that with the crowd of people who constantly ebbed and flowed through the Residency, there were several people who would know of Sophia's affection for young Charlie. A lady from London did not ordinarily spend time with children in a nursery—quite often their own mothers didn't darken the door until bedtime. The fact that Rachael and Sophia were often seen playing with the children and spending time on the third floor singled them out as unique.

"My goodness," Sophia was saying to Lady Pilkington, "I do not know how you accomplish it. Another party tomorrow evening?"

Charity Denney clapped her hands. "It is to be a midnight picnic! With dancing!"

Lady Pilkington placed a hand humbly on her chest. "As the wife of a prominent gentleman, such is my responsibility."

"I do not believe I've heard of a midnight picnic," Rachael said.

"Yes, please enlighten us, my lady," Lissa said to Lady Pilkington.

Sophia breathed the slightest puff of air out of her nose and managed to convey what she could not utter aloud. Anthony's lips twitched.

"Well, it is quite a glorious procession. When the moon

is full, as it will be tomorrow evening, we travel to the temple ruins with all the accommodations necessary for the finest of meals, followed by dancing beneath the stars. I do not mind sharing that multiple happy young couples have fallen in love at one of my midnight picnics. Prince Ekavir is not well enough to attend, but his cousin and heir, Mr. Darzi, will be in attendance."

"That sounds glorious." Lissa flicked a glance at Anthony.

He surreptitiously reached under the table and clasped Sophia's hand, which was balled into a fist on her leg.

Presently, Major Stuart excused himself from the table. "And Lord Wilshire," he added as he stood, "you asked about your grandfather's paperwork with the Company many years ago. I am happy to say I located it in some dusty archives at the compound. Should you like to see it?"

"Indeed, yes, thank you."

Lissa's brow wrinkled in a frown. "Your grandfather was an earl. Why would he have labored with the Company?"

Drat Stuart for not thinking of a less detailed ruse.

Anthony spoke quickly. "His course took much the same as mine did. My grandfather was a second son who inherited by default." That much was true, at least. But as far as Anthony knew, his grandfather had never stepped foot in India.

He stood to leave and Lissa's mother, Lady Seadon, addressed him. "Surely you will return to the mansion this evening? We have enjoyed playing games after supper, and it is not the same without a fair retinue of gentlemen. Major Stuart, shall we see you as well?"

"Of course, my lady, it is always an honor and a pleasure."

Anthony bowed his head and left the table, a smirk crossing his face as Dylan caught up to him. His friend was as smooth as ever, said the correct things without fail, though it always amazed Anthony that nobody ever seemed to hear the thin thread of sarcasm that ran underneath.

He resisted the urge to look back at Sophia; he had intentionally avoided eye contact as he'd left the table. He did not have the luxury of allowing his feelings to show and he couldn't guarantee that they wouldn't.

"Thought you were out of your mind sitting next to that one at the table just now," he said to Dylan in an undertone as they made their way down the hall. "She has claws."

Dylan glanced at him, his smile wry as they exited the mansion and turned toward the stables. "She doesn't want a thing to do with a cavalry officer, Wilshire. She has her eyes set on you. Consider it a favor on my part."

"How so?"

"I shall endeavor to keep her occupied so you'll preserve any chance you might have with the delectable Miss Elliot."

Anthony flicked a glance at his friend as they reached the stables. Dylan requested his horse brought forward and an additional mount saddled for Anthony. "Delectable, is she?"

Stuart cocked a brow. "Is she not?"

"You needn't feign innocence with me; I see through you."

"The two of you seem to need a nudge. I do not know all of the details of your assignment this time around, but I do believe that you had best get things settled before Miss Elliot either comes to harm or leaves you for someone else."

His throat felt tight. "It is my fondest hope, of course,

that the first does not occur, and it is my firm belief that the second is no longer a concern."

Dylan gave Anthony a sidelong glance. "You have made amends with Miss Elliot?"

"Indeed," he said. "Though it is not yet official, so I would ask for your continued discretion and assistance."

"Then I shall aid you as best I can. We'll find Captain Miller's murderer, and I'll keep Lady Lissa from wreaking havoc."

"How do you propose to accomplish that?"

Stuart smiled. He appeared casual, almost bored. "I'll think of something, I'm sure."

Anthony would wager his title that Dylan was already three steps ahead.

Sophia, Rachael, Charity, and Beatrice strolled down the crowded market near the quay and looked for trinkets for Rachael to purchase and send home for her three nieces and two nephews.

They chatted as they walked, and Sophia eyed Beatrice with some surprise at an unexpected turn in the conversation. "Your father approves of the match?"

With Beatrice's permission, she had shared with Rachael Taj Darzi's interest in Beatrice, figuring three smart heads were better than two.

Beatrice nodded. "He mentioned after breakfast this morning that he had noticed Mr. Darzi's particular regard of me and suggested that the alliance could be advantageous to all. Mr. Darzi marries a British woman, securing an alliance, and I remain in India, which suits my desires." She smiled and flushed.

The women stopped walking and clustered around Beatrice. Rachael frowned and broke the silence. "I do not understand Mr. Darzi's intentions. There are prejudices on both sides that prevent such a union from being ideal. Your offspring, for instance. Assuming you produce an heir, any children who follow are ineligible for employment by the East India Company. Only British-born are candidates for salaries above a certain mark and station. The most your children could hope for would be to serve with a native Indian regiment, and being half-European, they would come under scrutiny from that side as well."

Sophia lifted a shoulder. "That much is true, however, consider Professor Gerald. He is of mixed parentage and has done very well for himself professionally."

Rachael nodded. "Yes, but he also attended school in England and has ties to an influential family." She turned to Beatrice. "I also know his road has been difficult, at times. As a friend who cares about you, I want very much for you to understand the challenges beforehand. The Company, the military, society—they can be horribly unjust."

Beatrice chewed on her lip. "I believe that is exactly the issue Mr. Darzi wishes to address. He has implied he hopes to see a reversal of the laws back to the early days of the Company when the two societies were not segregated and there were no stipulations on eligibility for high positions."

"He is an idealist, then?" Sophia asked.

"Or an opportunist," Charity grumbled, and Sophia's

attention flew to the younger sister. Charity had been unusually quiet during the afternoon, and her comment was oddly direct.

"Are you concerned?" Sophia asked.

She shrugged. "I want my sister to make a good match. I want so many good things for her." She looked miserably at Beatrice, who glanced away with a frown. "I do believe he cares genuinely for her, but I am concerned about the old traditions that still linger at the palace."

"You worry needlessly," Beatrice murmured.

"What does your mother say?" Sophia asked Beatrice.

"She is in agreement with my father. She seems hopeful for it."

"And yet our father is still insistent on *my* return to London." Charity looked near tears. Sophia eyed her with sympathy, realizing the girl seemed impossibly young. Her light brown curls blew softly against her face, and the wind molded her pale pink dress against her slender frame. She looked one step out of the nursery, and, Sophia mused, she probably was. The gentlemen who might pursue her in London could well be decades older than she, but she was pretty, of child-bearing age, and had a dowry.

Charity chewed on her lip, her eyes liquid and bright. "Of course I want to be with Beatrice, whether here or in England, but even if I must go back alone, I do not wish to leave her here with someone who will not care for her. Being an Indian princess sounds lovely, but the current prince, the members of his court . . ." Charity's lip trembled, and she wiped at a tear with her fingertip and folded her arms closely against her body. "At least Mr. Darzi is young, unlikely to die soon," she muttered. "She wouldn't have to worry about sati."

Sophia's heart thudded in alarm. She exchanged a glance with Rachael, whose eyes were wide.

Beatrice's face was pale, her lips nearly bloodless. "Charity! The Darzi family do not practice sati!"

"Prince Ekavir's father did, and that was only twenty years ago!" Charity dropped her arms to her sides with fists clenched.

Beatrice regained some of her color in slow degrees. "They have pledged with the Company to cease and desist. And as Mr. Darzi is committed to maintaining good relationships with the Company hierarchy and military, that is the last thing he would allow."

Sophia frowned and looked at Charity.

"Why would you expect such a thing might be a choice for Prince Ekavir?" she asked quietly.

She shrugged. "The servants talk. Both in our compound and at the mansion. I hear things. Prince Ekavir's wife is young, and some of the older servants have said she shames the family with her reluctance to . . ." Charity swallowed, and then she straightened and looked at her sister. "Her reluctance to be burned to death with her husband's body."

Her blunt statement hung in the air and remained undisturbed by the pronounced silence that fell over the four women.

"I shall mention these rumors to Major Stuart," Rachael finally said. "Though not much happens of which he is unaware, I suspect."

Sophia made a note to tell Anthony, as well. It seemed

intrigue was destined to follow the man wherever he went. Now that she was aware of his position with the government, she realized that activities of diplomatic and cultural significance could direct his responses. Would he be bound to take action should cultural traditions of a princely state directly oppose any prior understanding with British officials?

Beatrice wrung her hands. "I do not want Mr. Darzi to suspect I have been gossiping about him or his family. He is a good man—I wish you all could see it!"

"This has nothing to do with what you've told us." Rachael placed her hand on Beatrice's arm. "I shall merely call Major Stuart's attention to the servants' whisperings." She paused. "How ill is the prince? Does his family truly expect his death soon?"

Beatrice nodded. "Mr. Darzi is amazed Prince Ekavir still lives. I should not be surprised to receive word of his death before long."

Rachael quietly blew out a long breath between pursed lips and tapped a finger absently against her leg. Sophia scrutinized Beatrice with intense concern, and Charity was a study in misery. They blocked the small thoroughfare enough that people were forced to go around them, and Sophia realized they could stand there all day in that frozen tableau unless someone took action.

"Rachael, let us find presents for your family, and we shall discuss this again later at the mansion."

"Yes, let's." Rachael blinked and nodded definitively. She put an arm about Charity's shoulders and turned her toward the awnings and shops with a gentle squeeze. "We shall find an answer to the problem," she told the girl. "And in the meantime, I am in desperate need of advice. I'm told the toy you found for Charlie has been a smashing success and has made Sophia quite the heroine of the nursery."

Beatrice trailed the other two, deep in thought, and Sophia followed, running her gaze along the displays as she walked. Rachael's comments reminded her that she'd hoped to find another small horse for Charlie to give him in addition to Chestnut, who currently resided in Anthony's bedchamber within a large clamp borrowed from the carriage house. Abdullah had found a gooey adhesive used to adhere leather in the stables, and he and Anthony had then carefully smeared it on the two broken halves of the toy. Anthony hoped it would be set by evening. It wouldn't be perfect, he told Sophia, but it would be close.

Chapter 21

Sophia sat in the drawing room after the evening meal and tried not to be obvious as she looked repeatedly at Beatrice and Charity, who sat with their mother. Mrs. Denney spoke gently to her daughters; Beatrice's eyes had glazed over and Charity's mouth was set in a determined line that Sophia figured could only bode trouble. Sophia and Rachael had pulled aside Major Stuart before dinner and told him of Charity's concerns and of the prince-presumptive's interest in the elder Denney sister. He had listened intently and given a definitive nod when they asked if he would please keep them informed should he discover anything.

The entire situation concerned Sophia. Charity looked as combustible as a powder keg, and Sophia felt sympathetic affection for the young girl. She might have to petition Jack to provide refuge for not only young Charlie in the future, but the younger Miss Denney, as well. She felt her brow creasing in a frown and wondered if she'd done little else since her arrival but scowl at everything. India was fraught with intrigue, it seemed.

Music from the corner of the room lifted on wings and soared beautifully into flight. Lady Lissa not only played the pianoforte, but sang as well. And why should she not? Lissa executed both skills exquisitely, of course, to the clear delight of her beaming mother and a wary Lady Pilkington. For all that her sponsor was obsequious, she didn't seem to have forgotten Lissa's cutting remarks upon arrival, though the Resident's wife was not about to alienate family of a peer of the realm. The whole thing was but one more irritant in Sophia's slipper, and her scowl deepened.

"Of course she sings and plays beautifully," Sophia said glumly to Rachael, who sat next to her on the settee.

"Her ability to play and sing or not play and sing should signify nothing to you at all." Rachael glanced at Sophia.

"I do not trust her as far as I can throw her."

"You are fairly strong, you know."

Sophia glared at Rachael, who put an arm about her shoulders. "You've nothing in the world to worry about, Sophia. This business will be over soon, and you shall go home with the man you love. You shall live the life you've been waiting for."

Sophia smiled. "Is life ever simple, Rachael?"

Rachael chuckled. "Where would be the fun in that, sweet friend? Simple is boring and dreary, and boring and dreary we are not."

Sophia's smile widened into a grin. "Let's try it, you and I. Let's be boring and dreary and ordinary. We can rusticate at one of my family's country estates and while away the time picking flowers and playing with our nieces."

Rachael shook her head. "You would be fit to be tied

in less than two weeks. Perhaps one. As would I, truthfully. Besides, do you not have a school to oversee?"

Sophia nodded and pursed her lips, wistful. "I do miss it. I wonder how they fare."

"I suspect you will be ready to return when the time comes."

"We have been here barely outside a week. Should we not still be in the throes of grand adventure?"

"We have been on this grand adventure for much longer than just a week," Rachael said drily. "Or have you already forgotten the voyage itself?"

Sophia grimaced. "And to think we had the good of it. I hear some stories and feel we were positively pampered."

"I should say so. I spoke yesterday with Miss Jane Sla—" Rachael was interrupted by a throaty laugh that came from the music corner.

Lady Lissa was looking at Anthony, who had entered the room near the pianoforte, which was unfortunate. His gaze traveled the room until he found Sophia, and there it stopped. He smiled slowly, and she sucked in her breath.

"He has got to stop doing *that* if he wants to keep anyone from suspecting he has feelings for you," Rachael muttered. "Therein lies the problem. I'm not certain he cares one way or the other anymore about keeping it secret."

Sophia elbowed her in the ribs. "Do be quiet."

"He was fine to break your heart when his concern was keeping you safe, but now that he seems to have thrown caution to the wind—"

"Rachael." Sophia turned to her, prepared to lecture her

friend on the wisdom of *not* lecturing friends when she saw Rachael's smile.

"Which is why I have devised a plan for you to sit next to him for at least thirty minutes." Rachael stood and pulled Sophia up with her. "Lord Wilshire, you must join us," she said as Anthony reached them. "We are bound for the library where I understand there is a fast-moving game of whist at play."

Anthony's lips twitched. "A fast-moving game of whist? That truly must be a sight."

"Come, come," she said, taking one of his arms and leaving the other for Sophia. "Dylan is there already, and I promised not to keep him waiting long."

"And here I had assumed the two of you dallied for the music."

Sophia pinched the back of his arm as they exited into the hallway, and he pulled it away from her with an incredulous laugh and a look of remonstration she was certain he intended to be gruff but fell well short of the mark. She raised a brow at him in admonition, and he chuckled at her. When they were safely away from prying eyes, he winked at her.

There were a few groups of people already in the library when they arrived. Several officers from the military compound played vingt-et-un at another table and a few Fleet ladies filled the room with the comfortable, quiet hum of conversation.

The game of whist was, of course, not fast moving at all. In fact there hadn't been one in play until they reached the library and Rachael pulled Major Stuart away from his conversation with Lord Pilkington to begin one.

Clergyman Denney immediately took Stuart's place across from Lord Pilkington. If Pilkington's expression was any indicator, the conversation had begun with the evils of drink.

"Poor Pilkington," Anthony murmured to Sophia as she took her seat at a game table and patted the chair next to hers. "Though perhaps he is secretly relieved we have diverted Stuart's attention. I do believe the major is tightening the screws."

Sophia knit her brow. "Does he suspect Lord Pilkington of something nefarious?"

Anthony shook his head. "We are spinning our wheels, as it were. I believe he is as frustrated as I. We keep thinking that if we manage to overturn the correct stone we will discover something useful."

Rachael quickly took the seat across from Sophia, declaring, "Sophia and I must be partners, for you and I always lose, Dylan."

He cocked a brow at her but took his seat by her side. "I suppose that pairs us, old boy," he said to Anthony.

"We are not truly invested in this game," Rachael whispered.

"You don't say." Dylan glanced at Anthony, who slid his chair closer to Sophia's.

Sophia glanced about the room, and more importantly at the faces who were decidedly *not* looking in their direction, and leaned a few delicious inches closer to Anthony. He glanced at her from the side, his lips twitching in a smile. He angled his shoulder so it brushed against hers.

"That will be enough of *that*." Dylan snapped the cards

together and whispered to Anthony, his brows drawn close. "You will never convince anyone you don't care for her if you don't maintain some distance. Are you a lad fresh from Eton, Wilshire?"

Anthony cocked a brow at Dylan and smirked. Sophia regarded her would-be protector with a bright smile. "Come now, Major Stuart. Surely you're acquainted with the heady rush of new love?"

He narrowed his eyes at her. "I do remember, and therein lies the problem." He glanced left and right, and then leaned forward. "I must add it is a sad state of affairs when I, of all people, must act as chaperone."

Rachael sighed and nudged her cousin. "You have become rather a stuffy old fellow, darling."

"And what about after you're married?" Dylan persisted. "You should know how gauche it is to be demonstrative with one's spouse in public. I suggest you rein it in now, my friend."

Sophia turned a pout on Anthony. "So such will be the case with us, then?"

"I never have claimed to be *de rigueur*." He grinned. "In fact, I do tend to fly in the face of convention."

Sophia laughed, but then spied Amala Ayah at the door to the library, her face a mask of terror. The nanny motioned desperately to her, and Sophia stood so quickly she knocked her chair askew. Anthony grabbed it to keep it from crashing to the ground.

Sophia ran to the door, heedless of the starts of surprise from others in the room, and pulled Amala into the hall. "What's happened?"

"Miss Sophia, Charlie is missing!"

Sophia barely caught Amala as she crumbled, her face pale and her breathing shallow. The woman's eyes rolled back in her head, and Sophia lowered her awkwardly to the floor. She glanced up as Anthony, Dylan, and Rachael appeared in the doorway.

"She must have run all the way down here," Sophia said quietly, desperately trying to still the furious pounding of her heart. "Anthony, help me elevate her feet."

Anthony grabbed a stool that sat just inside the library door and placed Amala's feet on it. "Did she say anything?" His voice was low, tense.

"Charlie is missing." Sophia fought back a wave of nausea and put her hand over her mouth, taking a few shallow breaths through her nose.

"Here, now, what's this?" Pilkington entered the hallway, and a few curious faces peeked from behind his shoulder.

"Your nanny, my lord. She has distressing news, I fear." She looked down at Amala, wanting the woman to come to and give her more details.

"We must take her back upstairs," Pilkington said.

"My lord, if I may?" Rachael stepped around Pilkington, sank down next to Sophia, and reached into her pocket. "I have salts." She produced them and waved the small packet beneath Amala's nose.

The nanny breathed deeply, blinked, and coughed. Anthony placed his arms behind her shoulders, and Sophia pulled gently on her wrists to seat her upright.

"Amala." Sophia looked into the woman's wide and

unfocused eyes. She waved a hand in front of her face and repeated her name. "What has happened?"

Amala blinked again. Then she clutched Sophia's hand and looked up at the small crowd. Her face crumpled, and tears gathered in her eyes when her gaze landed on her employer. "My lord, Master Charles is not in his bedchamber. We have looked everywhere he might have gone but cannot find him." Amala sobbed a gasp and put her hand over her mouth. Her other hand clutched Sophia's so tightly her knuckles were white. "Please help me find him!"

Sophia nodded. "Of course." She looked up at Lord Pilkington, deferring to his position and expecting him to begin giving orders. He simply stared down at Amala, his face blank.

"Pilkington," Anthony said firmly, standing. "Where shall we begin?"

Pilkington seemed to search for words he couldn't find.

Dylan cleared his throat and Anthony stepped around Sophia to address Pilkington directly. "Major Stuart can dispatch runners to the post and bring reinforcements. We'll begin an immediate search."

"Probably just hiding . . ." Pilkington managed to say, and cleared his throat. "Charles likes to play hide-and-seek. He must be hiding. Amala Ayah, you must look in all of those places! I cannot fathom that you would cause this sort of worry without looking there first!"

Amala's eyes widened, and Sophia felt her tremble. From the set of her mouth, she knew the nanny's reaction had nothing to do with fear of her employer and everything to do with outrage. "I did look," she bit out, and Pilkington blinked at her firm tone. "He is not here." She fumbled awkwardly and tried to stand. Rachael and Sophia aided her, and Amala smoothed her hands over her sari and took a deep breath.

"My lord, I have searched every single hiding place where Charlie used to play, but hasn't for the past week. I have even searched places he likely would never have thought to hide. He is not in the house. We must have additional help searching for your *son*." Amala's face was still deathly pale, but she stood straight and did not blink away from Pilkington's shocked attention.

Sophia noted the slight tremble that still vibrated through the woman's frame, but realized that she and Rachael alone were likely the only two to see it. The nanny was fierce, and, in spite of Sophia's thick, suffocating fear for Charlie, she internally cheered Amala Ayah.

Pilkington seemed at a loss—undoubtedly a servant had never spoken so firmly to him before, and Sophia hoped Amala would still have a position come morning. Of course, if they couldn't find Charlie, the point was moot.

Sophia drove the thought away and put a trembling hand to her forehead. She looked at Anthony. "The first step. What shall be our first step?"

Anthony addressed Pilkington again, as the man was still as befuddled as a fish out of water. "With your permission, my lord, I'll set the plan in motion. Suppose you go to your study and pour a glass of whiskey. I'll join you straightaway once I've conferred with Stuart, here."

Clergyman Denney addressed Anthony. "We would be better served to remain here in the library where there is more room to gather people."

Lord Pilkington frowned. "But my best whiskey is in the study." It was as though the man could focus on only one small, inconsequential detail at a time.

Denney glowered at Pilkington. He opened his mouth, likely to blast a rebuke, when Anthony held up a hand.

"Take him to his study," Anthony told the clergyman in an undertone. "I shall meet you there presently." Then he and Dylan stepped aside, their heads together in low conversation.

"Come along, my lord. I shall accompany you." Denney took Pilkington's arm and led him away. The remainder of the guests milled about and whispered.

Sophia turned to Amala, struck by a sudden thought. "The study!"

Amala shook her head. "I searched already. I couldn't imagine him going there but I looked anyway."

Rachael turned to Amala, patting her on the arm. "Can I get you anything?" she asked quietly.

Amala shook her head, and enormous tears pooled in her eyes. Sophia handed her a handkerchief while Rachael helped smoothed the woman's dress.

Sophia glanced down the hallway, which was slowly filling with more and more people, questions bouncing around in the air. She felt the moment word began to spread. It was a wave, crashing through the entire house and filling each corner with worry and tension.

Think. Think.

"We will need a command post, of sorts," she said, thinking of the clergyman's suggestion. "Lord Pilkington's study is not as big as the library."

Amala agreed. "Perhaps half that size."

"Suppose we gather people—" Sophia paused as Lady Seadon, the matron, let out a small shriek from her position at the drawing room door. The news was traveling fast. "Suppose we gather *useful* people here in the library," Sophia said to Rachael. They maneuvered Amala into the library and sat her in a chair by the hearth.

Amala rubbed her hand along her forehead. "I put him to bed. Lady Pilkington hasn't done it for some time, and I've worried Charlie will feel as though he isn't important. I tuck him in and sing a song my mother taught me as a child." Her voice broke. "Tonight I retired to the servant's sitting room. An hour later, I checked on him, and he was gone. I don't know how long he has been missing."

Sophia nodded. "I shall find Antho—Lord Wilshire—in Lord Pilkington's study. He may have more news for us by now."

"I will stay here with Amala." Rachael brushed Amala's hair away from her face. "We will find him, dear lady. He is little—he cannot have gone far."

"Unless someone has abducted him and taken him in a carriage," Amala whispered.

Sophia fought back a new wave of panic that image produced.

She left the library on shaking legs and spotted Abdullah, who stood in the main hall with Himmat, his face creased in worry. She gave the butler instructions to provide tea to Amala Ayah in the library and asked Abdullah to gather as many servants as were available. She then wound her way to the study.

She approached the study just as Major Stuart exited the room. He gave a grim head-nod in her direction and walked quickly down the hall.

Anthony was in the study with Lord and Lady Pilkington. She was as baffled as her husband, and Sophia suspected that once the shock of the pronouncement was no longer fresh, emotion would flood. Beneath her exterior, and sometimes notably closer to the surface, Lady Pilkington was a nervous woman.

Sophia knew she loved her son and had high hopes for his future. She suspected that was partly the reason she had stayed away from Charlie of late; he was in pain, bothered so profoundly by something she was at a loss to explain that she left his care entirely to others and instead immersed herself deeply in things she did understand, could control.

Sophia stepped just inside the study door and stayed against the wall where she could unobtrusively observe. *He cannot have gone far. He cannot have gone far.* She hoped if she repeated the sentiment enough times in her mind, it would be true. She couldn't think in terms of an abduction, or worse. Not yet.

"Once Major Stuart returns with reinforcements, we shall divide into teams and begin searching the rooms and the grounds." Anthony addressed the Pilkingtons, but also Clergyman Denney and Professor Gerald, who had followed closely on Sophia's heels.

"You are certain the child is not in the mansion?" Gerald asked.

Anthony looked at Sophia, a brow raised.

She shook her head. "We cannot be certain as the

mansion is extensive, but the child's ayah has searched every place she thought he might be. I have asked Abdullah to begin gathering servants in the library in order to give instructions to everyone at once and also have a designated gathering place to report when finished searching."

Anthony nodded. He spoke again with Lord Pilkington, and Sophia slowly approached the large desk where Amala had found Charlie hiding the night of the costume ball. She hoped to see his little body crouched there again, but as she leaned to peer underneath, the space was as empty as she had known it would be.

Anthony finished his conversation with Pilkington and made a slow perusal of the room, stopping to examine the statues of two Hindu gods on the mantel: Vishnu, the preserver, blue with multiple arms, and Kali, the goddess of death, her tongue dripping blood and adorned in a necklace of human skulls. Sophia frowned. Lady Pilkington had mentioned once on a tour of the mansion that her husband favored his décor in groupings of three. The man was fairly exacting in his habits—she would hazard a guess that there should have been three statues on the mantel. A missing god statue?

She frowned at the mantelpiece, thinking back to the multitudinous statuary she had seen at the marketplace. The statues were usually beautiful carved by the locals and painted with the brightly colored dyes the country produced in vivid abundance. There were dozens of Hindu gods, but Sophia knew a few of the most easily recognized ones.

Vishnu, Kali, . . . and Brahma? She didn't know why the detail mattered. It probably didn't signify anything at all, except that a man had been murdered in this room with a heavy object, and finding it might lead them to the attacker.

She joined Anthony at the hearth, passing both Clergyman Denney, who looked like a nasty thundercloud, and Professor Gerald, who was speaking with the Pilkingtons. On a whim, she pushed lightly on the statue of Vishnu. It sat solidly in place until she put greater pressure on it, using both thumbs. It budged a quarter of an inch.

The statue stood perhaps just under a foot tall, and though she wasn't an expert, she presumed it was carved from sandstone since she was able to nudge it herself with relative ease. There was some heft to it, and she bit her lip in thought, feeling a rush of cold through her limbs despite the stuffy air in the study. She couldn't wield it as a weapon . . . but perhaps if she were threatened? In some sort of altercation? She could grab it with both hands and swing. She fought down a shudder and realigned the statue, then surreptitiously nudged Kali. They were likely produced by the same artist—the dimensions matched.

"What are you doing?" Anthony whispered.

"How heavy are these, do you suppose?" she whispered back, still looking at the statues as though admiring them.

He paused—glanced at the Pilkingtons—and then moved Kali, lifting it slightly from the mantel and placing it gently back down. "Fifteen, twenty pounds, perhaps."

She scooted closer to him, and he leaned his head down to hers. "Could you kill someone with one of these, Anthony?"

"Please do not touch the statues," Pilkington said suddenly, and Sophia jumped back, knocking her head against Anthony's nose.

"Forgive me, my lord. We were admiring them."

His eyes were wide and he shook his head. "I prefer they not be touched."

"I've told you they are not appropriate for display in the home of a man of faith, Pilkington," Clergyman Denney said, eying the statues on the mantel with clear disgust, his color high.

"Mr. Denney, I'll not have you dictating to me in my own home!" Pilkington's own cheeks were flushed.

"George, I believe we are all overwrought." Lady Pilkington's voice was thin. She moved to her husband's side and firmly took hold of his arm. "We are beside ourselves with worry for our son. I am certain you all understand."

"Of course." Sophia nodded. "We join you in that concern, my lady."

Himmat appeared at the door and cleared his throat. "Mr. Taj Darzi, my lord."

"Sir, I have heard the news of your son." Mr. Darzi entered the room and clasped Pilkington's hand. "I am happy to provide whatever service you may need in locating him. Please, Lord Pilkington, allow me to help you. I have heard whisperings of recent trouble here in your home. I would not have you face such things alone, without your ally."

The significance—likely unintended—was not lost on Sophia: that the "trouble" Mr. Darzi spoke of had begun in this very study. She looked at the spot on the floor where copious amounts of blood had once pooled; it was now covered with a new rug. Also significant, she mused, was the fact that many of those who had been in attendance the night of the costume ball were present in this room, or would soon arrive at the mansion to help look for the missing child.

Pilkington cleared his throat. "Major Stuart and Lord Wilshire are investigating the matter, Mr. Darzi. I suppose they could provide details."

Anthony stepped forward and shook Mr. Darzi's hand. "Our first matter of business, of course, is to find the child. Any help the palace can provide would be most appreciated."

"Yes, of course. Whatever you need is yours."

"Right now, we are gathering people to search the grounds and surrounding areas while the domestic staff continues to monitor the home itself."

Mr. Darzi nodded definitively. "I shall have several of the palace guard dispatched immediately here for instruction."

"Thank you." Anthony managed a smile, put his palms together and bowed, touching his thumbs to his forehead.

Mr. Darzi did the same, then left the room and spoke softly to the two men who stood sentry for him in the hallway.

Anthony released a sigh. "Extra hands will help," he said.

"Seems foolhardy to risk so many in the dark of the jungle. We'd be better served to wait for daylight." Clergyman Denney's pronouncement hung thick in the air.

Lady Pilkington found her voice first. "My son is out in that jungle, sir, and I will take advantage of as many willing hands as I can." She glared at him. "Truly Christian gestures, and from those who are not even Christian! George, I shall be in the library." She turned and left the room.

Denney's jaw clenched visibly, but he refrained from further comment.

Sophia figured the man owed Lord Pilkington an apology at the very least. His callous dismissal of the Resident's son was in poor taste.

Denney left the study, followed by Gerald and Lord Pilkington.

As Anthony and Sophia headed for the door, he dipped his head toward the mantel. His jaw was tight as he glanced at her. "Yes. I could definitely kill someone with one of those statues."

Chapter 22

As dawn approached, the mansion's inhabitants were either fit to be tied with anxiety or exhausted. Sophia was jittery enough to have consumed a dozen cups of coffee. Anthony watched her pace the length of the library for what must have been the hundredth time and, in truth, had he not had years of experience pretending to be calm when he was far from it, he might have joined her.

Servants and guests had split into teams and combed every inch of the house, but to no avail. The front hall, atrium, and library were teeming with people who speculated endlessly on the fate of the boy and tried to share opinions that were positive for the sake of Lady Pilkington, who sat next to Amala Ayah on a sofa at the hearth. They spoke rarely, and when they did, it was to utter a word or two, or answer a question posed by Dylan. For all that Sophia was a bundle of raw energy, Charlie's mother and nanny were drained.

The two Denney sisters had joined in the search, and Charity had worn a track in the flooring behind Sophia as she paced. They collided twice, and Anthony nearly laughed out loud at Sophia's thunderous expression. Beatrice stood near the window and looked out, wringing her hands, her face strained. At one point in the evening, one of Mr. Darzi's aids found her and handed her a letter, which she opened as soon as the young man left. Whatever the contents of the letter said, her expression softened, and the ghost of a smile played around her mouth.

What business did Mr. Darzi's aide have with Miss Denney? Anthony turned the puzzle over in his mind as he approached Sophia and attempted to distract her. He halted her midstride. "Did you note that exchange?" he asked.

"What exchange?"

He gestured toward the elder Miss Denney with his shoulder.

"Oh." Sophia nodded. She dropped her voice to a whisper. "I forgot to tell you. Mr. Darzi has a *tendre* for Beatrice. She is receptive, but uneasy."

"Uneasy, why?"

"She is concerned about Charity's feelings and worries, potential social situations, and her parents' reactions, although her father seems to support the idea."

He frowned. That did not align with Anthony's understanding of the man's behavior. Of course, the marriage of his daughter to a prince may coincide nicely with Denney's apparent dreams of grandeur. He had dressed as a cardinal for the costume ball, after all.

"Does that not strike you as odd?"

Sophia nodded. "Perhaps he has abandoned all hope of the girls finding husbands in England."

"Lord Wilshire!" Private Thomas, one of Corporal

Mailor's aides, ran to Anthony's side and thrust a paper at him, his face all smiles.

Anthony scanned the contents and found his heart pounding, this time with joy. "Charlie has been found near Prince Ekinar's palace. He is well, aside from hunger and fatigue," he announced to the room, which erupted in a cheer.

Sophia put one hand to her abdomen and grasped the back of the nearest chair with her other. She closed her eyes.

Anthony felt a surge of relief, and he released it on a sigh. What the boy was doing near the palace—two miles away—and why he had run away were questions that remained unanswered, but he went to Lady Pilkington and the nanny and clasped their hands with murmured good wishes.

The women on the sofa shared tears and embraces. Lady Pilkington peppered him with questions for which he had no answers, but he promised to tell her as soon as the child and his rescuers returned.

Himmat left the library to spread the news, a relieved smile on his weathered face.

Anthony crossed the room to Sophia and placed a hand solicitously at her elbow when what he desired to do was haul her into his arms and kiss her soundly.

She smiled, but it was strained and he knew the reason. As relieved as she was for Charlie's safety, her speculation about the statues in the study had been in the back of his mind ever since, and was clearly still on hers. Anthony wondered if Pilkington's awareness of his missing statue as Miller's likely murder weapon fed an irrational fear of his son being harmed.

"You are well?" he asked Sophia quietly.

She nodded, but swayed on her feet.

"Shall I carry you to your bedchamber?" His lips twitched, and she smiled.

"Yes, please, my lord. Perhaps if I should faint, you would be obliged."

He leaned close to her ear, taking advantage of the distraction now spilling through the house. "And then I should be obliged to loosen your stays so you might regain your breath. Strictly for your well-being, of course."

She choked on a horrified laugh and blushed, laying a light smack on his arm, though had it been anyone else, she would have aimed for his face. He grinned in spite of the tension and worry and mysteries still unsolved and gave her elbow a gentle squeeze before releasing her arm and threading through the library to the front hall.

Guests and servants alike passed around smiles, and Mr. Griffen, the indigo plantation owner, produced a bottle of champagne which he shared liberally. Anthony smiled, but held up his hand when someone offered him a glass and instead made his way to the study.

The small room was empty and still unlocked—an anomaly since his arrival—and he entered. Light from a lamp on the mantel illuminated the space in a soft glow, but it wasn't nearly bright enough for what he hoped to see. He picked up the lamp and brought it closer to the statues. Sophia had assumed they were sandstone or limestone, and he couldn't be certain, but it seemed likely. Marble or granite would have been much heavier, and closer examination showed no telltale seam from a mold.

He glanced at the open door and closed it, then crossed

the room to the edge of the large new area rug. Part of Pilkington's desk anchored the rug in place, and opposite that, a chair, which Anthony slid out of the way. He lifted a corner of the rug and rolled it toward the center of the room.

Light from the lamp pooled ahead of him, and as he reached the desk, he noted a dark stain on the hardwood. He shoved the desk back and rolled the carpet to the end of the stain. He then rolled the rug back toward the hearth, glancing up at the statues and down again at the floor. If they were made of something less substantial than granite or marble, they might break if used as a weapon. Holding the lamp close to the floor, he looked carefully at the flooring slats between the hearth and desk. As he made a second pass, he noticed a gold item approximately one inch in length that had fallen in a crack between the hearthstone and flooring. He tried to pick it up but found it wedged in place.

He retrieved a quill from the desk drawer and used it to pry the thing from its spot on the floor, and then held the light close to where it lay in his palm. Painted in gold, one end cleanly broken off . . . he held it up to the other statues and rubbed his forefinger along each one, and then the shard.

A loud ruckus sounded from the front of the house. Stuart must have returned with Charlie. He quickly pocketed the shard and shoved the furniture back into place on the rug. Giving the room one last glance to assure everything had been properly returned, he set the lamp on the mantel and left the room as he'd found it, door open.

His cravat was too tight, and the starch on his shirt collars irritated his neck. Surely there must be a contingency rule somewhere about being allowed to shed outer layers of clothing when one had been awake for twenty-four hours and dealing with a missing child. He scratched at his neck and ran a hand over his face. He was scruffy and wanted a shave, a quick bath, and then a long nap.

Major Stuart stood just inside the front door, looking down at Lady Pilkington crouched down and clutching her son. Amala Ayah stood behind her, arms folded and teary eyed, and Anthony felt a stab of sympathy for her. She was not the child's blood mother, but a nanny in a British household usually spent more time with her charges than the mother ever did. Amala clearly adored the boy but was forced to wait for her own tender reunion.

Lord Pilkington spoke briefly to Dylan and then crouched down by his wife. He patted Charlie awkwardly on the shoulder and murmured a few words, and Anthony's eyes narrowed. The man had been distraught, certainly. But his lack of emotion and his unwillingness to bend the dictates of manliness even just a little reminded Anthony of his own father, and the distaste sat uncomfortable and unwelcome in his gut.

Sophia stood near Amala and whispered something to her. Anthony suspected it was a word of comfort. Amala smiled weakly at Sophia and nodded. He wanted to go to Sophia, but Dylan called his name and motioned, pulling him aside from the group.

"What did you learn?" Anthony asked him.

"He was with a young girl, twelve years of age, whose mother works in the kitchens. She was distraught, babbling. I couldn't make out everything, but between my understanding of the language and her broken English, I pieced a few things together. Wilshire, someone paid her to lose the boy in the jungle."

Sophia looked blearily at her reflection in her vanity mirror as Briggs wound a strand of pearls through a long clump of hair and then wove it all together in an elaborate configuration that Sophia would never have been able to manage during her days as a lady's maid.

"That is amazing, Briggs, and most impressive." Sophia turned her head from one side to the other and admired the young woman's handiwork.

Briggs beamed. "Thank you, Miss Elliot."

Sophia narrowed her eyes. "And how is it that you are so chipper this evening? We were both up all night and, to my knowledge, I had more of a nap than you did."

"Bah. I do not need much sleep, miss. Never have!" Briggs smiled brightly and tidied up the vanity while Sophia stood and stretched.

"I am green with envy." And she was. She was quite useless without sleep, and during her years of servitude, there had been many an early morning she had gone about her duties with a scowl and her eyes half closed. Now it was evening and she wanted nothing more than to crawl into bed. Charlie was safe, but Sophia had spent nearly two hours by herself in her chamber that morning crying and crying until she finally fell into a puddle of exhausted sleep. Her eyelids were still puffy even after Brigg's application of a cold spoon, and her face was pale.

She pinched her cheeks and smoothed her hands over her dress. It was the color of honey, and it matched her hair and eyes to perfection. A beautiful dress couldn't disguise a pallid complexion, but it did much to raise her spirits.

Since all the details for the midnight picnic at the ruins had been arranged weeks in advance, Lady Pilkington had insisted the party remain on the evening schedule. Sophia did learn that "midnight" was a rough estimate; it was already dark outside, nearing the ten o'clock hour, and the procession would soon be underway.

Sophia bid Briggs a good evening and followed a general hum of noise down to the front foyer and atrium, where lovely dresses blended with crisp suits and army uniforms of gray and white. The Seadon women were present, and Sophia dearly wished to ask where they had been the night before when the entire household was turned on its ear looking for a missing child. When word of Charlie's disappearance had circulated, Lissa had bustled her mother and cousin up to their rooms, claiming her mother had a "bear of a headache."

Sophia searched through the small groupings of people, circled through the atrium, and finally spied Lady Pilkington and Anthony near the front door, speaking with a gentleman Sophia did not recognize. He was of middle age, his blond hair turning to gray at the temples, his physique fit, his smile warm.

"Lord Braxton, of course! And how is Lady Braxton?" Lady Pilkington smiled at the gentleman as Sophia approached.

"Ill, I am afraid. London air is always difficult for her, so she recuperates at Bath."

Lady Pilkington's expression was appropriately sympathetic. "And your daughter?"

Braxton smiled at the woman, his eyes seeming to twinkle. "She has her first Season in a year. I can hardly believe it."

Lord Braxton's eyes landed on Sophia as she shifted closer to Anthony. His attention returned to Lady Pilkington, a brow expectantly raised.

"Yes," Lady Pilkington said and put her hand on Sophia's back. "Lord Braxton, Miss Sophia Elliot. I am her sponsor."

Sophia curtseyed and allowed Braxton to lift her fingers and bow very nicely over her hand. He kissed her gloved fingers and regarded her with rich brown eyes. "I know your brother, Earl Stansworth, of course. Such a pleasure to make your acquaintance."

"Likewise," she murmured. Handsome, charming—possibly too much charm. She had seen his kind in spades from afar as they wandered through her former employers' balls and soirees. She and the other maids had often labeled such men as "Don Juan," from the old Spanish tales, and the majority of the time, the moniker held true.

She felt a brush against her back and realized Anthony had stepped close to her. Too close, really, but when she tried to subtly shift, she felt his hand grasp the fabric at the small of her back.

"Lord Braxton is here for business, unfortunately, not as a sightseeing traveler." Anthony's voice sounded just behind her, and she strove to keep her face blandly polite.

What on earth? Tension vibrated from Anthony's frame, and she imagined it traveling from his hand up her spine. He was on edge, and it made her restless.

"I do hope you find the time to see some of Bombay." Sophia smiled. "Is this your first visit to India, my lord?"

Braxton's eyes flickered from Anthony and back to her. He smiled, and the nickname solidified in her head. He was most assuredly a Don Juan. "I have been to Calcutta twice, but, as I mentioned to Lady Pilkington, I am here for diplomatic training with the Bombay Presidency. I am a guest of the Governor General and had business to conduct through the day."

"When did you arrive in Bombay?" Sophia asked.

"Only this morning. When I received word of Lady Pilkington's famed midnight picnic, I knew I couldn't miss a moment of the fun. Perhaps we shall commandeer a coach and ride together?" He smiled at Sophia as if they were alone, and then made an examination of the room. "Ah, I see Major Stuart is here as well."

Braxton motioned to Major Stuart, who had been waylaid by Mr. Denney. The Denney sisters had abandoned their parents in favor of Rachael Scarsdale's company, who had again captured the notice of Professor Gerald. Sophia wanted to ask Beatrice and Charity about any new developments concerning Prince Ekavir and Taj Darzi before they arrived at the picnic because Mr. Darzi and retinue were also supposed to be in attendance at the ruins.

It would have to wait, she supposed, as Anthony threaded her hand through his arm and the assembled guests funneled out the front doors. As promised, Lord Braxton secured the largest vehicle available, a spacious coach, and he, Major Stuart, and Anthony sat facing Sophia and Rachael. Sophia was directly across from Braxton, and Anthony's face might have been hewn from granite for all the expression—or lack thereof—upon it. She wondered what had made him so tense.

The footman closed the door and rapped on the side of the carriage.

The carriage lurched forward, and Sophia looked out the window at the darkness beyond. The trees and vegetation were thick and rather frightening at night. It was as though man had carved just enough space out of the jungle to nestle in his own habitat, yet the land constantly fought to regain control. The land between the Residency and the ruins, and the ruins and the palace, was thick and tangled. Wildly beautiful, but threatening.

An animal howled, and the sound carried on the wind as if to punctuate her mood. The tension in the carriage was suffocating. Anthony was clearly uncomfortable with the man, and even Major Stuart, who was affable to everyone, seemed unusually guarded. She wished someone—anyone—would speak.

Anthony broke the silence. "Major Stuart, would you please inform Lord Braxton of what you have learned regarding young master Charles's kidnapping?"

"Now see here," Lord Braxton said with a note of warning in his voice. "Shouldn't we avoid such an unpleasant topic in the presence of fine ladies? I'm sure the discussion could wait."

Anthony clenched his jaw. "Major?" he prompted.

Stuart hesitated, then nodded and cleared his throat. "I

secured a translator and spent the bulk of the day questioning the young girl, Chakori. She was approached by an unfamiliar servant who paid her a healthy sum to lure Master Charles from his bed and lose him in the jungle no closer to the Residency than the ruins. The area from the ruins northward is expansive enough that a young child of his stature might have easily either fallen victim to an animal or lost his way in a swamp or river."

Sophia shook her head. "It makes no sense to me, Major. Did she say how she was to accomplish this? Charlie doesn't trust anyone other than Amala Ayah. I would have wagered my brother's title that he would never have willingly gone somewhere with anybody else. I don't know that he would come with me if I coaxed him, and I've spent considerable time with him in the nursery."

"Fortunately for your brother's title, you were nowhere near a bookmaker." Braxton smiled at Sophia, and she made an effort to keep from narrowing her eyes.

"You do understand what I mean, my lord. These days, the child is terrified of his own shadow."

Stuart nodded. "He is, and Chakori knew what to say. She told Charlie that Amala Ayah was outside and needed him right away and that she had sent Chakori to fetch him." He frowned. "Chakori also had in her possession one of Amala Ayah's bangles. When she showed it to the child as proof of her good intentions, he went with her."

"Where was the ayah?" Braxton asked.

"In the servants' sitting room."

He frowned. "Might she have been complicit in the crime?"

Sophia shook her head. "Amala adores Charlie. As much as his mother does, I daresay."

Stuart added, "Chakori did not implicate the ayah in any way. She maintained over the course of several hours that her only point of contact was with this stranger."

Sophia took a deep breath and tried to make sense of the riddle. Why would someone pay to have Charlie go missing? Perhaps because it was cleaner and simpler than killing him outright in the house? Or perhaps the guilty party didn't have the stomach for killing small children. She shuddered.

"And I am to understand that the boy's nanny believes he was witness to Captain Miller's murder?" Braxton asked.

"You know about that?" Sophia asked.

Braxton nodded. "Lady Pilkington mentioned it to me. And, if I may say, I am surprised that you know about it as well. I would have thought that Lord Wilshire would have spared you the details." He gave Anthony a sharp look that seemed to carry more meaning than expected.

"You should know that there are no secrets here, Lord Braxton," Anthony replied. "We are among friends."

Sophia drew her brows together. She wondered again what the relationship was between Braxton and Anthony.

Lord Braxton frowned. "I see," he said. After another moment of strained silence, he seemed to rouse himself and return to the conversation. He looked at Sophia with a smile. "So, the nanny believes the boy witnessed something, and you believe her. That is enough to convince me."

Chapter 23

Anthony braced his arm against the coach window and rubbed his temple. Kill the man. He was going to kill Braxton. He had multitudinous questions for his superior, not the least of which was "*Why in blazes are you here?*" Braxton had upended Anthony's life, had him following bread-crumb clues all over the globe, and now decided to swoop in like a hawk and muck around in the work Anthony had worked so hard to do? At *his* insistence!

It was bad enough that Anthony had begun sleeping with one eye open, fearful that whoever had the Janus Document had had time to start deciphering the code. Anthony's information, his friends' information—everything was listed, according to Braxton. Why the murderer hadn't come forward with a blackmail threat made no sense, unless the code was still intact, of course. But why threaten Sophia with Charlie's broken toy? Why lure Charlie away from home to his potential death? Why not deal directly with Anthony, or Pilkington, even, who both had money and influence? Why did the perpetrator's actions seem to focus only on covering up Miller's murder rather than on the larger issue of the document?

And by all that was holy, if Braxton did not stop leering at Sophia, Anthony was prepared to put his fist in the man's throat. Sophia, bless her, had eyed Braxton with thinly veiled mistrust from the moment she had joined them in the foyer. Once again, her instincts were spot-on. As a woman who had been propositioned and harassed by Braxton's type in the past, she likely recognized a Lothario when she saw one. Even now, Braxton had extended his leg in the cab of the spacious coach and inched it closer to Sophia's skirts. She was looking at Dylan, but she subtly gathered the fabric of her dress and tucked it beneath her legs. He was torn between pride in her ability to keep herself free from men of Braxton's ilk, and fury that a man of Braxton's ilk would take liberties with a woman if left unchecked.

The coach came to a stop, and he stepped out, taking a deep breath. He told himself to pull it together, that none of them could afford mistakes. He would act as he had since his arrival in Bombay. He was on extended holiday, and he happened to meet up with his friends after a protracted separation, and as a group they were attempting to help Major Stuart with his investigation into the mysterious disappearance of a merchant seaman. Until someone came forward either publically or privately to expose his connection with the War Department, he would not acknowledge it, and Sophia, Rachael, and Dylan would remain the only people who knew.

Braxton stepped from the carriage and eyed Anthony warily. And well he should. They had not had a moment to chat alone since Braxton's unannounced arrival at the mansion.

"What a surprise to see you here," Anthony said quietly. "On orders to work with the Bombay Presidency. And now investigating the death of a sea captain."

Braxton brushed a hand down his sleeve and straightened his suit coat. He looked at Anthony evenly. "You've been away for some time. I thought you might appreciate support."

Anthony bit back a quick retort and turned instead to help Sophia down from the coach.

"How wonderful to reacquaint yourself with friends from home, Wilshire." Braxton smiled at Sophia as she moved a few steps away. "You must have been delighted when Miss Elliot arrived."

"Implying something, Braxton?" he murmured.

"Wondering if you've kept your focus."

"Have not wavered."

Braxton glanced at Sophia, his eyes flicking from her face to her bodice, and back to Anthony. "I wonder."

Anthony narrowed his eyes, his temper close to boiling over at the man's crude insolence. "We should speak. Later."

Braxton turned as the next carriage rolled to a stop and settled his smile back into place. "Well, bless me, if it isn't Lady Seadon! And the young Lady Seadon, and Miss Vale!" He left Anthony and Sophia without word or gesture, which was the height of rudeness, especially to Sophia. He helped Lady Seadon, the mother, from the carriage and bestowed his blinding smile upon her as she stammered and fussed about what a pleasure it was to meet him.

"He is . . . oily."

Anthony looked down at Sophia's pronouncement. She had returned to his side and observed the show with an impassive expression, her shoulders straight, her gloved hands lightly clasped at her waist, her hair shining like silk in the bright moonlight, her jaw curving gracefully into the elegant line of her neck. Her bearing was impeccable, her sense of self firmly fixed. She was more of a lady, had always been, than most of the women he knew.

"I love you." He whispered it, but she still turned to him abruptly with wide eyes. She flicked them wider in surprise, as if asking if he were sane.

He smiled. "I do. You are glorious, and I love you."

"*There* you are." Rachael marched over to them and grasped Sophia's hand. "Sophia, you simply must look at the hors d'oeuvres spread. Were you aware that Lady Pilkington had everything set up beforehand? I vow, she is incredibly organized. We must ask her . . ."

Sophia glanced back at him, and as he stood in profile to Braxton and the Seadons on his right, he winked at her with his left eye. It was dark; he wasn't certain she saw it. But she smiled.

He moved to join the others at the center of the ruins but was, regrettably, too slow. A hand threaded around his arm, and he looked down to see Lady Lissa Seadon attached to him like a barnacle. His smile was tight; she had to know he didn't care for her, had been all but rude in the past, but she was tenacious. Desperate, perhaps, given her mother.

"Lady Seadon."

"Lord Wilshire." She smiled up at him, and he was again struck by the fact that, beautiful as she was, he hadn't a spark of interest. "I have been waiting interminably for an opportunity to chat with you. Miss Elliot quite seems to occupy your time."

"I enjoy Miss Elliot's company." He prayed Miss Elliot would not turn around and see them. He was only just beginning to earn her trust after she'd lived through two years of sordid rumors.

"But it is quite unfair of her to monopolize so much of you. She simply must share." The perfect mouth curved in a perfect smile.

"Where have your travels led you these last many months, Lady Seadon?"

"Ah. Seeking to distract me, are you? Very well, I shall play along. We began on the Continent and traveled through Europe, the Mediterranean states, coastal China, now we find ourselves here."

"And you plan to remain here indefinitely?"

"Do you return home soon? Do you hope to see me there?" She affected a very sympathetic face. "We are here, mostly, in hopes of finding my dear cousin Adeline a husband. She's had no luck at home, and is unlikely to." She glanced over her shoulder and pulled herself even closer to his arm. "Her face and form have little to recommend them, you see, and she has no fortune. Papa will settle a small dowry on her, but only out of the goodness of his heart."

What a woman could do to another with a few carefully placed words. He shook his head. "I've always found Miss Vale quite pretty, and she is delightful company. We partnered once at whist."

"Oh, Wilshire, you are such a gallant." She looked over her shoulder again and sniffed. "The poor dear."

They reached the courtyard, and Lady Seadon could not have timed their entry through the flowering arch more perfectly—or more likely she had intended a show for Sophia from the beginning.

Sophia was chatting with the Misses Denney, and she looked up at Lady Seadon and then at him.

Anthony wished for a way to detach his arm from his shoulder.

The length of Lady Seadon's body pressed against his side. "I am certain a man with your bloodlines can appreciate a woman whose own are equally impeccable. We are well suited, you and I, Anthony. We are cut from the same cloth. No surprises, no unexpected complications. Marriages are much more efficient between parties who are well-versed in the realities of a *ton* union. Emotions are such an unnecessary entanglement."

He smiled tightly and pried her hand from his arm. Very deliberately he separated himself from her and bowed lightly. "I leave you here, Lady Seadon. You'll forgive me, but I must thank our hostess for this wonderful adventure."

Her mouth curled. "Of course. I shall avail myself of Lord Braxton's company." She glanced again at Sophia. "Do remember, society is not tolerant of upstarts."

He watched her turn and head back through the arch, angry and irritated and not trusting her for an instant. She approached Braxton, who had her mother and cousin on either arm, and she nudged her cousin ever so slightly. Adeline immediately released Braxton and Lissa replaced her. Braxton laughed at something she said, and Anthony's gut clenched. Sophia's description of Braxton also applied comfortably on the young Lady Seadon's shoulders. Oily. It was appropriate.

Sophia watched Anthony watch Lissa Seadon. Surely, no. He could not possibly be interested in her. But he had turned to watch her walk away.

I cannot do this again.

The thought swam insidiously through her head, and a sense of panic started in her chest and threaded through her until her fingertips felt cool and she was light-headed.

He loves me. He only just told me he loves me. Please, please, please, I cannot do this again.

Anthony sought out Lady Pilkington, and with effort, Sophia pulled her attention back to Charity Denney.

"Miss Sophia, are you unwell?" Charity tilted her head. "You suddenly seem most peaked."

She swallowed. The smells of the food surrounding them on buffet tables assaulted her nose, and she fought back a gag.

Please. Please.

Beatrice touched Sophia's arm. "Sophia?"

Sophia looked at the young woman, focused on her face. Brown eyes, light brown hair, such a kind face. She inhaled carefully and exhaled slowly, willing her heart to relax. "I felt quite faint for a moment. I daresay all the excitement since last night has me quite exhausted."

Beatrice nodded. "I understand. It was quite awful, was it not? How is little Charlie now?"

Sophia was grateful to have something else to focus on. "Amala Ayah has not left his side, of course, and Lady Pilkington spent the bulk of her day with him. He does not seem frightened, and has communicated in his quiet way when asked questions. Apparently the girl said nothing to hurt or alarm him; she did wander off a time or two but he stayed on her trail." Sophia smiled. "He is a smart little fellow."

Charity nodded. "Most assuredly, the dear. Mama retired early to her bedchamber when she heard Charlie had gone missing. I do believe it worried us all."

"Do you know who would have done such a thing? Why harm Charlie?" Beatrice asked.

Sophia lifted a shoulder.

Charity's eyes grew wide. "Perhaps it was a kidnapping for ransom, but Major Stuart and the prince's men found Charlie before the demands could be made."

Beatrice looked flatly at Sophia. "She has been reading lurid novels just arrived from England."

Sophia laughed. "Ah, Charity, I should hate to think of a world where you are different than you are right now."

Charity smiled at Sophia and shot a scowl at Beatrice. The girl's attention shifted to the entry arch and her face lost all traces of humor. Taj Darzi had arrived with some of his attendants, and Lord and Lady Pilkington welcomed them with all due aplomb. Beatrice's breath quickened, the color in her cheeks heightening becomingly.

"Why must he show his face everywhere we are?" Charity grumbled.

"Shh." Sophia linked their arms together. "Beatrice is an

intelligent girl and knows what is best for her life." She glanced at Beatrice, her steady demeanor, and found herself believing it.

Dinner was lavish and formal in its presentation, yet guests were encouraged to select their choices of food and sit at whichever table they chose. "Which is lovely," Charity told Sophia, "because now we can enjoy one another's company at a meal other than breakfast!"

"Indeed." She smiled. Charity's enthusiasm was infectious, and when she saw Anthony heading toward her, all was very nearly right in her world again. Lady Seadon the younger, however, was on a collision course with him, and when he realized her intentions, he quickly sat at a table that was full except for one seat. He had placed himself neatly between Clergyman Denney and Professor Gerald, who spoke to a blushing, smiling Rachael Scarsdale. Blushing and smiling? Sophia was happy for Rachael, who had mentioned earlier that she would welcome the gentleman's suit, should he declare it.

A splash of color on Anthony's black suit coat caught Sophia's eye, and her breath stilled in her throat. She felt the burn of tears forming behind her eyes, and she blinked them back. He had placed flowers in his lapel. At home, before he'd left, he would place flowers of different kinds and colors in his lapel so that she would know he was thinking of her even when she was swamped by suitors and grasping debutantes anxious to ride along on her coattails. It had become a game; he would wear a flower, and when she returned home, she would look in her reference book, *Le Language de Fleursand,* to translate the meaning. Before long, she'd memorized entire pages.

Tonight he'd pulled flowers from the cracks in the ruins. The types of flowers were likely all wrong, but the colors were clear enough. Lavender for *devotion,* and blood-red orange for *I love you.* The colors were vibrant, and under the light of the full moon, she saw his messages clearly.

He held her gaze and put his hand to his heart. As his fingertips brushed against the lapel, the small boutonniere turned, and she noted a sprig of green. If he intended it as a stand in for mint, as he'd done once before in London, he was communicating *warmth of feeling.*

Her tears threatened to return. How on earth had she ever believed a word of his fateful letter? He had been giving her signs indicating his interest in her from nearly the beginning of their association. She considered the wretched nature of his duty—of what it had demanded of him—and for the first time felt the stab of hurt and dismay he must have experienced, knowing what was expected of him, what he had to do to her. Even knowing the truth the last few days, she hadn't examined the issue from his point of view. She hadn't considered that he had been as much a victim as she had.

Sophia placed her hand on her heart and smiled. She blinked and a tear fell. She wiped it away with her finger. She would have gone to him, but there were no more seats at his table.

Charity sighed and laid her head playfully on Sophia's shoulder, oblivious to the silent communication traveling across a crowded space. "I do believe I hear wedding bells for our dear Miss Scarsdale."

"I do believe I also hear those bells." Sophia rested her head against Charity's and matched her sigh, which made Charity giggle. "And the professor is so handsome, is he not?"

Charity fluttered her eyelashes. "Ever so handsome. Come, Sophia, we must retrieve our dinner from the buffet tables."

Charity pulled her along, and Sophia took another moment to scan the crowd as they walked. Lissa Seadon had been forced to sit with her mother, cousin, and Lord Braxton, who still made the hair on the back of Sophia's neck rise. Sophia looked back at Anthony, who raised a champagne flute in her direction. His entire regard was focused completely on her, and for a moment it seemed as if there was nobody else in the courtyard. The corner of his mouth lifted, and he took a sip of the drink.

Her heart lifted, and she very nearly sighed for herself.

Charity pulled Sophia over to Beatrice as Taj Darzi approached with the Pilkingtons. The royal cousin bowed, his palms together, thumbs touching his forehead. His attention was clearly aimed at Beatrice, who curtseyed and flushed.

"Mr. Darzi has asked that you join our table, Miss Denney," Lord Pilkington said. "If you would?"

"Of course, I would be honored." Beatrice smiled and again Sophia was struck by the gentle transformation it made to the girl's face. "I would ask that my sister and Miss Elliot join us as well?"

"Most certainly. We would be honored." Mr. Darzi smiled, the small wrinkles at his eyes crinkling with obvious use. He was tall next to Beatrice, but Sophia could envision the two fitting together, rather like pieces of a puzzle. He carried himself well with a quiet confidence, every inch the royal heir. He complimented Beatrice on her appearance, and she smiled, ducked her head, and thanked him.

Sophia squeezed Charity's arm and whispered, "My dear, I do believe Beatrice shall be very much cherished, should she accept Mr. Darzi's suit."

Charity turned her troubled blue eyes to Sophia. "I so wish we could be certain."

Sophia smiled. "Does life ever promise guarantees of success?"

Charity frowned, but lifted a shoulder.

"Come along, do," Lady Pilkington called back as they made their way to a reserved table near the arch.

"Miss Denney," Sophia said to Beatrice, "would you like your parents to join us at this table?"

Mr. Darzi awaited Beatrice's response as he held her chair. Beatrice glanced across the courtyard at her father and looked back at Sophia, her eyes widening in a clear plea. "Oh, no, my father is already settled and our mother is at home tonight. She is feeling ill, I am afraid."

"As you wish, Miss Denney," Mr. Darzi said and tucked Beatrice into her chair. He sat beside her then, and said, "I do hope your mother's illness is not a serious one."

"Nothing some time away from our father wouldn't cure," Charity muttered in Sophia's ear, and then clasped her hand over her mouth.

"Charity," Sophia whispered, "does your father hurt your mother?" She was grateful for the light conversation that flowed among the other four diners.

Charity shook her head. "Not in the manner you suggest."

She frowned. "But he is not kind to her. And she is not strong. Not as you are, or Miss Rachael."

Sophia clasped the girl's fingers. "Or as you are, and Beatrice. The two of you are very strong, and very talented. You must remember this."

Charity nodded, solemn. "I shall, Miss Sophia."

Mr. Darzi spoke easily with Lord Pilkington, who was all things lively and conversant. The Resident's air of command was quite at odds with his behavior from the night before. But perhaps, Sophia mused, she was judging him harshly. His son had been missing, after all.

Sophia made her way through the dinner and observed those around her quietly. Mr. Darzi spoke of a new dawn, of fresh beginnings, of strong alliances between neighbors and friends. He offered suggestions for additional activities between the local populace surrounding the palace and the British citizenry.

"I must say," Mr. Darzi said as the group began eating, "that when I learn of the early days of the Company that began more than a century ago, I wish relations were not so different. The two cultures mixed freely, and they did not seem to suffer from the discord we often see now."

"Quite right," Pilkington said and tackled his dinner.

Sophia glanced between him and the heir-presumptive and felt slightly awkward at the stalling of a pleasant exchange.

Beatrice lightly cleared her throat. "Mr. Darzi, if I may, I must applaud your intentions and your efforts toward such a noble goal. I find it splendid and inspired."

Mr. Darzi beamed at Beatrice. "Do you indeed? Oh, I am so glad. How wonderful to be of a like mind."

Lady Pilkington nudged her husband, and he started. "Yes, yes, of course, how right you are, Miss Denney. Very noble goals indeed."

"Might we schedule a meeting soon, Lord Pilkington, to exchange ideas? I would bring my aides, of course, and would fully expect to see representatives from the Bombay Presidency, should you wish it." Mr. Darzi regarded Lord Pilkington patiently, and Sophia realized that the man understood full well Lord Pilkington's limited capacity for leadership.

Lady Pilkington was also clearly cognizant of the undercurrents. Her husband nodded in response to Mr. Darzi's suggestions, but had stuffed his mouth full of food. "Of course, such meetings would be not only appropriate but welcome," Lady Pilkington said with a smile. "And please do continue to visit the Residency. Our door is open always to you and your family."

"I thank you, madam."

"I regret that we've not seen the prince of late," Lady Pilkington said. "I do hope he does not suffer."

Mr. Darzi's expression tightened fractionally. "I do not expect him to be with us much longer, but I thank you for your concern."

"The silver lining, I suppose, is that you will perform much more effectively in that role," Lord Pilkington added. "He clings to the old ways, does he not?"

Lady Pilkington briefly closed her eyes, and Sophia acknowledged that there was more to her sponsor than readily visible. Of the two Pilkingtons, she would have been by far the better diplomat. "We all approach customs and traditions differently, do we not?" Lady Pilkington added.

Mr. Darzi smiled at her, and Sophia knew that he had probably reached Sophia's conclusions about the Pilkingtons long ago. "We do indeed, my lady. And my cousin does hold to some of the older traditions that I and my other family members do not."

The midnight picnic continued, the guests laughed, the moon shone brightly down on the ruins, and the champagne—the finest from French vineyards—flowed generously. Dessert passed, tables and chairs were cleared, and a seven-piece ensemble began to play so that the guests might dance.

Sophia looked occasionally for Rachael and Professor Gerald as well as Anthony but the random seating arrangements had placed them in different areas. She finally spied Anthony, who locked eyes with her and mouthed, "Stay there."

She remained in that spot as he dodged his way through soldiers, tea planters, and Fleet women, until he was at last before her.

He grabbed her hand. "A waltz," he said. "Finally." He led her to the center of the courtyard and pulled her close with what sounded very much like a relieved sigh. "The last waltz, the one at the costume ball, does not signify. We shall pretend it never happened. Though after this dance, I must ask others to dance, and you must fill your dance card, because we are nothing more than friends, of course."

She smiled. "Of course."

He sobered. "Keeping you safe has been the hardest thing

I've ever done in my life, Sophia. It continues to be the hardest thing I've ever done." He dropped his voice and deliberately shifted his hand higher on her back from where it had comfortably, familiarly, dropped. "Acting as though there is nothing . . ."

"I shall be fine, and we shall finish this soon. And as we are to dance with others, might I suggest you save one for Charity Denney?"

He tipped his head in question. "She is not the sort you usually point me toward. Is she suffering in some way?"

"She is very pretty and vivacious, however she is concerned for her sister and anticipating loneliness should this association with Mr. Darzi escalate quickly." Sophia lifted a shoulder. "I believe she would benefit from a lovely dance with a handsome gentleman. And then I would suggest Miss Adeline Vale. Her cousin is atrocious, and I suspect Miss Vale is never allowed to shine."

He arched a brow, his lips lifting at the corners. "I am wounded you would deliver me so casually to potential rivals with no apparent pangs of jealousy."

Sophia mirrored his small smile. "Are you suggesting I should be jealous?"

His expression was all things benign. "Certainly not. I am, after all, practically in my dotage, especially in comparison to the young Miss Denney. She would find me quite ancient, surely."

Sophia couldn't halt the smile from growing across her face. He had opened himself so beautifully for a perfectly aimed jest. "I am not so many years older than she, my lord. And you are of an age with my *elder* brother."

He chuckled and gave her hand a playful squeeze. "You are ageless, my dear. I was quite undone from the moment I met you over your brother's sickbed. You possessed a maturity I'd never seen in a debutante."

Her response was wry. "Likely my life experiences have given me a different perspective than other debutantes."

He nodded, his eyes softening. "I cannot say I am glad for that, but I readily admit you are incomparable. Strong. And I am honored to be held in your good esteem."

Her eyes burned. "My, my. Much more of such talk will have me blubbering like a ninny."

Anthony gave her hand another gentle squeeze and glanced casually around at the other couples and the people thronging the courtyard and beyond. Ever aware, ever vigilant. Sophia had to admit it was a comfort. She felt safe.

His mouth tightened, eyes narrowing slightly before returning his gaze to her. "Sophia, I teased you about Miss Denney, but on a truly serious note, please know I will not seek out Lissa Seadon's attention or favor, ever. Should she corner me, or insinuate anything the least bit suggestive, you must know it is untrue. She is manipulative and conniving. And very much envious of you." His expression was earnest, focused. "I do not care for her company, even casually. Do you trust me in this?"

She nodded, and a warm glow settled in her chest. He knew the other woman had rattled Sophia's confidence and so he addressed it directly. "I do."

They settled into a rhythm that was so much like her dreams that Sophia nearly cried. He was back. He was home. This was how it had been, how it had felt, although now there was a depth to their relationship, a better understanding than before, and perhaps she was that much more grateful he was who she had believed him to be all along.

"You're thinking," he murmured.

"I am remembering. This is exactly how it was. This feeling."

"Yes." He paused and exhaled. "I have missed it. I have missed you so very much. I have dreamed of this since the night I left London, and there were times I feared it would never happen, that you would marry another, which would have been completely justified and understandable."

She swallowed, met his eyes. "I wanted to, and I could not."

"I shall thank God daily for that from this day forward."

She laughed. "Which one? You have several now from which to choose—Brahma, Vishnu, Kali, *Shiva*!"

"Your personal favorite, is he?"

"No, that's—" She glanced around quickly. "That's the statue I believe is missing from Pilkington's study."

His brows drew together in thought and then his mouth slackened and his pace slowed.

"What is it?"

"Shiva, the destroyer."

They had all but stopped in one place and blocked other couples. She tapped his shoulder, and he resumed, his hand applying light pressure on her back as he led her out of the way. They continued dancing, and he said quietly, "I found a shard in the study the other night."

Sophia took a breath. "And you believe it is a part of a Shiva figurine?"

"It is painted gold—Shiva is often portrayed with a trident in one of his hands. If the statue matched the other two in proportion, I believe the piece I found could be part of that trident."

They were silent for a moment, lost in their own thoughts.

"Do you suppose the killer destroyed the rest of it?"

"Possibly."

"It might explain why Pilkington was so insistent we not touch the other two—he is superstitious. He must have his belongings in threes, and the fact that the statue is missing is unsettling for him."

Anthony frowned, dropping his voice to nearly a whisper. "On the surface Pilkington has seemed somehow complicit in this whole affair—he is odd and obsessive in his behavior—but I am not certain circumstances are anything more than they seem. Aside from the fact that one of his statues was likely a weapon of convenience, I cannot find a legitimate tie from him to the crime. He had access to his own safe any time day or night. Had he sought to take the item from his study he could have without raising suspicion. There would be no need for an altercation."

Sophia nodded, thoughts swirling. "Could he have been interrupted in just that act, though?"

Anthony lifted a shoulder. "During the costume ball when his house was stuffed full? And he, hosting with his wife?"

"What better cover? Distraction, nobody to take note of his whereabouts?"

He knit his brow in thought. "It makes no sense to me."

Sophia was frustrated that so many pieces of the puzzle

still seemed to be missing. The music finally came to a close, and Anthony slowly released her, his attention focusing again on her with a smile. "Where is Miss Denney, then?"

Sophia narrowed her eyes in mock recrimination as she craned her neck. "Over there, near the arch. But as people rarely escape your notice, I suspect you already know where she is. Go, now, and behave yourself."

He bowed and placed a kiss on her hand.

"Who shall I dance with, do you suppose?" She blinked at him innocently.

His grin gave way to a scowl. "Preferably the oldest man in attendance. Someone who paints me as a veritable adolescent in comparison."

She laughed softly and curtseyed as he brushed past her.

"*You* behave yourself," he muttered and shifted his way through the crowd to the arch.

Chapter 24

The mansion was hushed; most people were taking a late afternoon rest. Anthony had gone to the cantonment to talk to Dylan, whose superior officer had contracted malaria and foisted several duties onto his next-in-command. Taj Darzi had accompanied Anthony in an effort to strengthen relations and perhaps lend resources to help find Captain Miller's killer. To Sophia's knowledge, Anthony had not divulged the nature of the dark reason behind the death to anyone but her, Dylan Stuart, and Rachael Scarsdale.

Sophia flopped on her stomach across her bed and opened a novel she'd tried to read five times already. Too many thoughts swirled and tumbled about her head, and she couldn't focus. Anthony was a spy. Sensitive information had been stolen, but as long as the thief did not have access to the code, they were probably safe. But now someone had killed for it. That same someone didn't realize a young boy had witnessed the crime until his nanny spoke of it, trying to find a listening ear. Someone had threatened Sophia and tried to kill the boy . . .

"Ugh," she moaned and tossed the book on the floor, feeling juvenile and out of sorts. It was as though the mansion was anchored in the doldrums and there wasn't a hint of wind anywhere. They would all die there on the equator, sunburned and shriveled.

"Mercy," she muttered. "What is the matter with me?"

A rapid knock came at her door—panicked. She opened the door and realized why.

"Charity?"

The girl's eyes were huge. But then, the girl's eyes were often huge.

"Sophia!" Charity pushed into the room and slammed the door. "It's Beatrice," she breathed and grabbed her middle. "Beatrice—" Her face crumpled, and her voice caught on a sob.

Sophia pulled her to one of the chairs by the hearth. She crouched in front of it and patted Charity's knee. "Breathe. There's a good girl. And another deep breath—there we go. Now. What has happened to Beatrice?"

"She overheard the servants talking in the compound today as they laundered clothing. Many of the families' servants gather to do the chores. It makes the task so much less tedious, you see."

"Yes?" Sophia twirled her hand in a circle, encouraging Charity to speak more quickly.

"Right, yes. So she was outside with her watercolors and overheard them talking. Someone had heard from the trail of servants between here and the palace that the prince died this morning." She gulped a breath. "But the palace is keeping the news quiet, and they are following the directive of the late prince's advisor. The short one who always smells like cheap tobacco, which is odd, because they have so much money."

Cheap tobacco?

"I've not met the advisor, so I cannot speak to the truth of it, of course, but Beatrice heard all of it, and she understands the dialect perfectly."

Sophia put her hand to her forehead. "Do you mean to suggest that Mr. Darzi is unaware that the prince has died?"

Charity nodded, curls bobbing. Her eyes teared. "The servants said his funeral would be tonight, that 'things would continue as planned' so that he—Mr. Darzi—would lose favor with British officials." Her voice broke. "The short advisor—the one with the cheap tobacco—he is hoping to enflame relations between the Indian princely states and the British military. A revolution, he calls it."

Sophia felt a measure of alarm. "The gossip is that the funeral pyre will happen tonight?"

"Yes," Charity gasped.

Oh, no. No, no, no. "Did they offer any specifics about this ceremony?"

"No!" Charity wailed. "But you and I both know what it means, Sophia!"

Sophia was afraid she did.

"And then, and *then* they said the dowry would be worth every penny, that it was a small thing to take the woman with it, that once suspicion had been cast on Mr. Darzi and the British imprisoned him, the advisors would rule the state as one body. They would have the dowry money by then and would have no further use for either Mr. Darzi or his new bride."

Charity shuddered on an indrawn breath, and Sophia's heart was torn in two. One half ached for the girl who cared so much for her sister that she hurt when her sister hurt, and the other half was bent on murdering a short advisor to a dead prince who smoked cheap tobacco.

Sophia took a deep breath and reached for Charity's hands. "I am so sorry, sweet girl. Some people are quite cruel. Was Beatrice very afraid?"

Charity nodded miserably. She faced Sophia and clutched her hands tightly. "And why on earth would Beatrice tell me all of these things? She knows I cannot keep a secret to save my life! Why would she tell me all of this?" She gulped. "She said she needed to warn Mr. Darzi of the nefarious plans. And then there is our father!"

Sophia's heart beat faster. "What of your father?"

"He ranted at Beatrice last night after the midnight picnic for advancing things too quickly with Mr. Darzi. He said he had not yet secured the key to her dowry, that he had to find some code, and that the prince's advisors would not want something they couldn't sell. He said he was to receive half of the profits, but now he didn't know if the advisors would honor the agreement. And then he ranted about not having the same pool of resources as the prince's advisors or the captain and that he would never find a buyer on his own." Charity shook her head. "He sounded like a madman! And when Mother tried to reason with him, to make sense of his ramblings, he shouted that the dowries were at stake and . . . and he hit her!" Charity bit her lip, her gaze stricken. "We were so afraid—Beatrice and I! He . . . he . . ." Her lip trembled, eyes full of misery and disbelief. "He is a man of God! How *could* he?"

Sophia winced. How indeed? She had seen her share of violence against women and children on the dirty streets of London, and it horrified her every time. Her heart went out to Charity, who gasped back another sob and placed her fingers against her mouth.

"I didn't want him to hit her again, so I shouted at him and ran to my mother. He left the house, and has not returned." Charity's eyes had grown huge again. "I am so afraid, Sophia, and I do not understand any of this. What would possess him to be so completely . . . completely insensate? Nothing makes sense, nothing. The dowry money was supposed to come from his uncle. What has that to do with the prince or his advisors or something for which he needs a mysterious key and a code? And another buyer—another buyer for what?"

The puzzle pieces suddenly snapped together for Sophia, and she felt panic settling in. She asked for the one thing Charity had yet to tell her. Perhaps Beatrice had known her searching out Mr. Darzi on her own would be dangerous, and she knew Charity would tell someone. "Where is Beatrice now?"

"At the palace."

Sophia sighed. "Of course she is. And none of the gentlemen I trust are in this house at the moment."

"I suppose we do need a gentleman." Charity's face fell.

"Yes, especially as Mr. Darzi is not at the palace."

"What?" Charity leaped to her feet. "Beatrice knew he had plans away from the palace this morning, but surely he is returned by now!"

"He is at the military compound with Major Stuart and Lord Wilshire."

"Are you certain? Perhaps they have left."

"Lord Wilshire told me he would speak with me directly upon their return. I have yet to see either of them." She frowned. "And if Mr. Darzi has returned to the palace, he may be in danger as well. If these advisors are intent on enacting their plans tonight without his knowledge or interference, they will, at the very least, incapacitate him."

"Beatrice will die of a broken heart if something befalls him!"

Sophia didn't tell Charity that Beatrice was in far worse danger than dying of a broken heart. She also couldn't bring herself to tell the girl that her father had probably killed Captain Miller and was now in possession of stolen British state secrets.

"We shall have to tell Lord Pilkington about this. We can insist he take us to the palace so that we might retrieve Beatrice and Mr. Darzi, if he is there—although we have no legal right to demand they surrender him."

Sophia hurriedly put on her shoes and sat at her vanity table. She scribbled a note to Anthony explaining that he must come immediately to the palace, that Beatrice Denney might be in danger, but he was not to tell her parents. She also mentioned to keep Taj Darzi with him if they hadn't already been separated, that the man was in danger if he returned to the palace.

Charity read over her shoulder and wiped her nose with a handkerchief. "Why can he not tell my parents?" she asked, her nose pinched and voice funny.

"Well—" Sophia scrambled. "We do not want them to worry. Not yet."

She folded the note and hustled Charity down to the front foyer to find Himmat. The butler was out front, settling a dispute between two of the kitchen servants, one of whom was now unclean after handling dishes the Residency guests had eaten from. Charity bounced on the balls of her feet, and Sophia impatiently waited for a break in the flow of angry words. She did not want to compound matters by being disrespectful.

Finally, a lull. "Himmat," she said quickly, and the butler turned around and bowed to her, palms together.

"Where might I find Lord Pilkington, do you know?"

"Miss, my lord is hunting."

She blinked. "Hunting?"

"Yes, miss. He hunts duck with Lord Braxton."

"Wonderful," she muttered. Sophia tapped the folded paper against her leg and scrambled for an alternate plan. The sun had moved lower in the sky. While most of the mansion's guests would soon be awake from their naps, there wasn't one person inside whom she believed would be useful in gaining entrance to the palace.

"Fine, then." She handed the folded paper to Himmat. "Would you please see this delivered immediately to the First Cavalry Light Brigade post? It is imperative that Lord Wilshire receive it straightaway."

"Yes, miss. I shall have Abdullah take it."

"Oh, Abdullah! We will need him to take us somewhere. In a carriage, or bullock cart—whatever is most readily available."

His old brow wrinkled. "Would you care to ride a mount?"

Sophia brightened and turned to Charity. "Do you ride?"

"Not so well. I fell off a pony when I was but ten and have since been terrified."

Sophia looked to Himmat, who nodded. "I shall send for Abdullah and a carriage."

Sophia paced back and forth from the large banyan tree to the porch while Charity alternately bounced and wrung her hands. Sophia's worry grew by the moment when she thought of Beatrice attempting to confront the late prince's advisors by herself.

Himmat appeared at the porch, his face grave. Sophia rushed to him, her heart sinking. Now what could the problem be?

"Abdullah is at the bazaar."

"For the love—" Sophia spied a familiar figure crossing the foyer and called to her. "Rachael!"

Rachael came to the door and shaded her eyes against the ever-sinking sun.

"Is Professor Gerald here?"

"No, he is at the University."

"Oh!" Charity stomped her foot and tears filled her eyes.

Rachael looked at Sophia, brows raised high. As Sophia told her the story as quickly as she could, Rachael's expression turned from grim to horrified. She grasped Sophia's arm. "We must go right now."

"We are trying to, but Abdullah isn't here and Charity cannot ride."

Rachael turned to Himmat. "Please, will you have a curricle readied?"

"You drive?"

Rachael nodded. "I do. I believe the Pilkingtons' is a two-seater, but we can manage." She looked at Charity. "As she is the smallest, she shall be the tiger."

Within a matter of minutes, the three women were settled into the curricle, Charity situated behind in the seat normally reserved for the driver's groom. The palace was roughly two miles away. Rachael had ridden to it on horseback with several ladies and a handful of soldiers the afternoon before, though they had not entered the palace compound.

Rachael handled the curricle and team of matched grays admirably, and Sophia was impressed. They left Malabar Hill and headed toward the palace on a road that was fairly well groomed for most of the journey. They had traveled fifteen minutes in tense silence when Rachael pulled on the reins at a fork in the road.

"We have a decision to make." Rachael looked at Sophia. "The groomed road takes us directly to the palace and, from what I gather, directly to the outer courtyard. We shall likely encounter a show of force by way of soldiers and possibly a tiger or two." She glanced back at Charity. "An actual tiger."

Charity lifted a finger. "I should like to hear the second option."

"The path to the right circles around the palace and approaches from the side. When I came here before, we took that path, but it grows quite thick with underbrush. We could go with the horses only so far before turning around. On foot, we could have pushed through."

Sophia took a breath and blew it out. "What are the dangers, do you suppose, of approaching from the side?"

"As much as we were able to tell, there were no tigers circling the perimeter outside the palace walls. The horses were not spooked, at any rate, and the tigers we did see inside the walls were contained with long lengths of chain. We did not encounter soldiers, but the wall around the compound is quite high so I cannot say for certain what sort of defenses lay beyond it."

Sophia nodded. "The logical thing to do is approach the front gates and request an audience as Beatrice suggested she was going to do."

Rachael shook her head. "Supposing we are detained? They would certainly separate us. Once inside, we are utterly defenseless."

"My sister is in there," Charity whispered.

Sophia made a decision. "By this time, or surely before long, my note will have reached Lord Wilshire. He will return to the mansion, gather fresh horses or possibly Lords Pilkington and Braxton, if they are back from their hunt, and come here. We needn't go in ourselves at this point. I suggest we secure the curricle, take this path to the right while we still have some daylight, and see what we can on the other side of the wall."

Rachael nodded once. "Excellent." She drove the curricle some distance down the path, which did, indeed, become rougher with each turn of the wheels. Some distance into the trees, she reined in the horses and set the brake. She secured the horses and vehicle while Sophia and Charity ventured slowly ahead. Rachael caught up to them, and Sophia set a brisk pace along the path.

The farther they traveled, the more the walls of trees and plants closed in around them. Animals sounded to the left and right. Birds squawked at the invasion, as did several angry monkeys who swung from branch to branch and chattered. Charity pulled her arms close to her body and walked right next to Sophia, who was irritated and yet strangely comforted by the contact. She didn't want to be afraid, but once under the thick of the jungle canopy, what little light still in the sky dimmed significantly.

"Not much farther." Rachael walked ahead and shoved at branches, holding them aside for the other two. Her dress snagged, emitting a horrible ripping sound. She looked down and then back at Sophia with a wry grin. "My petticoat is exposed, but not my ankles. My modesty is preserved."

Sophia laughed, grateful for Rachael's presence. Had she come alone with Charity, they would probably have been eaten by the tigers at the front gate.

They continued to walk until Sophia was convinced Rachael had been confused in her directions. As she was considering suggesting they turn back, Rachael called out in triumph.

"Aha. Ladies, I give you, the wall." Rachael looked at Charity with an encouraging smile, and Sophia realized the other woman's aim all along had been to keep Charity busy, to distract her from fretting herself into insanity.

"Excellent," Sophia said. She examined the bank of trees that grew up, over, and into the stone structure. The roots were gnarled, exposed, and great knobby protuberances stretched from the wall into long branches that hung on either side of the property. The wall itself stood fifteen feet off the ground, which meant that one of them needed to climb the tree. Sophia remembered her experience with the elephant and exhaled slowly. She wanted to be the heroine but doubted her ability to stay in the tree once up high enough.

The air was humid; she was sticky, filthy, and exhausted. Animals scuttled, insects chirped, and the air—already cooler under the canopy of vegetation—seemed to drop degrees steadily.

Rachael examined one of the trees, fumbling in the dark and slipping as she stepped on a low hanging branch.

A breeze blew across the jungle canopy, and Sophia put her palms together and thanked Vishnu, the preserver, for the tiny relief. The falling twilight illuminated the small space, and another gust of wind showed a bright moon rising and settling over the jungle. The smell of coming rain permeated the air, and the leaves overhead continued to rustle. Light danced over the trees, casting flickering shadows on the wall.

Low music and chanting from within the compound propelled Sophia forward, and she took to the tree beside the one Rachael had claimed. The music from the palace was rhythmic, steady, and stately, and Sophia's heart climbed into her throat even as she climbed higher into the massive tree.

Charity's words echoed in her head. *Prince—dead—ritual.* The acrid smell of smoke filled the air, and Sophia remembered a summer evening the year before when her family had visited one of the estates and enjoyed a village bonfire.

No, no, no . . .

Sophia reached the wall and shimmied onto a thick

branch that rested atop the stone. She started at movement beside her and nearly lost her grip, only to see Charity perched on the branch next to hers. She looked to her left at the next tree over and realized she was close enough to grab Rachael if she stretched—somehow it brought a measure of comfort.

The sun had fully set, and the sky deepened by degrees from the horizon. Directly overhead, stars popped into view and began filling the sky as she watched. She shifted for a better view of the palace grounds, leaning to her left toward Rachael, who leaned to her right.

The grounds were pristine, and a procession lined beside a funeral pyre set on a bed of carefully groomed logs. The fire had already been lit, and the wrapped form atop the pyre was far enough away that exact details were unclear. There was nobody else on the pyre, however, and Sophia hoped desperately it would remain that way. Her pulse pounded, and she looked at Rachael, who met her gaze, her eyes mirroring the uncertainty Sophia felt. She turned to her right to ascertain how much Charity was able to view, and her heart sank to see the girl's attention riveted, focused.

Sophia shifted closer to Charity and saw that the tree branches parted to offer a clear picture of the funeral ceremony below. The musicians continued to play, the whine and drone of the instruments so unique to the strange land. *Strange to me, of course,* Sophia thought and rested her chin on her hand. *Meaningful, special to those who revere it.* There was a reverence to the ceremony, a tribute to honor a fallen ruler. She could only imagine that the speed with which the ceremony was happening was to keep Mr. Darzi from putting a halt to it, and she prayed that the new prince was safe from his late cousin's men.

Movement to the left of the pyre caught her eye, and Sophia noted a procession of men who carried a *palkhi* on their shoulders, in which sat a veiled woman dressed in red.

Sophia's pulse thudded, and she hoped desperately that the widow was simply there to observe. Her hopes were dashed as the men lifted the palkhi high and, with great care, set it atop the pyre next to the wrapped body already laying there.

Get out! In her mind, she called to the widow, screamed to her. *Get out! Run!* Sophia felt the exact moment when Charity realized what was happening. The young girl sucked in her breath, and as the flames continued to climb steadily upward, Charity's breath came in gasps.

Rachael's eyes showed clear desperation and fear, but her focus remained on Charity, who had started shifting on her tree branch. Rachael gestured toward the girl. "Watch her."

"Charity," Sophia said. "Charity!"

The girl's eyes were trained on the fire, and Sophia braved another look at the scene. Flames had reached the top of the pyre, and the figure in red sitting so still was eclipsed by shafts of yellow and orange that danced and flickered. The processional and musicians stepped back from the pyre, but still the music played.

"No!" The scream tore from Charity's throat, and Sophia lunged at her as she crawled out farther on the branch. "No!"

Sophia pulled desperately at Charity's shoulder, trying to find a good grip while maintaining her own perilous hold on her branch. She slid forward, braced her foot on the stone wall, and hauled Charity up against her, clamping her arms down against her body as the young girl began to sob.

"It isn't Beatrice!" Sophia tried to tell her.

"She's . . . she is . . ."

"Charity," Sophia managed as she pulled both of them back toward the trunk of the tree. "Sweetheart, it isn't your sister."

"I know," Charity cried, and the grief in her voice was nearly Sophia's undoing. It wasn't Beatrice, but it was someone else's sister. Daughter. Even mother, perhaps? She was *somebody* with a life. And her end was painfully, horribly barbaric.

"Sophia." Rachael's voice whipped through the air, and Sophia glanced at her as she continued pulling Charity back, inch by slow inch, so terrified of the height she herself was nearly paralyzed.

"Someone is coming." Rachael reached the lower branches of her tree and dropped to the ground. "Slide her down to me. Now."

"Charity, we must go or we will be caught." She murmured the words fiercely in Charity's ear, and the meaning seemed to penetrate. Charity began moving on her own, shimmying back toward the trunk and then down. Sophia followed suit, her hands slippery with sweat and her dress catching and impeding her efforts with every movement. She also reached the trunk and began her descent, wondering if she should be grateful for the darkness that hid exactly how high she really was.

A flash of light illuminated the jungle floor, followed by a tremendous crash of thunder. Sophia was ten feet off the ground and stepping to another branch when her foot slipped, and she threw her arms around the branch closest to her. Slipping again, she scrambled for purchase and slapped her hand down on a thinner branch, which emitted a loud croak. Her hand smeared along a soft, compact body, and she realized with horror she had touched a toad.

A startled gasp and squeak squeezed from her as she released her hold on the tree and fell the rest of the way to the ground, landing hard on her side. Pain sliced through her hip and shoulder, and the breath had been driven from her lungs so fiercely it hurt.

Rachael and Charity scrambled to her side and hefted her upward.

"Sophia," Rachael gasped, "we must run. Now. I am afraid the guards are coming."

Sophia tried to propel her legs forward as the other two women held her on either side and stumbled forward. Her breath returned by degrees, gasping and wheezing through her lungs. Her stomach and chest hurt horribly, and the pain in her shoulder and hip had her seeing stars. Finally, finally, she was able to move on her own, and she lifted her skirts and stumbled after the others, stopping to help one or the other when tree roots hampered their progress and sent them sprawling.

There were shouts from behind, but the noise was swallowed by thunder and the mad screeching of monkeys who were irritated at the mayhem. Sophia looked quickly behind her as she ran, but could see nothing but a black void. Branches whipped across her face as she turned forward, stinging and bringing forth tears.

It felt to Sophia as if they had run ten miles, though she knew that perception was a result of the fear she felt. Eventually the vegetation thinned, and the path widened considerably. The disappearing canopy allowed for more light that came now, unfortunately, from flashes of lightning as the moon and stars had been completely obliterated by storm clouds.

A whinny signaled their return to the curricle, and Rachael soothed the terrified horses as Sophia untangled their leads from a nearby tree.

"They may not cooperate," Rachael said over the wind. "We haven't a choice but to try."

Sophia boosted Charity into the curricle seat, insisting she sit in front, and she took one horse's reins from Rachael. They led the horses for a time on foot until they came to the fork and the groomed path. Sophia gave Rachael a quick hug for good luck, then climbed on the back of the curricle in the tiger's perch. She faced forward, as Charity had, and held on to the seat back as Rachael climbed in and clucked at the horses.

Chapter 25

To Sophia's amazement, and possibly with help from Vishnu, Allah, or the Christian God she'd been raised to believe in, the horses ran. It was entirely possible that they were too spooked to do anything but run, but they stayed on the path and Rachael, through much straining of muscles and a few words that would have made Jack blush, guided them back to the mansion.

The sight that greeted them was an uproar that rivaled the storm breaking outside. Lady Pilkington directed the Seadons, a few Fleet ladies, and Corporal Mailor with his entourage to the drawing room. She assured the small crowd that all would be well, that her husband and the brave men of the military would save the day and prevent heinous things from occurring at the palace.

Sophia, Rachael, and Charity stood just inside the doorway, looking numbly on the scene. Sophia refused to think about what they had witnessed. It would have to wait until later when she had time and privacy. There were too many things still unsettled.

Lady Pilkington turned and caught sight of them. Without taking her attention from them, she directed the staff to gather toweling and blankets, and then sent instructions to the kitchen to prepare more tea. She approached, finally, wringing her hands. Sophia stepped forward and figured she should say something, but she struggled to find anything useful.

"Oh, my dears," Lady Pilkington said, and her eyes filled. She stepped closer to Sophia and whispered, "Did you see . . . Did the men arrive in time to stop it?"

Sophia shook her head, her throat tight. There wasn't time, she did not have time to dwell on it yet.

"And Miss Denney?"

Sophia slowly exhaled a trembling breath. "We did not see her."

Himmat arrived with an armful of blankets, and she gratefully accepted one. She wrapped it about her shoulders. "Will you tell us how things stand?" she asked the butler and Lady Pilkington. "The men are riding to the palace?"

Himmat nodded. "They gathered reinforcements from the neighboring infantry division and likely have arrived by now. I had hoped they would be in time—but at any rate, Mr. Darzi is safe and with them."

"Beatrice is in the palace," Charity murmured, her brow creased. "We must notify them."

"They will find her." Rachael held her own blanket around her shoulders with one hand and snugged Charity's closer about her chin. "They will find her and bring her home."

"Oh, my dear," Lady Pilkington said, "your father was here earlier, and your mother is here now." She paused and pursed her lips, looking at Charity as though weighing a decision. "Whatever has happened, please know that you have a home here."

Charity frowned. "I don't understand."

"He left a note for you and Beatrice. Himmat, do you have it on your person?"

The butler nodded and reached into his pocket. He handed Charity a folded paper, and the girl stared at it as though she couldn't comprehend what it was.

Sophia moved to her side. "Shall I help you?"

Charity handed her the letter. Sophia unfolded it and held it so Charity could read it.

> *There is still time, but if I fail, I should rather my own flesh and blood have access to these documents than another. All I have done, I have done for my family. To my daughters: live respectably and beware of vices and temptations of the devil. When you were small, frolicking in the heart of the orchid was appropriate, and although I have forbidden it for some time, I tell you now there are still treasures to be found there. Conduct yourselves with temperance and circumspection. If you are submissive and respectful to your husbands, as your mother has been to me, you will find favor in Heaven. Only once have I been forced to discipline her, and it pained me to do so. Since Eve led Adam astray, however, man has been compelled to set the world to rights.*

Charity looked at Sophia, her head tilted, her expressive eyes showing confusion. "What on earth does he mean?" She read the letter again, and Sophia held her tongue, wanting to proceed carefully.

"Charity, I fear . . ." She trailed off. How much could the poor girl handle in one night?

"What? Is my father in danger? What has happened? What has he done? And my mother?" Charity shook her head, her brow drawn.

Sophia found it infuriating that the man would blame his wife for his behavior. The man was delusional. He committed murder for greed yet didn't acknowledge his culpability or express remorse.

"My dear, I am afraid your father may have had a hand in Captain Miller's demise." Sophia wished more than anything she could spare her the news.

Charity's mouth dropped open. "Why would you say such a horrible thing to me?" She looked at Rachael and back again at Sophia. Lady Pilkington and Himmat were awkwardly silent. "I thought you were my friend. Why, how . . . why?"

Lady Pilkington lifted a hand to the girl and then let it fall back to her side. "Charity, your mother is upstairs in one of the guest rooms." Her voice was hushed, pained. "Dear, she has confirmed it. I am so sorry."

Charity stared at the woman, her eyes luminous, the bright blue of them intensified by the moisture that gathered there. Lady Pilkington moved forward and placed a hand on Charity's arm. "Sweetheart, look at Sophia. She is scratched and bruised, her dress is torn—she looks a right mess. She risked her life for you, for Beatrice." She paused, adding gently, "You were all in more danger than you could have imagined in the jungle. Sophia and Miss Scarsdale, I, myself—none of us have anything to gain by being cruel or telling you lies. Your father has made some choices that have not been wise."

Charity dropped her arms and her blanket fell to the floor. She gestured with the letter as she spoke. "You are telling me, then, that my father, a man of the cloth, *killed* a man?"

"His intentions may not have been so drastic in the beginning." Sophia took a breath. "I am surmising, but I believe your father wanted something that Captain Miller had. Perhaps they had entered a partnership, but they must have argued, and in the end, the captain died and your father—"

Charity narrowed her eyes and looked again at the letter in her hands. Her mouth fell open and she drew a shaky breath. "I know where he is. Dear heaven, I know where he is." She looked up at Sophia. "I must talk to him, stop him! He doesn't know Beatrice is at the palace. He doesn't know she and Mr. Darzi are in danger—"

Sophia pitied the girl with her whole heart. Beatrice's safety was probably Denney's last concern. "I will get word to Major Stuart. He and his men can locate your father. They will—"

"They will kill him!" Charity's face was ghostly pale. She may have lost her innocence with all she'd witnessed tonight; she might never again bounce or blurt secrets or read lurid novels.

"Where do you believe he is, dearest? I shall speak personally with Lord Wilshire. He is kind and good, as is Major Stuart. They will not kill your father in cold blood."

Charity blinked and tears fell fresh. "He is at the place where we frolicked with our mother when we were small. It is the heart of the orchid."

The ruins. Of course.

"The courtyard, then?"

Charity shook her head. "The central building—the one

we avoid." Her voice broke. "We called it 'the heart' because it seemed to be the center of the ruins to us. But we never went in there because it was dangerous." The tears continued. "He will be bitten by a snake or eaten by a bear. He is not . . ." She paused. "He is not a loving father, but he still *is* my father."

Lady Pilkington put an arm around Charity's shoulders, surprising Sophia. The woman wasn't running from the sadness this time. "Come to the drawing room. I shall fix you tea, and then we will see your mother. The bedchamber next to hers is empty, and I shall have it readied for you."

Charity moved with Lady Pilkington as though in a trance. Sophia looked at Rachael with true regret. "I wish we could have spared her that. Earlier—everything."

Rachael raised a brow at her. "I wish we could have spared *ourselves* that. I fear it is an image that will never fade."

"Perhaps it was quick. Perhaps the widow was not conscious before the flames—" Sophia gagged and tried to disguise it with a cough. "Himmat," she managed, "we are not finished yet, unfortunately. Please tell me there is a man in this house who is proficient with a firearm."

"I can shoot a gun," Rachael said wearily.

Sophia turned slowly to her. "Why on earth can you shoot a gun?"

"I was raised in the country with brothers. You're a city girl, Sophia. Why do you need someone who can shoot?"

"As it happens, miss," Himmat said, "Abdullah is here, and he is quite proficient."

Sophia frowned. "He is so young, Himmat. I would hate for him to come to harm."

"We are not in our dotage, you know." Rachael eyed her

flatly. "Abdullah is quite competent. He can accompany us, at least—"

Lady Pilkington rushed to the foyer, her face red. "She is gone. I cannot find her anywhere!" She wrung her hands. "Why do people go missing so much lately?"

Sophia's heart sank. "Charity?"

"Yes! I left her in the drawing room, went to instruct a maid to open a room for her, and she is gone! One of the servants saw her slipping out of the servants' entrance."

Sophia sighed. "Do you have a firearm, Rachael?"

"Not with me."

Lady Pilkington cleared her throat. "I have a gun."

Sophia and Rachael turned to face her.

She lifted a shoulder. "Well, it is my husband's. I shall retrieve it."

The lady rushed off, and Sophia unwound the blanket from her shoulders, immediately feeling a chill. She folded it neatly and handed it to Himmat with a weary smile. "I suspect we shall need these again later."

"Where are we going?" Rachael asked, folding her blanket.

"The ruins."

Lady Pilkington returned presently with a flintlock pistol, and Sophia eyed it dubiously. "Will that work?"

Rachael took it comfortably into her hand and Sophia shrugged. "Perhaps we shall only need it as a deterrent. Lady Pilkington, I do not know how long the men will be occupied at the palace, but should any of them return before we do, please send them to the ruins. My aim is not to waylay Mr. Denney, I want to retrieve Charity."

And that blasted document.

Chapter 26

The Residency descended into further chaos as neighbors and friends gathered and plied Lady Pilkington with questions. The stables were inundated with new arrivals and a few carriages, and it took many long minutes for Sophia's and Rachael's horses to be readied. Sophia swung into the saddle with a groan she couldn't contain. Everything on her right side hurt, and her feet were in agony from running and climbing trees in shoes meant for sitting in a drawing room. She glanced at Rachael, who was scraped, bruised, and filthy, and was glad to have made such a good friend. She did not have many, and Ivy was very far away.

Rachael led the way out of the stable, and Sophia wished they would have thought to put on a light pelisse. For all that it was India, it was winter, and still raining. It wasn't torrential as in monsoon season, but steady enough that by the time they neared the ruins, Sophia was soaked and irritated.

The thunder and lightning continued intermittently; occasionally the sky split and the horses shied. Grateful her mount wasn't nearly as tall as an elephant or a stone wall surrounding a palace, she controlled it with relative ease. She wasn't the horsewoman Rachael was, but she had done her fair share of riding in two years.

They passed the courtyard ruins, and Sophia looked through the rain hoping to see Charity. The letter, though, had said "the heart," which Charity had identified as the frightening building beyond the courtyard. If the clergyman had hidden the stolen document somewhere among the ruins, it would have to be a fairly sheltered spot. She and Rachael guided their mounts slowly through the buildings, skirting fallen statuary and bending down to ride under arches and around tipped pillars as they approached the enclosed sanctuary.

"I was hoping we might see them out here," Sophia admitted. "At least Charity. We were delayed in leaving, but she was still on foot. She must already be in there, and we have no torch, no light source at all."

Rachael drew her mount alongside Sophia's. "She was upset; even in the dark she could easily have made it here in twenty minutes. It took us almost that long to get saddled up." She drew a deep breath and exhaled, shoving wet hair out of her face. "We can assume if Denney is in there, he will have a torch or lamp."

Sophia nodded and followed Rachael. They drew closer to the imposing structure, charmingly haunting in the daylight but terrifying at night. She dismounted, tied her horse next to Rachael's, and wiped the rain out of her eyes. She was cold, and wet, and so very tired. She wished for the ability to send Anthony a message with her mind, and she realized she was fatigued enough that her thinking was muddled.

Come save me, my gallant knight on a black stallion. I am tired, and I want to be carried home like a princess.

She blinked, fuzzy-headed, and for a moment was certain she saw two of everything. She stumbled and tripped on the muddied hem of her dress.

Rachael turned around, her arm protecting a leather bag that held their only weapon. "Are you well?"

Sophia pushed her hair off her forehead with numb fingers. "Yes. Just tired."

"Here." Rachael grasped her hand and continued moving toward the building. They entered slowly under a huge arch and walked forward. "Look," Rachael whispered and pointed to a second arch, beyond which lightning flashed, illuminating a wide courtyard open to the sky and filled with vines and leaves. Huge trees grew inside the area, and those outside leaned over, suspending long vines and branches to the interior. As on the palace wall, the tree roots extended above ground and pushed their way over and under the stone structure, becoming part of it and transforming the building into a living thing.

A snarl and hiss sounded from behind, and Sophia jumped. Rachael urged her forward, mumbling something about not wanting to be eaten by a snake, and she weaved a bit too, causing Sophia to wonder if the blind were leading the blind.

They crossed the courtyard, skirts heavy and dresses plastered to the skin. Sophia pulled out the few pins that remained in her hair and dropped them on the ground as she walked, allowing her hair to fall free. It was soaked, and everything ached from head to toe. She realized that there was a circle of hell Dante had overlooked.

Once on the other side of the courtyard, they passed under another arch and walked slowly into the suffocating dark. "I do not think we should venture too much farther without light," Rachael whispered, and the sound echoed off the walls.

Sophia agreed and was prepared to turn back when she spied a sliver of light ahead and to the right. "Do you see it?"

She felt Rachael's answering nod, and they pushed forward. Sophia closed her eyes when she heard a rustle and a hiss—if they didn't step on a snake, or worse, she would count herself lucky. It was then she heard the muted sound of voices.

The light grew as they reached a narrow doorway and turned a corner into a large square chamber that contained a waist-high wall roughly three feet from each exterior wall. Each corner inside the low-walled square supported a pillar that was larger than Sophia in circumference. The space was dimly lit by a lantern, and Sophia spied Charity's muddied, light blue dress. She pulled Rachael down behind the wall and edged carefully along it until she was behind the pillar closest to the girl.

Charity was out of breath. She had likely only just beat them there. "Papa, I do not understand why."

The clergyman's voice was heavy. "I did it for both of you."

"But why offer it to the prince's corrupt advisors? Why offer up Beatrice?" Her voice broke. "Do you know what they do—what I saw tonight? If they remain in power, uphold the old customs, even Mr. Darzi would be unable to protect her."

"The two of you were willful and refused to select husbands in England! The monetary potential of this document would have bought you men of consequence and placed me in political power."

"I suspect you couldn't have cared less about buying us 'men of consequence,'" Charity said bitterly. "You wanted money and power for yourself. You are the very thing you preach against each Sabbath!"

"I am not!" The roar echoed through the room, and Sophia winced.

"You killed the captain!" Charity's voice rose to a squeak.

"No. Not intentionally. Miller assumed I had contacts within the palace that could help facilitate the sale of the document, and he offered me half of whatever it sold for to arrange it. When I realized Darzi had an interest in pursuing your sister, prospects for the plan's success seemed even better." The man sighed, and Sophia heard a shuffling of feet. Could it be he was actually feeling the sting of a conscience?

"I frequently spend time with Lord Pilkington in his study. I know the combination to his safe. The night of the costume party, the captain asked me to meet him in the study to retrieve the packet of documents. He worried incessantly and was convinced it wasn't safe unless he had it with him at all times. He figured that as the party was in full swing, Pilkington would be busy with his guests, and the study would be unoccupied. We were to review our plan."

There was a pause. Charity finally broke it, and her voice was flat. "What happened to the plan?"

"He hadn't told me that the document was encoded. He hadn't found the key to decipher it and told me I had to discern it. As if I should know! He planned to set sail within three days and return it to London, forgoing the rest of his voyage. He said someone in a position of power—possibly a peer—had tried to sell it once already. But I knew if he left India, the partnership was lost and I would never see my half of the money. I had already made contact with Prince Ekavir's advisors. The ball was rolling, and it was too big for me to stop by that point."

"So you killed him."

"We fought! I defended myself." There was a shuffling of feet again. "I hardly need to explain myself to you, girl. That you would stand here in judgment of me is beyond the pale!"

"And yet I do!" Charity shouted, her voice ringing against the cold, damp walls. "I do judge you, Father, and find you lacking! You have not treated me or Beatrice well, let alone our mother! There has never been an ounce of softness from you."

"That is what a mother is for! A man is not to be soft."

Charity laughed. "I had assumed that perhaps Taj Darzi would not be good enough for Beatrice, but he is gentle and kind and very strong. All of the things you are not."

"I do not know who it is you think you talk to, Charity, but—"

"I am talking to a murderer and a man who strikes women." Charity's voice broke. "A man who hides his weaknesses behind a cloak of feigned righteousness."

Sophia slowly lifted her head and peeked past the pillar. The clergyman paced in a tight circle, occasionally pulling at his hair. He held a deadly looking blade in one hand and a packet of papers in the other. "You should never have come here, Charity. I was going to hide this and then disappear for a time."

"Where is his body? His family needs to know." Charity moved closer to her father, and Sophia chewed on her lip. She didn't want the girl venturing too close to the knife.

Rachael slowly opened her satchel and pulled out the pistol.

Sophia closed her eyes, hoping the weapon would prove unnecessary. She didn't want Rachael to kill a man; she didn't want Charity to see her father die.

Denney was silent for so long Sophia decided he wasn't going to answer his daughter's question.

"I buried him with Mr. Carter."

Stunned silence followed his pronouncement. Sophia frowned. Who was Mr. Carter? She glanced at Rachael, whose eyes were wide. She had her hand over her mouth.

"You buried him in the same grave as a parishioner who had just *died*?" Charity's voice was a combination of dismay and anger. She put her hand to her forehead. "That was why you had Faiyaz dig Mr. Carter's grave a day early. You put . . ." She choked. "You put the captain's body in it and then covered it with dirt. When they lowered Mr. Carter's coffin, nobody was the wiser that there was a man already in that grave!"

"Charity, do not judge me! I had no other choice."

"You had a choice." Charity's tone was bitter, and Sophia felt a moment of sadness. She had hoped to never hear Charity Denney sound bitter. "You could have at least left Captain Miller in the study. He could have had a proper burial."

"I was not thinking clearly at the time." Denney's voice cracked like a whip. Even still, he saw himself as morally superior to everyone. "And things grew increasingly complicated. I was not aware that there had been a witness to Captain Miller's death."

"Who?"

"The boy."

"The boy?" A pause, then a gasp as Charity connected the pieces. *"Charlie?"* She began to cry, and it broke Sophia's heart. "You had that girl lure him away into the jungle! I suppose we should be grateful you weren't awful enough to kill a child outright."

"We waste time. Before long, others will discover where you've gone to. I am leaving, and you know the truth of it all. It matters not to me what you do with the information. I shall be gone where I will never be found."

"I cannot allow you to take that document with you, Father. If it is as valuable as you suggest, if it contains secrets, that means innocent people could be hurt if it is in the wrong hands."

Sophia closed her eyes and eased back down until she was sitting with her back against the low wall. Her foot bumped a rock and it skittered away. Sophia winced at the sound it made.

"Who is there?" Denney's shout echoed through the room. "Who is it?" He had rounded the corner before Sophia could blink. She pulled herself to her feet with a wince, and Rachael stood, the gun pointed at the man's chest.

"I do not wish to use this, sir." Rachael's voice shook, evidence of her exhaustion.

"Rachael," Charity said, her voice barely more than a whisper.

"She will not use it unless she must. Charity, you must be brave. I want you to leave this room, take one of the horses, and return to the mansion. Have Major Stuart and Lord Wilshire sent here straightaway. They are good and fair men, and you know they will not hurt your father unjustly."

"I cannot. I cannot leave you here with him."

Sophia smiled at Charity. "Sweet girl, it will be well. You go. Rachael and I will wait here with him. We are armed, and shall be fine."

Charity gave her father one last look and left.

Denney eyed Sophia and Rachael, his eyes clouded with calculation. He still held the packet of papers in his hand, and when Sophia moved to take it from him, he whipped the blade up and snarled. "Do not touch it."

"It needs destroying, Clergyman Denney," Sophia said evenly.

"It is worth a *fortune*."

She nodded. "And people I love will be in danger if it is not either burned or locked up in the King's bedchamber. We speak of treason, sir."

He eyed her speculatively. "You have a vested interest in taking this from me, do you? But I cannot let that happen. I have come too far. And as for you, Miss Scarsdale, I do not believe you will shoot me."

"I sat in your last sermon, Clergyman. I listened to you preach about righteous behavior and the evils of sin. And all the while, you had killed a man and put him in another man's grave. You were prepared to sell your daughter to madmen who care for nothing but their own gain, and now apparently you are willing to risk innocent lives for *your* own gain. I will not let you harm Sophia, and I will not let you leave with that packet."

"Well done, Miss Scarsdale," a soft voice from the entryway said. "I shall take your place, now." It was Lord Braxton, and Sophia's despair rose. The night had rapidly progressed from bad to worse. She didn't believe they could trust him any more than the murdering clergyman.

Chapter 27

Rachael stepped slowly to the side, and Sophia wondered how to warn her to stay close without tipping her hand. She didn't trust Braxton—hadn't from the first moment.

"Here is your culprit then, Lord Braxton," Sophia said, wary. "He has confessed to the murder, and there were three witnesses to hear it."

Braxton nodded. "Well done, Miss Elliot. Now I'll ask you to move slowly away from the clergyman."

Without warning, Denney wrapped an arm around Sophia's body from behind—over one shoulder, across her body, and beneath her other arm—and clamped tight. With his other hand, he pressed the point of the knife to her throat. "Let me leave, or I will kill this lady. We are going to walk slowly around this way," he said, pulling Sophia with him and taking her to the center of the room. Denney clutched the packet of documents in his fist under her arm, documents Anthony had spent two years trailing. They were pressed against her, so close to her hand, and yet she couldn't take them.

"We shall go out that way. Miss Scarsdale, I would ask you to move," Denney panted.

Rachael slowly slid closer to Braxton, who shook his head at Denney, and said, "Do not be a fool, man."

"I am not a fool. I am a desperate man with nothing left to lose. I've killed a man and negotiated a sale of a stolen government document." He laughed. "One more death means nothing to me now. But it will be on your head." The blade dug into Sophia's neck and it stung.

"Stop moving, Denney."

"And why should I do that?" he yelled, but did indeed halt.

The knife blade pressed harder against her throat, and Sophia felt a warm trickle down her neck that signaled blood. She swallowed, the movement painful against the unyielding metal. She and Anthony had only just found each other again, had only just put their relationship to rights. She envisioned Jack and Ivy receiving news that she had died in India. She pictured her niece, Catherine, whom she would never again hold, who would never again squirm to get away while she tackled her with kisses.

Braxton was speaking, Denney was shouting back, and Sophia felt as though she heard the whole of it from down a long tunnel miles away.

Catherine, squirming . . . Catherine, wiggling when she wished to be set down on the floor . . . Catherine, lifting her arms straight up and allowing her dead weight to impede the adult trying to pick her up when she was determined to do something else . . .

I will not die here. Not today. Not like this. Not at this man's hand.

Sophia immediately allowed her body to slump as Catherine's often did, turning toward the arm that held her tight even as she shoved at the hand holding the knife to her throat. As Denney stumbled forward a step, she dropped all of her weight straight down, still shoving with all her might at his knife hand.

He cursed, unbalanced, and she took advantage of the moment to push his slackened arm away from her body, ripping the packet of papers out of his hand as she dropped onto the floor.

The shot that echoed through the room made Sophia's ears ring, and she flinched, stunned. For a moment she wondered if she'd been hit by a bullet, but as she placed her hands over her ears and looked over at Denney, she noted the hole in his forehead and the vacant stare in his eyes.

Denney fell to the ground.

Sophia looked at Rachael, who also covered her ears, and at Braxton, who lowered his weapon with a grim sense of triumph.

"You shot him?" She managed to ask past the ringing in her ears. "You shot him while I was not inches from him?" She stared in horror at the dead man, her thoughts tumbled and confused. "He . . . he . . . But I told Charity he wouldn't be killed! I promised her!"

"Miss Elliot," Braxton said as he secured his weapon. "You find fault with the way I saved your life?"

Sophia gaped. "I knocked him off balance, you had only to subdue him. You didn't have to kill him!"

"He was a British citizen who killed another British citizen in cold blood. He would have met the gallows."

"That is not for you to determine or decide!"

Sophia looked at Denney, at his limp, empty hand, and at the knife that had clattered to the floor. She pressed the packet to her chest with shaking hands, determined to see that Anthony receive it. If one good thing came from the hellish night, that would be it.

Braxton smiled as she struggled to her feet, still clutching the packet close. "Thank you, dear. I'll handle that from this point."

She shook her head. "No. I'll deliver it to Anthony myself."

He raised a brow. "Well then, you should know that Anthony works for me. It will come to my hands ultimately."

Oily.

"No. Again, I shall keep it with me. Nobody should see it."

He laughed. "Nobody should see it? Miss Elliot, I *wrote* it."

She narrowed her eyes, swaying on her feet but maintaining a death grip on the packet. "You wrote it?"

"Yes, and it was stolen from my office."

She wished she weren't so tired, that her ears would stop ringing. She couldn't think, couldn't reason. The only thing she knew for certain was that Braxton was not to be trusted.

She said as much to Rachael.

"I wondered." Rachael still had her firearm, and she pointed it at Braxton, although it wavered dangerously and Sophia worried Rachael might shoot herself by accident. "You should leave Miss Elliot alone."

"You're threatening a peer of the realm, Miss Scarsdale? You don't seem to understand I have the power to destroy your whole family. From Kent, are they not?"

Rachael's lips tightened, and her eyes blazed. "Do not threaten my family."

He moved so quickly it was a blur, raising his gun and striking Rachael's temple with the butt of it. Rachael fell, her gun clattering next to her on the stone floor.

Sophia gasped and felt her knees buckle. "You *killed* her!"

"No, I didn't kill her. I put her to sleep." He advanced on Sophia, and she backed up until her legs hit against the short stone wall. "You look tired, Miss Elliot." With that, his arm came up, she felt a crack against her temple, and all was dark.

Anthony watched Sophia crumple to the ground as though it happened ridiculously slowly. He was winded and sick with fear. When Lady Pilkington had told him not to worry, that she had dispatched Lord Braxton straightaway to the ruins to rescue the women, he hadn't been able to move fast enough, to commandeer a fresh horse quickly enough.

Dylan rushed up behind him in the dark hallway and took in the scene. "What has happened here, my lords?"

"This man is my employer," Anthony ground out and moved slowly across the room, giving a wide berth to the body of Clergyman Denney.

Braxton's eyes widened at the open admission. He recovered quickly enough and brandished his weapon. He snatched the packet of papers from Sophia's limp hands and stood. "Do not come another step closer, Anthony. I do not want to, but I will shoot."

Anthony smiled. "You do not have time to reload." He

rushed Braxton, using his momentum to drive the man backward, his energy fueling a storm of fury. He twisted Braxton, shoving his face up against a pillar and noting a satisfying thud as he did so. Using one hand, he twisted Braxton's arm high up behind his back. The older man gave a grunt of pain, but Anthony did nothing to ease the discomfort. He used his thumb to dig into Braxton's wrist, and forced him to relax his grip on the gun. Anthony ripped the weapon from Braxton's fingers and tossed it to the ground, where it clattered against the stone floor, slid, and then came to rest against the wall.

Anthony ground the barrel of his gun into Braxton's temple and felt a vein in his own temple throb. He glanced down at Sophia, relieved to see the rise and fall of her chest. "You are lucky she lives, else I would end you right now. As it stands, I will give you a chance. Who stole the document, Braxton? Who initially set out to sell it to the French? It wasn't Harold Miller."

"Major Stuart, this man is mad. I demand you arrest him immediately. The clergyman confessed to killing Captain Miller. I dealt with him, and I insist on the return of my property." Braxton choked as Anthony shoved his neck against the pillar.

"Who—stole—it? Who are you protecting? You should tell me now, Braxton, because I'll tell *you* something. Captain Miller left a diary. In it, he wrote that his nephew names the guilty party in this very packet." He reached beneath Braxton's fingers which held the documents flush against his waistcoat. He pried it away, his gun still pressed against the man's head.

"Stuart, come here, if you please."

Dylan walked to them, his weapon also trained on Braxton.

"If he moves, shoot him."

"Understood."

Braxton snarled but remained still.

Anthony bent down to Sophia, placed two fingers against her throat to check for a pulse, and was relieved to feel it steady and consistent. Her skin was so pale. She looked as though she'd gone rounds with a bad sort in an alley. He tilted her head to the side. There was a goose egg on her temple that he knew had come from the butt of Braxton's gun.

He opened the packet of papers and found the Janus Document itself, which was several pages long. It was indeed written in a familiar code—one deciphered through the use of specific passages in Shakespeare's *As You Like It.* Anthony had committed the pattern to memory, as had every government operative, former and current. He located his name, Jack and Ivy's information, details about Sophia. Where she liked to *shop*. The names of his associates past and present and their information filled the pages, details so finely determined Braxton must have used a small army of his own to gather the intelligence. It would take some time to decipher the whole of it. Anthony wasn't certain anyone should.

At the end of the packet was a letter signed by Harold Miller. Not only did it outline exactly what had transpired, but it named the man responsible.

Anthony's anger was so palpable he thought he might choke on it. "You." He stood and faced the man he'd not necessarily always liked, but ultimately had trusted. "You were the point of contact negotiating the sale. You took Harold Miller to France, intended to use him as the scapegoat when either the information became public or when your people started dying."

Braxton remained silent.

"How . . ." Anthony paced away from him, not trusting himself to not cause more harm than good when Stuart had a pistol trained on the man already. "You were prepared to watch us all die or be blackmailed. Our families used against us, killed, tortured?" He flipped through the pages again. He gave a bitter laugh and looked at Braxton. "You told me you were in danger, that your information was listed here also. Which, of course, I would wager it isn't."

"You are a smug one, aren't you, Wilshire? Your family coffers have always been full. You have no idea what it is like to have the family property, all your holdings, gambled away by a wastrel father. Do you think I have *worked* all these years by choice? Only to realize that in my retirement my pension will not support me, let alone my estates?"

"If Major Stuart were not here right now, Braxton, I would kill you." He approached the lantern Denney had left on a ledge. Rolling the papers into a tight cylinder—all except for Harold Miller's statement—he held them to the flame and watched the hated document burn to ashes.

"I hear the others," Anthony said to Stuart. "Reinforcements. I am going to get the women out of here." He bent to Sophia, scooping her up and cursing Braxton when he saw the huge bruise that was developing around her temple. Her head lolled listlessly against his shoulder, and he felt a stab of fear that he tamped back down.

"I'll not go to Newgate, Wilshire!" Braxton shouted.

"No, not for long," Anthony agreed without turning around as he carried Sophia to the entrance. "You'll hang."

Chapter 28

Sophia floated in a strange haze. People spoke in hushed tones, and small sips of water or broth were held to her mouth. When she fought, a low, masculine voice in her ear told her to behave, and when she fought more, he forced her chin down. She was also force-fed an awful, sickly-sweet substance that made her gag and sputter.

She fought the haze, but it was like clawing her way through clouds. The fog never moved out of her way, never cleared. When she thought she would go mad from it, strong arms held her still and brushed her hair away from her face. She was so incredibly tired.

Finally, the haze lifted. Sophia opened her eyes and then wished she hadn't. The shutters in her bedchamber were open, and the light pierced through to the back of her skull. She held up her arm and heard a startled, "Oh!"

"Briggs?"

"Miss Sophia! Oh, goodness, you're awake! How do you feel?"

"The shutters—"

"Oh!" A scuffle of feet, a loud slap of wood, and the offending light was dimmed.

Sophia lowered her arm and looked around. There were bottles, cups, and spoons on the nightstand and a wrinkled cravat and suit coat over the back of her vanity chair. "This is my room?"

"Yes." Briggs sat gingerly on the bed next to her. "Do you not remember the room? We are in Bombay. India." Briggs spoke slowly, enunciating very carefully.

Sophia tried to smile but it hurt. Everything hurt. "Water?"

Briggs reached to the nightstand and poured water into a small cup.

Sophia took it, but had to use both hands to hold it steady. "Briggs, what happened?"

Her maid eyed her warily. "What happened since we left London?"

Sophia rolled her eyes, and that hurt as well. "No, what happened since Braxton killed Clergyman Denney at the ruins?"

"Ah, I best leave the telling of that to his lordship."

"Lord Pilkington?"

"No, Miss Sophia. Lord Wilshire. This is the first he's left your side since bringing you in here like a rag doll yesterday morning."

"Yesterday?" Sophia looked in vain for her timepiece. "What time is it now?"

"Nearly six o'clock."

"People will be up for breakfast soon, then. I should like to check on Amala Ayah and Charlie."

"No, miss. Six o'clock in the evening."

Sophia blinked. "I've never slept so long in my life."

"They kept you loaded up with laudanum. Doctor said it would be good for you to sleep some. You're a right mess of bumps and bruises."

She put a hand to her head and felt a lump the size of a small apple. "Oh, Briggs! Rachael! Braxton hit her so very hard—" A flood of images rushed back, and her head ached from it.

"She is fine. Woke up a few hours ago." Briggs smiled. "Most romantic mansion in the province, I'd wager. Lord Wilshire playing nursemaid in here, Professor Gerald doing the same for Miss Scarsdale. All properly chaperoned, of course."

"And Charity? Beatrice?"

A soft knock at the door interrupted them, and Briggs opened it to reveal Amala Ayah and Charlie. Sophia put a hand to her mouth and looked at the small boy, who had color in his cheeks and held his beloved horse, Chestnut, close to his heart. She beckoned to them, and Briggs allowed them entrance.

"Charlie!" Sophia smiled and hoped she didn't look so horrifying as to frighten the boy. "I am so happy to see you!"

"As I am happy to see you, Miss Elliot. I am glad you are well." He looked so solemn.

Sophia patted the side of the bed. "Will you show me Chestnut's healed wound?"

Charlie looked at Amala, who nodded and helped him climb gently onto the bed with Sophia. He held out the horse, and she saw he had kept the "bandage" around the middle that Anthony had tied on the toy after they adhered the two pieces together. She imagined Mr. Denney sawing the toy in half in the first place to frighten Charlie into remaining silent, and she felt a fresh wave of anger at the man.

"He looks splendid." Sophia touched the bandage with her fingertip and smiled at Charlie. "He is such a noble horse, after all."

Charlie nodded. "He was wounded in battle, protecting his master. It is very praiseworthy, don't you think?"

Her eyes misted. "I do, indeed."

"Chestnut is also great friends with Lightning, the elephant you gave me."

Sophia grinned, despite the fact that it hurt. "You named him Lightning?"

"Yes." His smile was wide. "Although he certainly isn't quick as lightning, the name reminded me of you, so it seemed fitting."

"Charlie, do I detect a small space between those two front teeth of yours?" Sophia widened her eyes dramatically.

He nodded and showed her his teeth, one of which was indeed missing. "Amala Ayah read me a story about a boy who lived in the Congo, and when he lost his tooth, he tossed it up onto his roof and made a wish. I did that very thing with Mama and Papa, although we had to toss it from one of the third-story windows."

She smiled. "Did your wish come true?"

"It did." He smiled. "You are recovered."

Her eyes burned with tears. "Oh mercy, sweet boy." She leaned forward and gently embraced him, ignoring stabs of pain that came with every movement. His little arms encircled her, and she kissed his head. "I believe you shall always be one of my dearest friends."

Sophia released him, and Amala tapped his shoulder. "Miss Elliot must rest, now."

Sophia reached her hand toward the nanny, who clasped it between her own. "Amala Ayah, I am so glad he is safe," she whispered. "When I have children of my own, I shall look to my memories of you as an example of motherhood at its most noble and purest."

The woman's eyes glistened. "You honor me, Miss Elliot."

Briggs asked if she could see Chestnut's bandage, and Sophia took advantage of Charlie's momentary distraction. "Amala, did he ever tell you why he did not simply name the clergyman? Surely he recognized him."

Amala nodded and released Sophia's hands to wipe at her eyes. "I asked him," she murmured, "and he said he was afraid of him. Every Sunday, you see, he attended the sermon with his parents, and the message relayed was always one of fiery death and eternal burning. I believe when he witnessed a violent crime at the very hands of a man who was so fearsome, he was absolutely terrified."

Sophia shook her head. "Little wonder, then, that he chose to keep silent. But we are beyond it now, and he has both you and his parents to love him."

The door opened, and Anthony stood at the threshold, attempting to tie his cravat himself. A clean suit coat was draped over one arm and he looked freshly shaved and bathed. She smiled at him and winced only a small bit.

"You're awake!" He rushed into the room and slammed the door shut behind him.

Her ears hurt.

Amala laughed lightly and took Charlie's hand. "We shall visit later."

Sophia nodded and waved at Charlie.

"Briggs, why did you not send for me?" Anthony demanded. "I specifically told you to send for me immediately!"

Sophia looked up at Anthony. "I do hope Rachael's maid is with her and Professor Gerald or the Resident's mansion will garner a reputation as a house of ill repute."

"That was funny." He sat on the edge of her bed, evidencing a level of familiarity that must have increased while she was unconscious. "That is most definitely good. You're saying funny things; you seem lucid."

"I am lucid, silly man."

"The doctor said you might be fuzzy for a time, but that your brain will clear up straightaway."

She reached for his fingers, and he stopped fiddling with the cravat. "I am not fuzzy," she told him gently. "Now that you all have stopped dosing me with laudanum, I am feeling remarkably alert."

He lifted a shoulder. "The doctor thought it would be best. You were so hurt." He paused and swallowed. His eyes clouded. "You were so hurt."

"But I am better now."

"You do still look as though you've gone the rounds at Gentleman Jack's."

"Thank you."

He flushed. "I am saying all the wrong things. Briggs, this is a private moment, please close your ears."

Sophia smiled softly when Briggs slipped out the door and stood in the hallway, but left the door ajar. "Bless her."

"Sophia, when I received your note about Beatrice and the palace I was terrified. I returned here to find you had *gone*—without help, without me. When we reached the palace, there was no sign of you but definite evidence of sati. Beatrice was perfectly safe; she had been detained in the women's quarters, and she provided testimony that warranted an arrest for Prince Ekavir's advisory officials."

Sophia nodded. Good. One hurdle cleared.

"Stuart left a retinue of soldiers at the palace, and then we returned here. Lady Pilkington apprised us of everything that had happened while we were gone, informed us that Braxton had arrived first and that she had sent him ahead to the ruin. Lady Pilkington thought she was doing a good thing, but . . . I was terrified."

She smiled and gave his hand a squeeze. "You did mention that."

He brought her hand to his lips. He closed his eyes and pressed a long, lingering kiss on the back of her fingers. When he looked up, his eyes were suspiciously bright. "Lady Pilkington has taken the Denney girls under her wing, along with their poor mother, who very much needs a strong friend at the moment, I should think."

Sophia smiled. "And little Charlie seems on the mend. When he was here just now he was very near the little boy I met when I first arrived."

"I have other good news for the both of us. The Seadon family has packed their bags. They are staying at the Governor

General's bungalow for the next few days until their ship arrives."

"To take them where?"

"I do not know, nor care. Matron Seadon lost interest in remaining here when I made it clear that I am not interested at all in her daughter."

He kissed her fingers again, rubbing his lower lip softly across her knuckles. He put her palm to his cheek and held it there. "Lady Pilkington, the Denney sisters, even Amala and Charlie—they have all camped outside your door awaiting news, praying that all would be well." He smiled and then sobered. "What is the last thing you remember about the ruins?"

"The last I remember is Braxton trying to take the documents from me."

"I needn't bore you with details. But Braxton is aboard military transport back to London and the Janus Document has been destroyed."

"Oh, Anthony. Braxton is to stand trial for murdering Denney?" She creased her brow, which hurt.

"Yes." He shook his head with a humorless laugh. He paused, the muscles in his jaw pronounced. "Additionally, since he was behind the theft in the first place, he will face charges of treason. He is the reason we are not now, as we speak, at the Wilshire townhome in London, married, with a baby in the nursery and hopefully another on the way."

She laughed. "Oh, everything hurts!" She clutched her stomach. "There are a few problems with your scenario, dearest."

"Such as?"

"Firstly, I would like a true proposal. And then I should

like for us to spend some time in the country being boring and staid and playing with Catherine and Ivy and Jack." She looked up at him, but frowned as something on her neck itched. She scratched, only to find a large bandage in place.

"What is the purpose of this thing?" She rubbed it lightly, which of course, hurt.

Anthony shook his head, his nostrils flaring slightly. "That blasted clergyman cut you with his machete."

She laughed. "It was not a machete."

"It looked like a machete. I saw it." He scooted closer to her so that his hip touched hers. "My sweet Sophia, I am so sorry. It is my fault you were hurt when I left, it is my fault that you're here now, still hurting, and it is my fault that my enemies nearly succeeded in beating you to a pulp. I can spend a lifetime attempting to make it right for you and never succeed." He kissed her lips softly.

She laid her palm on his cheek. "Silly man. I made the choices that have affected me. And I would do it all again. I love you; I never stopped loving you. And I am so very glad you are not a libertine."

He smiled and placed a kiss on her palm. "Will you marry me, Sophia Marie Elliot?"

"I will." A tear escaped, and he thumbed it away as she smiled. "I had promised myself to never shed another tear over you, Anthony Blake."

"Hopefully this is a good tear."

"The best kind." She leaned forward and kissed him, not minding that her aching body protested every movement. She decided love was worth a bit of discomfort.

Epilogue

Sophia sat on the sloping lawns of the Wilshire country estate on the shore and enjoyed the shade of the early summer day. Her daughter, Elizabeth, was five months old and cutting her first tooth. The only thing that seemed to help the child forget her aching gums was rolling around on the blanket under the shade tree.

"And how is our queen bee after her rest?" Anthony squatted down on the blanket, picked up Elizabeth, and nuzzled her tummy with his nose. It made her laugh, so he did it frequently. He kissed her cheek and set her back down on the blanket on all fours, where she rocked back and forth before collapsing on her stomach.

"She will be crawling before long." Anthony sat just behind Sophia on the blanket, knees bent on either side of her so he could wrap his arms around her middle.

She leaned back against his chest and closed her eyes. "Will she, now?"

He kissed her neck. "Mm-hmm. Jack told me Catherine began crawling at five months. Since you and Jack share the same bloodline, I would assume the same will prove true for Elizabeth."

"Their little David is six months now, and all he does is roll from side to side."

"That is because he is chubby. Are you happy, Lady Wilshire?"

She smiled. "So very happy. Content. I got exactly what I wished for."

"Look at what arrived in the post!" The call came from the door to the kitchens, and Charity Denney ran to them, clutching a letter. She flopped down on the blanket next to Elizabeth.

"Who is the letter from?" Sophia snuggled comfortably against her husband.

"Amala. She says Charlie is nearly as fluent in Hindi as she is, and his tutor at the Residency believes he shall move into his next reader before they return from the Hills at the end of summer!"

"I am so glad." Lady Pilkington had surprised them all by allowing Charlie to remain in India and learn from tutors and the local British schools. Lord Pilkington was not necessarily pleased at the thought that his son was receiving a "substandard" education like a middle-class working family's child, but Lady Pilkington had insisted so he relented.

"Is there a letter from Princess Beatrice Darzi?"

"No, but she did say in her last letter that she, Mama, and the prince are visiting a few more royal families while the summer is still in full force. We will hear from her again when they are not traveling."

"She seemed very happy in her last letter," Anthony remarked.

Charity nodded. "She is, and I am happy for her. I know much of my fear for her safety was also fear that she was planning her life with someone else and leaving me behind." She smiled. "But we must march forward and all that nonsense."

Sophia nodded. She, Charity, and Mrs. Rachael Scarsdale Gerald had shared experiences in India that bonded them forever, and while they didn't often discuss those events, they were as close as sisters because of them. Charity had come to live in England with Anthony and Sophia just after their wedding. She loved India and always would, but felt she needed some time and distance from painful memories. She was flourishing in England, and Sophia was glad to see happiness returning to the girl's eyes.

"Are you ready for your first Season, Miss Charity?" Anthony asked. They could have launched her two Seasons ago, but she'd said she wasn't ready, and they respected her decision.

"I am." She lay back on the blanket next to Elizabeth and looked up at the swaying leaves. "No sense in postponing the inevitable."

Sophia felt Anthony's smile as he nuzzled her earlobe with his nose. "You can wait one more, if you prefer."

Charity sighed. "I'm ready. And if all else fails, I shall be a nanny to this one for the rest of her life." She picked up Elizabeth and set the baby's feet on her own midsection. She proceeded to bounce the baby gently until she laughed. "And I shall read you silly novels and feed you sweets when your mother is not looking."

Sophia smiled, her eyes burning with tears of contentment.

Anthony looked at her and put a fingertip beneath her chin, turning her face to his. "Are those the good kind of tears?"

She leaned in and kissed him. "Yes, dear man. I am so very, very happy. And so very, very glad I waited for you."

"As am I." He produced a flower he'd been hiding behind his back and she smiled.

"An orchid." The tears continued to gather. "Reminds me of our wedding." Anthony and Sophia's wedding at the primary Wilshire country estate had been filled with orchids of every size and color. Anthony had told Sophia that he had learned the beautiful flowers were common in Indian weddings, that they signaled strength and wisdom, and represented a deep love and commitment between two people. Jack had overheard the explanation and then berated Anthony for making all other husbands in England pale in comparison to him.

Sophia touched a finger to the bright red petal with a smile, and Anthony popped the stem of the flower short. He tucked the flower behind her ear and kissed her temple, then settled his arms back around her, holding her close against his chest.

"I love you, Countess Wilshire."

Sophia laughed softly when he added, as he did every night, "And you are my very best friend."

Acknowledgments

Thanks go, as always, to my sweet family and friends for their love and support. I add again my heartfelt thanks to Lisa Mangum, Heidi Taylor, and the Shadow Mountain team, as well as Bob DiForio and Pam Howell for taking care of me and my career. You are all so good to me, and I am humbled and grateful.

Thank you, also, to the many readers who have emailed, messaged, tweeted, posted, or told me in person how much you're enjoying my books. Each time I am filled with a sense of awe and gratitude. I am truly living my dream, and that others find joy in it with me is the best thing a girl could ever want.

My love to you all!

(By the way, in chapter 23, I make reference to a book called *Le Language de Fleursand* although it wasn't published until 1819, which is actually a handful of years after this story is set. Communicating with flowers and plants became quite the thing to do in the nineteenth century, and it was fun to include it here.)

Discussion Questions

1. Sophia originally worked as a ladies' maid before being raised to a higher status in society. Do you feel that her humble beginnings gave her a different perspective of society? How do your past experiences influence your present circumstances?
2. Do you believe Anthony made the correct decision to write Sophia a letter saying they were "just friends"? Should he have told her the truth from the beginning? Is it ever appropriate to keep a secret from someone you love?
3. The Fishing Fleet was an actual option for ladies to find an eligible husband. How have dating and courtship practices changed over the years? How have they improved? How have they made dating and marriage harder?
4. One of the reoccurring motifs of the novels is the idea of wearing a mask. Anthony is unhappy at the necessity of working undercover and pretending to be someone he is not. A murder takes place during a masked ball. And Sophia has to pretend that she is not still in love with Anthony. Have there been times when you feel you have

had to "wear a mask" in a difficult situation? How did you feel? How often do you feel that you reveal your true identity to others?

5. Sophia and Anthony struggle as their relationship fluctuates between romance and friendship. Can you have one kind of relationship without the other? Discuss the ways in which their relationship was strengthened by the combination of both romance and friendship.
6. The story touches on the Indian practice of *sati*, which involves the living widow being cremated along with her dead husband. What are your thoughts about that practice? What are some of the customs in your country that may seem foreign to an outsider?
7. Sophia quickly makes friends with Rachael Scarsdale and the Denney sisters. What elements of her personality make her a good friend? What makes for a deep and lasting friendship between women? How is Sophia's friendship with Rachael similar or different from Anthony's friendship with Dylan?
8. Did you know much about India before reading this novel? If so, what details were familiar to you? If not, what did you learn about the culture or the country?
9. Children play an important role in the story. Compare the Pilkingtons' parenting of Charlie to the Denneys' parenting of Beatrice and Charity. In what ways are the parenting styles similar? In what ways could they be better parents to their children?
10. Where you surprised by the ending? What clues did you see in the story that lead you to suspect the person you did as the villain?

About the Author

Nancy Campbell Allen is the author of thirteen published novels, which span genres from contemporary romantic suspense to historical fiction. In 2005, her work won the Utah Best of State award. She has presented at numerous writing conferences and events since her first book was released in 1999. Nancy received a BS in Elementary Education from Weber State University. She loves to read, write, travel, and research, and enjoys spending time laughing with family and friends. She is married and the mother of three children.

FALL IN LOVE WITH A

PROPER ROMANCE

JOSI S. KILPACK

JULIANNE DONALDSON

SARAH M. EDEN

NANCY CAMPBELL ALLEN

Available wherever books are sold